John E. Taylor

Half-Hours in the Green Lanes

A Book for a Country Stroll

John E. Taylor

Half-Hours in the Green Lanes
A Book for a Country Stroll

ISBN/EAN: 9783337227241

Printed in Europe, USA, Canada, Australia, Japan

Cover: Foto ©Andreas Hilbeck / pixelio.de

More available books at **www.hansebooks.com**

HALF-HOURS

IN

THE GREEN LANES:

A Book for a Country Stroll.

BY

J. E. TAYLOR, F.L.S., F.G.S., &c.

AUTHOR OF "GEOLOGICAL STORIES," "HALF-HOURS AT THE SEASIDE,"
"THE AQUARIUM," ETC.

SIXTH EDITION.

LONDON:
W. H. ALLEN & CO., 13 WATERLOO PLACE,
PALL MALL. S.W.
1884.

PREFACE TO SECOND EDITION.

THE quickness with which the First Edition of this little book has gone off, has induced the Author at once to prepare another, in which all errors of letter-press, &c. have been corrected. This book includes so many subjects, on each of which volumes have been written, that the Author was necessarily obliged to be both discursive and brief. But if it has been the means of introducing young readers to higher-class works, in which the wonders of Creation are more detailedly set forth, or if it has developed a love for the multitudinous natural objects which surround us, his pleasant labours have not been in vain.

A*

CONTENTS.

—————◦◦◦—————

CHAPTER I.

BY A TARN SIDE.

CHAPTER II.

THE FISHES, MOLLUSCA, AND OTHER OBJECTS IN THE TARN.

CHAPTER III.

THE REPTILES IN THE TARN AND THE GREEN LANES.

CHAPTER IV.

THE BIRDS OF THE GREEN LANES.

CHAPTER V.

THE BUTTERFLIES AND MOTHS OF THE GREEN LANES.

CHAPTER VI.

THE BEETLES AND OTHER INSECTS OF THE GREEN LANES.

CHAPTER VII.

THE SNAILS AND SLUGS OF THE GREEN LANES.

CHAPTER VIII.

THE FLOWERING PLANTS OF THE GREEN LANES.

CHAPTER IX.

THE RUSHES, GRASSES, AND FERNS OF THE GREEN LANES.

CHAPTER X.

THE MOSSES, FUNGI, AND LICHENS OF THE GREEN LANES.

HALF-HOURS

IN

THE GREEN LANES.

———◦◦◦———

CHAPTER I.

BY A TARN SIDE.

WHAT naturalist is there who does not know the treasures to be found in a common pond? Animal and vegetable, here are to be met with objects that will find a twelvemonth's work for the microscope. But even without having to employ that useful instrument, the young student may acquaint himself with the structure and habits of many a strange organism. Of course, it is to no purpose our recommending creatures like these unless you have a love for nature. But if you have—and we pity the man or woman who has not—you are in possession of a faculty of enjoyment that will remain after fortune, friends, health, and even youth have departed. The power to throw yourself on the bank of some lonely tarn or stream, and give yourself up to communion with the inhabitants of that little world, to let your sympathies go out towards

B

them, as Hawthorne's "Donelli" did, is a gift not to be despised! And it is surprising, if you are really interested in your fellow inhabitants of nature, how soon they seem to recognise the fact, and to familiarise themselves with your presence, as though they knew you had a kindred feeling for them. As you recline on the flower-covered bank, shortly you see the birds following their usual avocations, quarrelling and making love, as if an individual of the genus *homo* were not present. The butterflies flit about you, the bees hum busily, the dragon-flies skim the surface, and buzz against your very face. The fishes rise at the flies, or bound above the water in frolicsome sport. The water-beetles spin and dive, and the flies and gnats drum around you, whilst overhead the summer sun is shining out of an intensely blue sky, just flecked with dappled white clouds. You shut your eyes, and allow your ears to drink in the many voices of nature. Bird and insect, wind and tree and rustling grass, all contribute to it. There is not a discordant note. How wonderfully all seem to blend and lose themselves in the joint and harmonious chorus!

We are not speaking now of the feelings of the mere hunter or collector of specimens, of him who values them not unless they are *rare*, so that his cabinet may be enriched by their grotesquely dried forms, and his selfish vanity be fed by the admiring envy of his friends when he exhibits them. If the study of and communion with Nature leads to no higher feeling than this, we are afraid that, instead of doing good, it will only accelerate the harm which mankind are so fond of appropriating out of the most innocent of objects. But we are referring to the sentiments of a man who feels that all things have a right to live by the mere fact of their being in existence—who loves them, not only for the pure joy they give him in sharing their vitality, but because they are, with himself, objects of the same providential care. With such feelings "collecting" is a secondary matter—only resorted to that we may know and admire more of the objects themselves. Coleridge has exactly expressed the sentiment of all genuine naturalists—

> "He prayeth most who loveth most
> All things, both great and small;
> For the dear God who loveth us,
> He made and loveth all."

We have never collected a flowering plant, insect, or egg, without feeling that if there were any other way of getting at the knowledge we seek, we should greatly prefer it. Life, however or wherever represented, is a sacred thing to the naturalist. The 'Loves of the Plants' are felt by him in a different way to that of which Dr. Darwin wrote. He knows that if a human mechanic could fabricate a small machine that should be able to fly, like the little gnat that has just settled on his hand, such a man would be lauded throughout the length and breadth of the land. Much more if he could place within it an internal apparatus for the development of an infinite number of machines like itself, and the power of providing for an offspring it will never see. Even then, it would be a mere machine, curious, nothing more. Why should we think less of the myriads of life-forms because they are constructed by a Divine instead of a human Architect? Do their wonderful structure, instincts, and habits or numbers detract from the wisdom that formed them, or the love that, so freely evolved them?

Such have been a few of our thoughts as we have reclined, like a lazy poet, drinking in the mere joy of existence, and thanking God for being allowed even physical life! We have made our selection of a "tarn" in preference to a "pond"—although both words are frequently used synonymously—because the former is a pond of nature's own making, whereas the latter may be of man's. In this sense the word is used by our older writers. Holinshed, in his 'Chronicle,' says, "The Air, or Arre, riseth out of the lake, or *tarne*, south of Dombrooke, wherein, as I heare, is none other fish than red Trowt and Perch." A "tarn" may therefore be of immense age compared with a pond, which simply means an excavation cut in the ground in search of clay or mould, and into which, when deserted, the waters have been allowed to drain. It is true, that even in such places, and within a very short time, there will spring up, as by magic, or rather as if the creative force had been specially and locally mani-

fested, a bountiful supply of life-forms. The fine
whirling dust will have peopled the water with
infusoriæ or diatomaceæ, the green scum of algæ
will mantle the surface, the larvæ of many aquatic
insects will sport in the water. But give us a
genuine tarn for natural history purposes—one
whose existence extends perhaps beyond the historic
period. There are many ways in which such tarns
may have been formed. In mountainous districts
they may, perhaps, be the result of glacial agencies
which scooped out the rock-basin of the tarn itself.
They may occupy the hollows of the land, as in some
parts of Cheshire, where the dissolving of the strata
of rock-salt beneath, and their removal as brine-
springs, has caused the overlying rocks slowly to
settle down. Or, still more common, and far more
widely distributed, they may have been formed, as
we have frequently discovered they have been, in
chalk or limestone countries, where the superficial
drainage has dissolved away portions of the soluble
rock, and thus formed "sand-pipes." In the hollows
thus left, whenever water has been capable of being
held, you may depend on a genuine tarn. It may
be centuries old, surrounded by low bushes, covered
with aquatic plants—a veritable microcosm, in which
the "battle of life" has long ago been settled, and
the animals and plants have adjusted themselves to
each other's needs. What myriads of agencies have
been at work to stock a little pool! The reptiles
and fish may have been originally brought, as ova,

adhering to the legs and plumage of aquatic birds from some distant river or lake, in which the birds last revelled. Many of the plants may have been transferred in a similar way, the wind bringing the rest. Even in the formation and stocking of the tarn, therefore, we cannot fail to observe the operation of purely natural laws, but they are none the less indicative of providential care and direction. Nature knows no sabbath—her laws are ever at work, but in their very operation declaring themselves but the visible operations of an active Deity. How true are the words of the poet :—

> "My heart is awed within me when I think
> Of the great miracle which still goes on
> In silence round me, the perpetual
> Work of Thy creation. Finished, yet renewed
> For ever !"

As if a new world had been created, this little tarn turns us to causes as powerful as the result, in this instance, seems to have been small. The geological phenomena which have resulted in the depression of a small area, the physical agencies which have filled it with water and turned it into a miniature lake, the vital operations that have peopled it, as though it were a new world—are all worthy the attention of the naturalist.

Wherever the thick sheet of boulder-clay occurs over chalk rocks, and some portion of the latter is dissolved away to form a "sand-pipe," there the clay will be depressed and form a hollow. The water-holding power of such a depression is evident, and in this way a tarn springs into creation at once. In the steepish bluffs which form the sides you may see imbedded stones and boulders. Some of them are angular, and indicate they must have been removed from their parent rock direct, and by some agent that could carry them without exposure to much abrasion. Others are water-worn, and show that they had been rolled about before their final removal to this spot. You are not long before you notice that many of these boulders, big and little, are strangers to the rocks of the locality, and have come from a distance, chiefly from rock strata lying towards the north. You are not wrong in your deduction, and a closer examination shows you that many of them are *scratched*, some to a considerable depth, and that others, of a harder texture, are polished. Here you obtain a glimpse of the nature of the conveying agencies. It was *ice*, and when the boulders were transported, the tarn occupied an inconsiderable space along the bottom of a wintry sea, where arctic mollusca lived and died, and over which icebergs brought their burdens of mud and stones, to form the boulder-clay of the neighbourhood. What wonderful changes have been wrought since then! This sea bottom has been elevated into dry land, has been scooped out into valleys, and sculptured into hills! The animals and plants of the old wintry period have departed to their original frosty zones, and more temperate forms have occupied these

regions since the climature became milder. It will
not take you long to find that a few square feet of
the exposed bank of a common tarn will teach you all
this, and a great deal more.

Perhaps you have made your way to this spot
along one of the old lanes which botanists and entomologists are thankful still remain, and where the
stiff boulder-clay crops out in cuttings or along the
bottoms of the high banks. There you may read off
the same lesson from the enclosed pebbles and
boulders as that to which we have drawn attention
in the banks of the tarn. This boulder-clay sheet
usually occupies the higher grounds, and forms the
"heavy lands" of the farmer. Consequently you have
been ascending some gentle acclivity in your way
along the old lands. If so, you may have noticed what
appeared to you evidences of an *old beach*, in the
sloping fields. Nothing could be more pronounced
than the terrace-like structure, and not a few good
geologists have fallen into the mistake of believing
and describing these terraces as the result of ancient
river or beach action! They are, however, nothing
of the sort, but they are none the less interesting.
And both the geographical and geological student
may learn something of the wear-and-tear of atmo-
spherical action on the solid land, by studying them.
Let us examine one of these hedge-rows that runs
more or less parallel with the valley. They have a
wonderful history, these old hedges, especially those
which shut in some of the green lanes. To the latter

however, we will return by-and-by. The first thing you notice is how much higher the ground is on the *upper* part of the slope against the hedge, than on the other side. In some cases it may be five or six feet—indeed, the latter is any thing but an unusual occurrence. How is this? It is certain that the original makers of the hedge never so banked up the soil; it would take no small time to do it. The real explanation has to be sought for in meteorological agencies. The rains of many generations have washed away the surface soils, especially in cultivated fields, and the slope of the ground has caused the material to be carried down. The hedge has stopped its further conveyance, and thus caused the upper side of the hedge to be so much higher than the lower. Destroy the hedge, as is often done when one field has to be thrown into another, and you will have running parallel with a valley a genuine terrace, which some geologist hereafter, ignorant of the true cause, may put down to having been formed when the river stood much higher than it does now; or, if he be more visionary, may see in it an old sea-beach, formed when the sea last came up this particular valley, and made of it an estuary!

Let us now return to the lanes. Many of them are deep, as if they had been cut, when in reality it is the ground on the other side the hedge which has been raised in the manner just described. How old some of these hawthorn shrubs really are we dare not say. The origin of the lanes is lost in antiquity. Many

of them are old "occupation roads," formed for the
convenience of the original cultivators of the soil
and without any reference to the wants of future
wayfarers, and depend upon it, certainly without
giving a thought to future botanists and entomologists! You observe the thick gnarled bases of the
hedges, some of which have been pollarded time out
mind. It is just possible that they were planted as
hawthorn sprigs by the first Saxon settlers in these
parts! Many of our old roads and lanes are the
boundaries of parishes which have retained their
present area since the Conquest, therefore many of
the hedges must have been in existence since then.
Only those who are acquainted with the manners
and customs of the first Saxon settlers, are aware of
the great value they set on the hawthorn fence as
a protection. Even now, when an Englishman
travels in France for the first time, it seems strange
to him to find what an absence of hedgerows there
is. Perhaps nothing appears in greater contrast in
the scenery than this. And should England ever
be attacked by a foreign foe, it is more than likely
we should, for the first time, realize the defensible
value of our hedgerows, and obtain from them that
cover and protection which their original planters
had in view when they stuck the first twig in the
ground. Every field and hedge would be disputed,
and an invader would meet with obstacles which
exist in no other country in the world. Whether
the first Saxon settlers brought the hawthorn with

them or not, it is certain they attached great importance to it. Their early towns—a mere collection of
huts—were surrounded with a strong hawthorn fence,
so that, in the terminal syllable of many of our
English village names, we have a reference to this
fact. *Ton* or *town*—as we have modernized it—is in
allusion to the forked branches of the quickset fence
and in the *tine* of an antler, and in the *tine* of a fork
we have the original word still applied. *Ton* is
merely a syllable from the same root, and is a silent
but expressive testimony to the ancient thorny and
forked character of the defences adopted by our
Saxon forefathers. Other village names end in *sett*,
as "Hethersett," from the Anglo-Saxon *sætan*, to
plant. In such cases the name is derived from the
ancient swine pastures, which were enclosed with
thorn fences, nothing else being capable of arresting
the migratory impulses of the "porkers." To this
day we call a hawthorn hedge, *par parenthèse*, a
"quick-*set*" fence, showing what vitality many of
these old words possess, and how much of genuine
history is silently locked up in their almost forgotten meanings. Indeed, the Anglo-Saxon student,
on his first introduction to the language, is surprised to find how largely the use of the hawthorn
has entered into the composition of our English
village names. Thus the old enclosures for the
purposes of the chase, made with this hedge, were
called "haighs" or "heys." In Lancashire, the
fruit or drupe of the hawthorn is still called
"haigh," whilst elsewhere it is termed "haw," and

thus the prickly plant itself "hawthorn." "Ham" is a very common termination of our village names, especially in eastern and south-eastern England, and was derived from the original settlements of the early Saxons being "hemmed" in chiefly by hedges. So that this shrub has more or less influenced that dearest of all English words, *home*, which has been undoubtedly derived from *ham!*

It may appear as if we had wandered from our place "by the tarn side," but if we have it has been merely to glance dreamily and lazily at the quiet history of the lanes and hedges through which we have passed on our way. All these objects are only so many beads, and it is necessary to have a string to connect them together. Now that we have once more arrived at our tarn side, we will proceed to note its inhabitants, animal and vegetable, which have possibly held possession longer than the lords of the manor over which we have been travelling. The quiet of the spot has a subduing charm, and it is in moments like these, when we give ourselves up to the influence of nature, that we feel a true companionship with all living things. Certainly, in this case, the tarn is inexpressibly handy to us, as enabling us, in our rambles in the "green lanes" not only to rest ourselves after our stroll, but to make acquaintance with objects we cannot find elsewhere; and therefore, we feel sure our readers will not be disposed to quarrel with a scheme intended to enlarge the circle of objects which we wish to introduce to their notice.

CHAPTER II.

NOW that we are well settled by some brook or tarn side, with a view to making ourselves acquainted with its living contents, animal and vegetable, we shall find our attention almost bewildered by the variety of material. It is only when you thus devote yourself systematically to its examination, that you wonder at the exuberance with which every spot capable of supporting it is peopled with life-forms.

Foremost among the inhabitants of such streams or tarns as it may dwell in is the Pike (*Esox lucius*). Well does it deserve its name of the "fresh-water shark." No object in nature has a more cruel, voracious look than this fish. Depend upon it, if there is one present, he is lurking this sunny morning just where the break occurs in the weeds that so thickly cover the surface of the water. There he will lie, as if in a comatose state, for hours, until some over-frolicsome young fry come almost within his capacious jaws. The pike rarely attacks

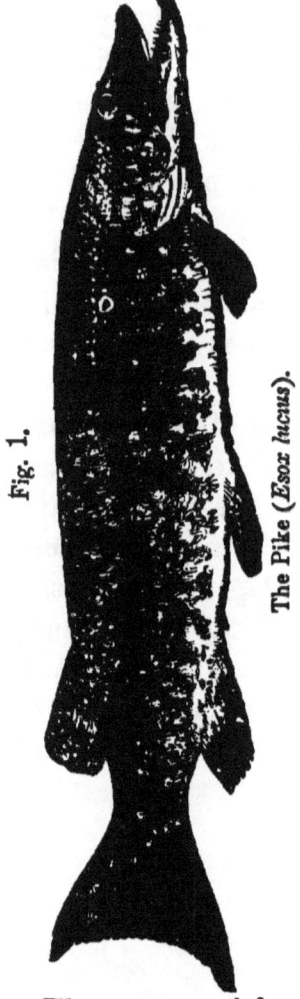

Fig. 1.

The Pike (*Esox lucius*).

the stronger fishes, unless he sees they are sickly, or in a difficulty; and still more rarely the perch, having a lively recollection of the way in which the latter sets up his back when assaulted! But let a roach be fastened to the end of a line as a live-bait, and the tyrant will then slowly swim round it, terrifying it into curious gyrations, and amus- ing himself by seeing how hopelessly helpless is the case of his victim! Little does he know that close against the glittering scales of his in- tended prey lie concealed a couple of hooks, destined to take hold of his own gullet. The pike never scruples to take his own kind—nay, you cannot lay a better bait for a large individual than a small one.

The young pickerel, or Jack, is even more vora- cious than his fat parent. Watch the gambols of a shoal of young roach—nothing is more amusing, and that time cannot be said to be lost which makes us more intimately acquainted with the lives and habits of God's creatures! All on a sudden the juveniles dart off in every direction, as if they had been fired by some central, radiating impulse. At first you see nothing to cause all this hurry; but, presently, your eye catches sight of a young Jack in the weedier parts of the pond, for well does he know that his dappled back screens him admirably from view, by resembling the shadows of the ripples and weeds cast on the floor.

Fig. 2.

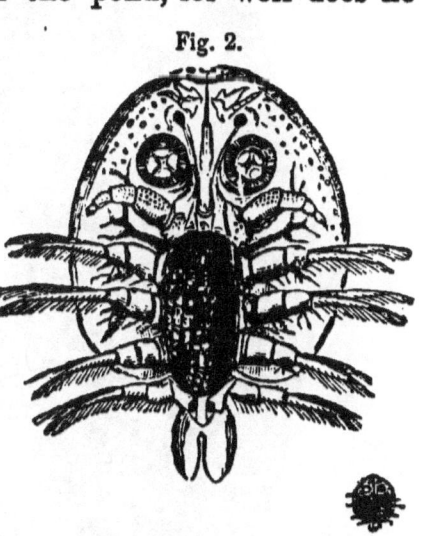

Parasite of Pike, *Argulus foliaceus*, natural size and magnified.

Strange tales are told of the rapacity of the pike, which it is not necessary to retail here. Also, concerning his longevity, there are facts and evidence sufficient to convert Mr. Thom and Sir George Cornewall Lewis to a belief in his being a centenarian, under certain circumstances. What a vast pyramid of life must he have destroyed before he can attain this great age! But the pike has not always an easy time of it. He is not unfrequently tormented by a tick-like parasite (*Argulus foliaceus*, Fig. 2), which roams at its will over his body, and feeds on his juices, so that pike are often weakly through the extra numbers of this particular torment. The

Fig. 3.

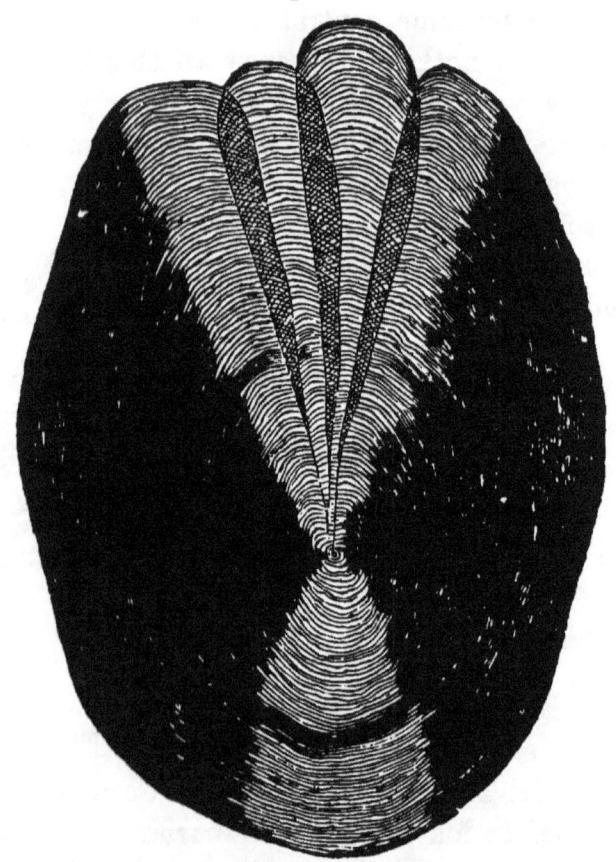

Scale of Pike.

same parasite, we may mention, is occasionally found on the carp, roach, stickleback, trout, perch, and even on the tadpoles of the frog.

Those of our readers who possess microscopes,

Fig. 4.

Scale of Perch.

will find in the scales of our fresh-water fishes, objects of great beauty and delicacy, which require only a low power to develope them. Fig. 3 gives that of the pike, and, although it is not so pretty as many, it is very attractive. The scales of the perch and tench are more ornamental, the denticulated margin of the former having been selected by Professor Agassiz for his order of *Ctenoid* fishes. In order to view fish-scales with the polariscope, it will be necessary to mount them in balsam. It will be seen that the scale of the tench differs materially from those of many other fresh-water fishes. Whilst dwelling on these, as objects for the

Fig. 5.

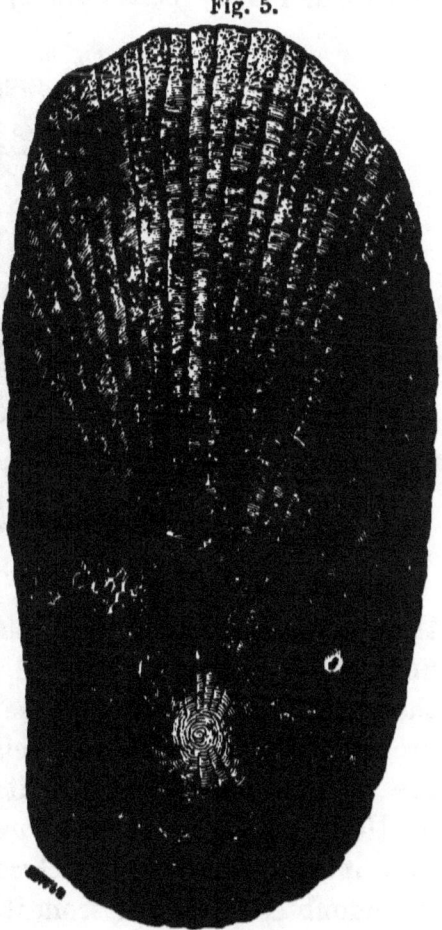

Scale of Tench.

c

microscope, it may be as well to introduce magnified
figures of others to the general reader or student
before noticing at greater length the fishes themselves. The Roach and Dace are well-known objects,
but their enlarged scales may not be so, and we
therefore give them. Let it be understood, however,
that the scales taken from the backs of all these
fishes differ very considerably in their form, from

Fig. 6.

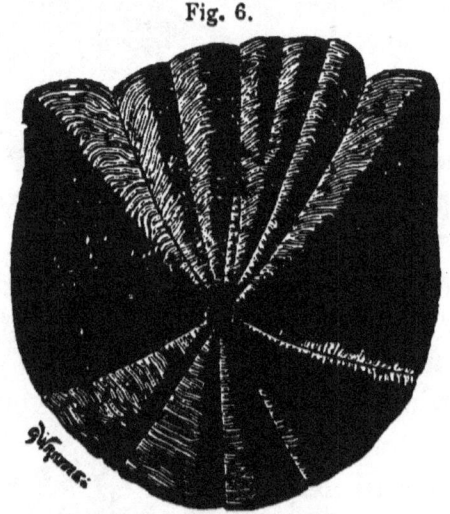

Scale of Roach, × 10.

those obtained from the belly. To thoroughly
understand them all, it will be necessary to get
them from both parts. Those given above are the
prevalent forms. Often associated with the roach is
the " Rudd," or " Rowd," as it is indifferently called
in Norfolk, where it is more abundant, perhaps,
than in any other part of Great Britain. Its name
is undoubtedly derived from its red colour, and it is

not unfrequently known as the "red roach," although it belongs to quite another genus, of which the common carp, and the introduced "gold-fish" are well known examples. On a hot summer's day you will always get this fish, if it be present, by dropping your baited line close to the dense patches of aquatic

Fig. 7.

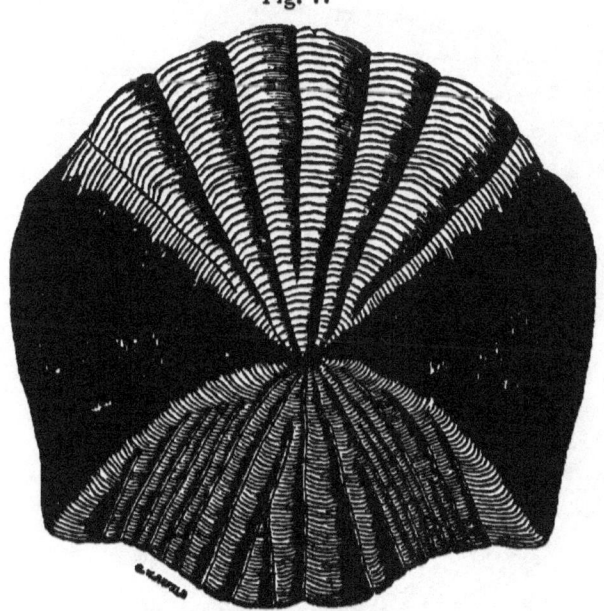

Scale of Dace.

plants which cover the surface of the water, and under which the rudd is cooling itself in a lazy fashion. If there be one near, you will not be long in a state of suspense, for the rudd will pounce on your worm, and dart away with it to its retreat at once, ignorant of the hook and line attached. "Bob" goes the float, and, if you are not looking, your line

will snap, or a jerk up to your elbow tell you of a
capture.   Connoisseurs say the rudd is better eating
than the generality of fresh-water fishes.   In the
deeper parts of many slow-moving rivers, also, may
be found the Bream, which, in Norfolk, often grows

Fig. 8.

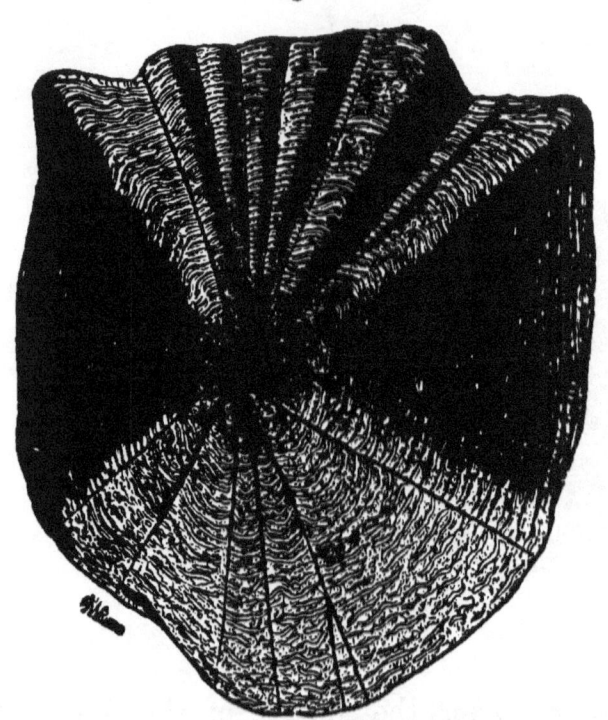

Scale of Rudd, × 10 diameters.

to four and five pounds weight.   In August and
September, anglers there always reckon their takes
of this fish by *the stone!*   We give examples of the
scales of these two fish, magnified ten diameters, a
power used whenever not otherwise stated.   The

Gudgeon and Minnow are fishes to be found in the clear running water of almost every streamlet, although the former does not disdain the tarn. Small as they are, their scales furnish good objects. The scales of the minnow are very delicate, but like every other true species of fish, they possess a distinctive character. This is an important fact to

Fig. 9.

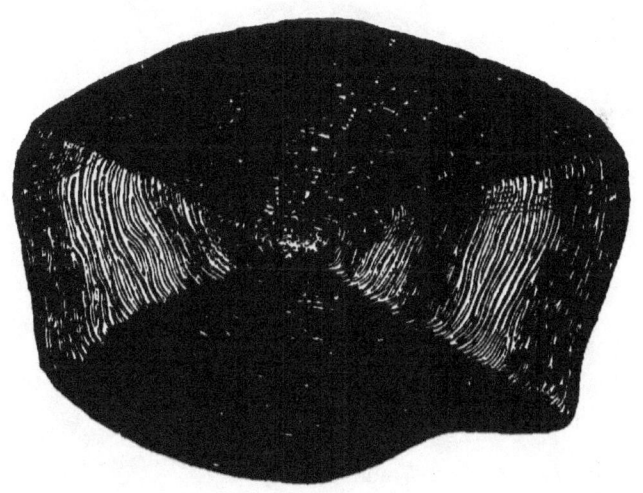

Scale of Bream, × 10.

be remembered, and one that cannot fail to throw light on geological questions, when the fossil scales of clycloid or ctenoid fishes are in question. The Common Carp (*Cyprinus carpio*) has long been domesticated for eating purposes, and its use, in the old Catholic times when long fastings were in vogue, is exemplified by the fish-ponds to be seen in the neighbourhood of our ancient monasteries, abbeys,

halls, &c. In these sluggish waters it would live to
a great age, and attain an immense size. Although
we consider its flesh undoubtedly coarse, yet the
carp has been a favourite article of food since the
days of Aristotle. The scales of the Common Carp
and the Crucian Carp are given below, and the
difference in their markings is plainly seen. The
latter sometimes goes by the name of the " German

Fig. 10.

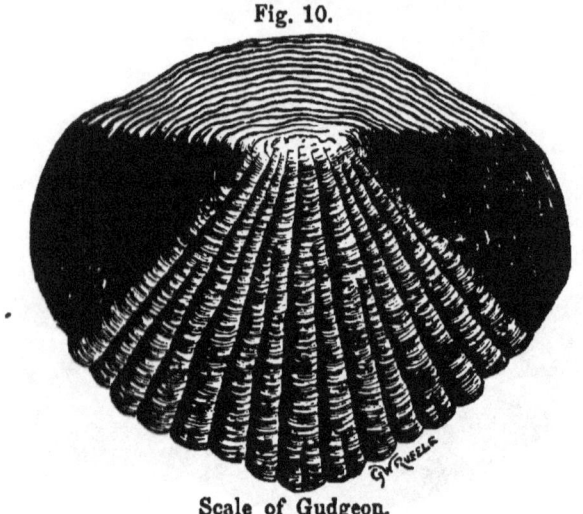

Scale of Gudgeon.

carp." Neither of them are indigenous to England,
but the exact time when they were introduced is
not known, although an old distich says—

> " Turkeys, Carps, Hops, Pickerell and Beer,
> Came into England all in one year."

Yarrell tells us that the common carp is mentioned
in the 'Boke of St. Alban's,' printed in 1496.
And, in a post-glacial river deposit at Mundesley,

in Norfolk, a bed of about the same age as our river or valley-gravels, the bones and teeth of the pike may be found tolerably common, showing that, so far as it was concerned, the affirmation in the couplet is decidely wrong. The term "Crucian," applied to the carp last mentioned, shades off, in

Fig. 11.

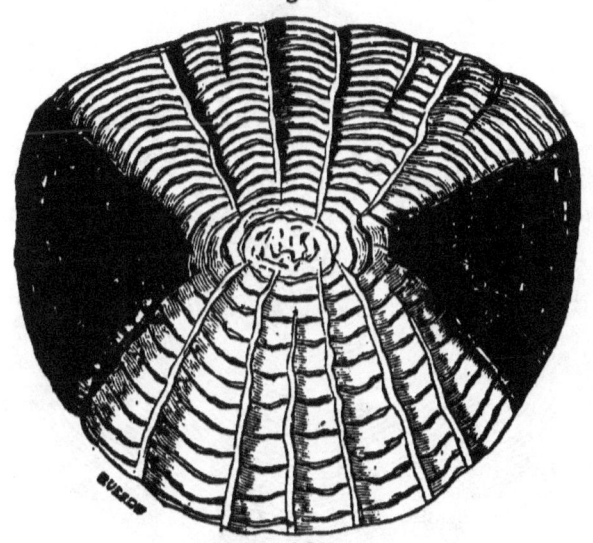

Scale of Minnow.

its phonetic sound, into French, German, and Swedish adjectives also given to it. In France it is *Carassin*, in German *Carouche*, and in Sweden *Karussa*. The scales of the Chub, and Grayling, which follow, are in marked contrast, and still further illustrate the difference resulting from the varied play of a few wavy lines. The chub is a river, rather than a pond fish, and, in those streams

where it does occur, you will be certain to find it in
the deepest holes. It is well known to Thames
anglers, who obtain it by "dibbing." The grayling
is a very elegant fish; indeed, with the exception
of the trout, it is perhaps the most comely shaped of
all our fresh-water fishes. It is very local in its

Fig. 12.

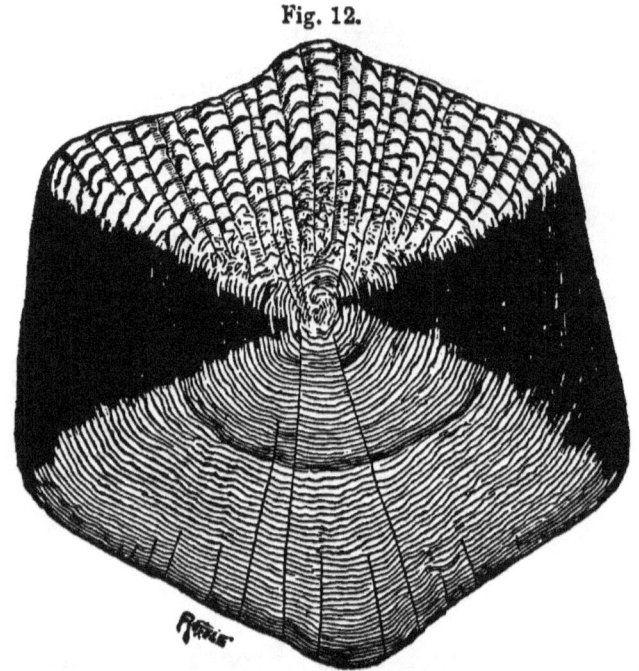

Scale of Common Carp.

geographical distribution, and so far differs greatly
from the perch, dace, roach, and gudgeon, which
are widely and plentifully distributed. Like the
chub, it prefers clear running rivers, with a gravelly
bottom, and is therefore a frequent companion of
the trout. Yarrell suggests that in some of the

streams near the ruins of large monasteries, it may have originally been brought by the old monks, who always took care to have a plentiful supply of fish by them, and those of the best kinds. The generic name of the Grayling was given to it on account of the peculiar odour of thyme which it gives out, just as the smelt emits that of the cucumber.

Fig. 13.

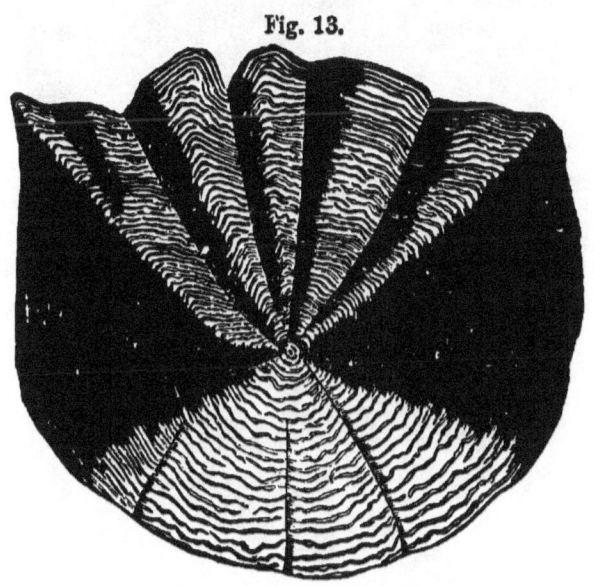

Scale of Crucian Carp (*Cyprinus carassius*).

The Barbel (*Barbus vulgaris*) is a fish fonder of warmer, or more equally temperate waters than those of our eastern and midland rivers. It is common, however, in the Thames, where it attains a great size. Its name is said to be derived from the *barbs*, or wattles atached to its mouth. This may be so, but it seems like catching at the first ex-

planation that offers; for other fish, fresh-water
and marine, have similar appendages to their mouths.
The magnified scale of the Barbel, as will be seen
by Fig. 16, is a very pretty object.   That of the

Fig. 14.

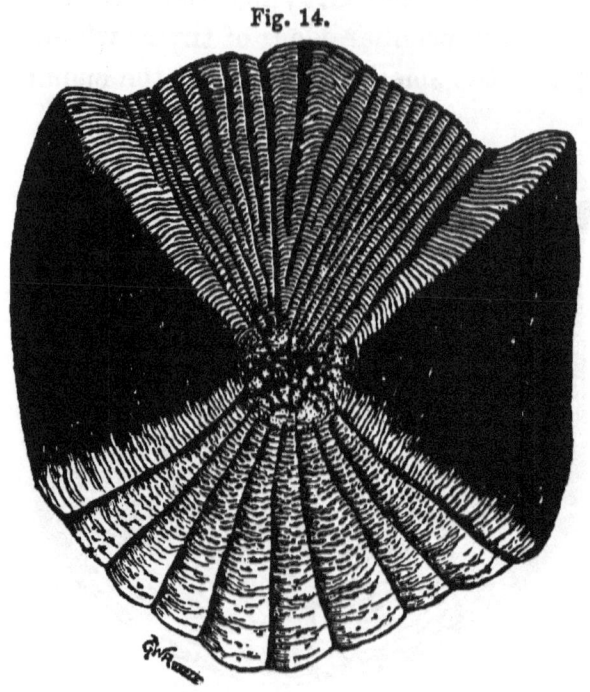

Scale of Chub (*Cyprinus cephalus*).

common eel (Fig. 17) is still more so, the markings,
instead of being concentric ridges, are like rings of
beads arranged outside each other. Some of our
readers may be surprised at hearing of the scales of
the Eel, for it is a popular notion, originating
doubtless in the smoothness of its skin, that the eel
has no scales. Perhaps, the best way of seeing

them is to obtain a portion of the eel's skin, from the belly, when the scales may there be observed in their natural position.

To omit notice of those common fishes, the Stickle-backs, would show how little the habits of these freaky creatures had been observed by us. Yarrell enumerates seven species as decidedly British.

Fig. 15.

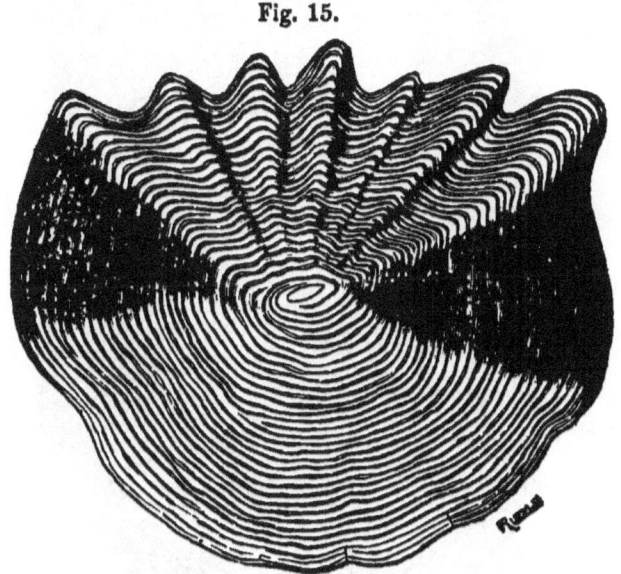

Scale of Grayling (*Thymallus vulgaris*).

Strange to say, many of these are purely *marine* in their habits, thus indicating a degree of special-isation, or adaptation to varying circumstances, on the part of the genus, which may have been the result of physical geological changes. Others, such as the Rough-tailed Stickleback (*Gasterosteus aculeatus*) live both in fresh and salt water, and so far connect the extreme habits. This is by far the commonest of its kind, and is to be found in every river, stream, and

Fig. 16.

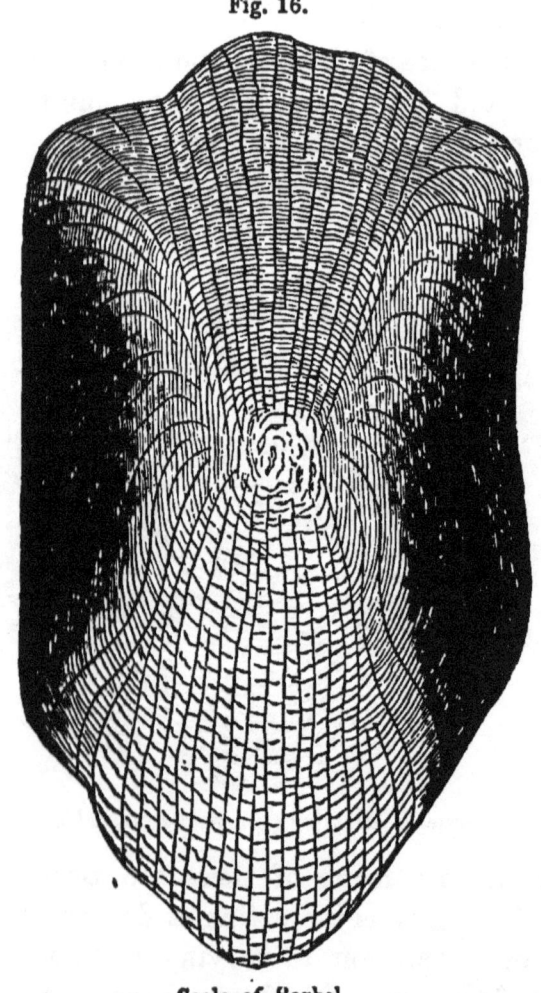

Scale of Barbel.

tarn, as well as all round the coasts, in Great Britain, from John o'Groat's to the Land's End.

The males are well known for their pugnacity, and
for the beautiful colours of scarlet and green they
put on in the spring, at the
time when they make their
aquatic nests. For, strange to
say, this and one or two others
are genuine nest builders!
Towards the middle of April
they may be observed (if kept
in a fresh-water aquarium),
collecting small pieces of stick
and wet moss, so saturated
that they cannot float. A pile
of these is made, with a hole
on the top. The stickle-
backs then collect, with their
mouths, fine sand, and trickle
it all round the little cone.
Woe be to any invader of this
little nest, after it has been
formed, and the female has
deposited her ova therein!
Small as the three-spined
stickleback is—indeed, perhaps, the smallest of all our
British species—it does not
hesitate to attack much larger
individuals, and will even tilt
at the stick you point towards
the little nest it is guarding! The ova hatch in

Fig. 17.

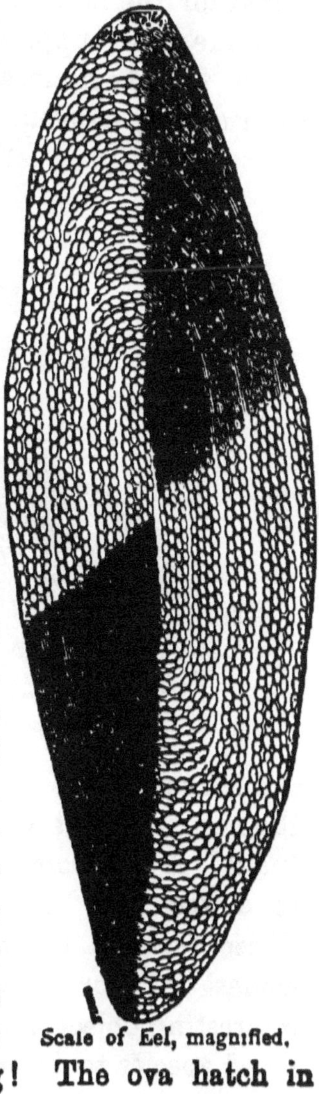

Scale of Eel, magnified.

ten days or a fortnight, the young remaining in the nest until the yolk-bag is absorbed. This is the signal for the male to leave them to themselves, for they are now supposed to be able to start in the world for themselves, and no longer to require paternal supervision. Not unfrequently, the con-

Fig. 18.

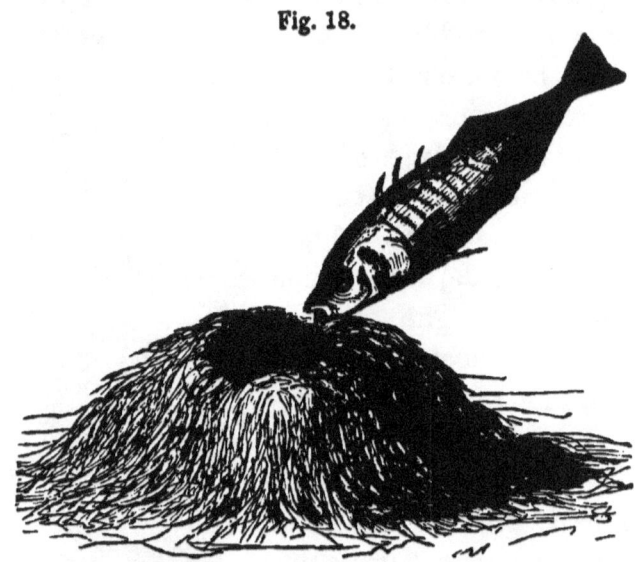

Three-spined Stickleback and Nest.

stant care on the part of the parents in guarding the nest when the young are there, results in death. Indeed, it is a common occurrence for the parents to sicken and die through overmuch watching. These facts in the history of, perhaps, the commonest of our piscine tribes, render it a most interesting object for the aquarium. Among other allied species to be met with are the Smooth-tailed

Stickleback (*G. leiurus*), in which the males exhibit similar variations of colour, generally crimson and purple; and the Ten-spined Stickleback (*G. pugnitius*), which also lives alike in fresh water and salt, migrating up our rivers in shoals in the spring. All the sticklebacks are most voracious, as every boy who has angled for them is well aware.

Space does not allow us to do more than point out the evidence our fresh-water fishes, shells, and aquatic plants afford of the very recent separation of Great Britain from the main-land of Europe. And what they indicate is abundantly verified by the strata of the most recent deposits. We have no aquatic plants, or mollusca, or fresh-water fish, that are not common to continental rivers, lakes, and ponds. And our English stock must have extended over English latitudes before the formation of the German Ocean, for they could not have crossed the salt sea, and been imported in that way. Hence, although geologically speaking these familiar objects have been in existence, in England at least, only a comparatively short time, if we reckoned their occupation in numbers of years we should nevertheless be startled at the amount. Consider the great physical changes that have taken place since they extended hither—the depression of the lowest levels on the eastern side of England to form the German Ocean, the submergence of the great plain to the west, to form the Irish Sea. Both these seas are shallow, and indicate recent formation. And the occurrence

of remains of pike, perch, &c., in deposits as old as
those containing evidence of man's first occupancy
of the earth, prove what a great antiquity, in point
of actual time, is possessed by our fishes and mollusca,
and tell plainly of the great changes that have taken
place since they overspread these areas, after the
gradual toning down of the rigorous climate of the
Glacial epoch.

Passing now to another group of objects of a
lowlier kind, but not less differentiated and adapted

Fig. 19.

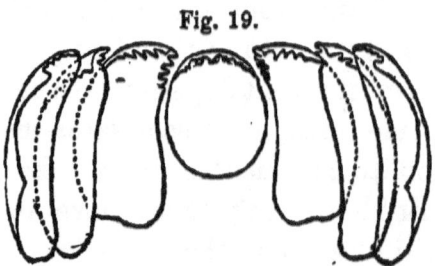

Teeth of *Paludina vivipara*.

to an aquatic life, we come to the fresh-water
molluscs. The student is sure to find species in
every streamlet and tarn. In the latter, especially,
underneath the vegetation floating on the water, or
at the bases of the sedges, rushes, and grasses which
fringe the sides, a careful examination will discover an abundant harvest. The Fresh-water Snails
(*Lymnea stagnalis*) creep about, the epidermis of
their shells covered with a green scum that affords
most interesting material to the microscopist.
Other Lymneas—*pereger, auricularis, glaber*, &c.—

are to be found in similar situations. The coiled shells (*Paludina*) cannot be mistaken, especially the biggest, *P. vivipara*, which flourishes most in large, slow-moving rivers. We have known this species to be collected in the dykes of the Norfolk rivers, and sold and eaten as marine periwinkles! The teeth of all the fresh-water mollusca are charming objects when prepared for the microscope. Perhaps the most complex dental structure of this kind is that possessed by the *Neritina fluviatilis*—a beautiful little zebra-marked shell, with mouth half-

Fig. 20.

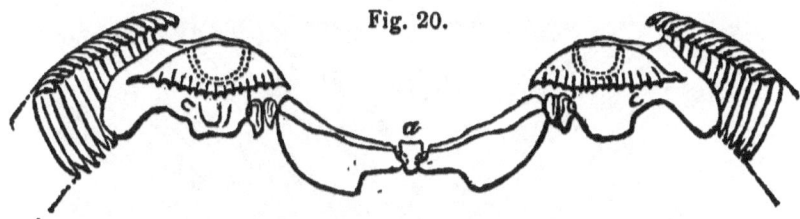

Teeth of *Neritina fluviatilis*.

closed, to be found adhering to the piles, under water, in many of our larger rivers. In the lingual teeth of this species, the central tooth *a* is minute; the teeth of the lateral areas (*pleuræ*), termed *uncini*, are about sixty in number. The first is very large, and of a remarkable shape; the rest being slender, hooked, and toothed. As a rule, the teeth of the fresh-water snails are remarkable for their fewness, those of land snails being, on the contrary, marked for their extraordinary number. In marshy spots, such as those bordering a natural pond, may be found the peculiar mollusc *Testacella*, which in some respects connects the shell-bearing snails with the slugs. It possesses only a rudimentary shell, which is placed at the further or tail end of the body. This shell appears to be the dwarfed representative of one that was once much larger, and few naturalists doubt that the original ancestor of the *Testacella* had a large shell, into which it could retreat at pleasure, like the ordinary land and fresh-water snails. The specific name of *haliotidea* is given to our common species on account of the shape

Fig. 21.

Part of the Lingual Ribbon of *Testacella haliotidea.*

of the rudimentary shell resembling that of the well known " Venus' ear " shell (*Haliotis*), of the Channel Islands. The *Testacella* does not possess horny jaws, and its lingual ribbon is very large and wide, being composed of about fifty transverse, oblique rows. The teeth diminish in size towards the centre, each row numbering about fifty teeth. The *Succinea* is another snail, delighting in moist or marshy situations. Its shell is exceedingly delicate, and on this account, difficult to preserve. But it is a very beautiful object, and richly deserves the necessary pains which are required to prepare it for the cabinet. The teeth in this species are not so complex as in that just mentioned, and are usually three lobed. For microscope purposes, the teeth of another fresh-water univalve, *Ancylus fluviatilis,* are worth obtaining. This shell is commonly known as the fresh-water limpet, and you may find it with its base attached to the pebbles in any neighbouring streamlet or brook, for it is fond of clear, running

Fig. 22.

A transverse row of the Lingual Ribbon of *Succinea putris.*

Fig. 23.

Portion of a transverse row of the Lingual Ribbon of *Ancylus fluviatilis.*

water. It well deserves its popular name, for it is the counterpart of its marine relative, on a smaller scale. There are about one hundred and twenty transverse rows in the lingual dentition of this mollusc.

In the little runnels leading to our tarn, you may find along the bottom, numbers of a small univalve shell, not unlike the *Paludina* in general form. This is the *Bithinia tentaculata,* which forms such an active and elegant object in the aquarium.

D 2

Equally well-fitted for the same place are the flat-coiled shells, termed *Planorbis*, which abound in various species, ranging in size from a pin's head to the diameter of a shilling, on the under side of such aquatic plants as the pond-weed (*Potamogeton*). The largest of these is *Planorbis corneus*, which has about five whorls, with a broad, shallow hollow, or umbilicus, on the under side. It is a capital mollusc for clearing away the green scums that will accumulate in the best kept aquaria, and is much sought after for the purpose. In the summer time you may find it in dried up ponds, with a thin film spun across the mouth of its shell to prevent the moisture of the animal being dried up, whilst the creature itself is in a torpid condition. *P. vortex* is a species very commonly distributed. It is a flatter and thinner shell than the forementioned, and has more whorls, the outer being sharply edged or keeled. This easily distinguishes it from *P. spirorbis* which may be found in the same localities, for the whorls of the latter are rounder, and the entire shell is not so flat. *P. albus* is another very common species, taking its name from the whitish colour of the shell, by which, and by its five whorls, the last one of which is disproportionately enlarged, it may be readily identified.

The *Paludina*, *Bithinia*, and *Valvata* have a different internal structure than the others mentioned. This is especially noticeable in their breathing organs, which are adapted for obtaining the air from the water, as in the gills of fishes. *Valvata piscinalis* is almost certain to be met with in an old tarn, and it is a species not difficult to distinguish. It has four well defined whorls, of a brownish yellow colour, and a deep hollow beneath, called the umbilicus. It is about the quarter of an inch in size. You may find it not only at the bottom of the water, but on the aquatic plants, up whose stems it frequently crawls. The teeth of this species form an exceedingly beautiful microscopic object, the central portion, *a*, being relatively larger than in many fresh-water molluscs. The common genera *Lymnea, Planorbis, Ancylus*, &c., are

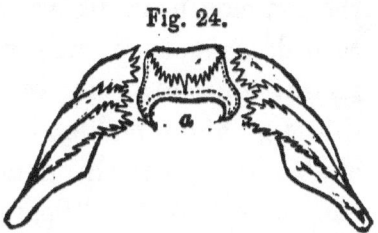

Fig. 24.

Teeth of *Valvata piscinalis.*

water-air breathers—that is to say, although they live in water, they are compelled by the peculiar structure of their branchial organs to rise frequently to the surface to breathe. The eggs of many of the above mollusca may be found attached to the under sides and stems of aquatic plants, the egg-sacs imbedded in a transparent jelly. It takes about a month to hatch them, at which time the young may be seen protected by a miniature shell.

In the rich black mud at the bottom of the tarn, lie hundreds of the shells of bivalve mollusca, such as *Anodon, Unio*, &c. The former takes its name from the absence of any toothed projection near the

beak, the valves being kept together by a ligament.
This will always enable the student to identify it
from *Unio*, in the hinge of which there are distinct
and well marked articulations. The "Swan mussel,'
(*Anydon cygneus*) is the largest of all our fresh-water
shells, often attaining the length of four or five
inches. The heron you may have disturbed on your
approach to the tarn, had most probably been making
a hearty meal off the swan-mussels, for both it and
the common crow are very partial to them. Pennant
records that they will carry the closed shell to a
height and drop it, in order to break it open in
this ingenious fashion! There are several species
of *Unios* in British ponds, of which, perhaps, the
commonest is the "painters' mussel," (*Unio pic-
torum*), so called because its valves were formerly
used by the Dutch painters for holding their colours.
The pearl mussel (*U. margaritiferus*) is fonder of
running water, and is generally found in rivers in
the neighbourhood of mountain ranges. In the same
runnel leading to the tarn that you found *Bithinia*
you will doubtless find both *Cyclas* and *Pisidium*,
small bivalve molluscs, with nearly globular shells.
The latter genus is noted for its single siphon. In
the stream, just where the bend has drifted fine sand
into a heap, you may surely reckon on meeting
with myriads of their empty shells, which have been
swept here by the current.

Whilst collecting or noticing the habits of these
humble creatures, one cannot but remember the

important part they have played in the economy of our planet. All of them have a geological antiquity far transcending that of the human race! The anodons have been in existence since the Devonian period, and the fossil specimens from the upper Devonian green sandstones of Kilkenny are seen to possess all the characters which still distinguish the genus. It would seem that when certain classes of animals have attained the characters best suited to them, evolution is arrested, and the form becomes stereotyped. *Paludinas* are so abundant in the upper Secondary fresh-water strata, especially those of the Wealden, that they form thick beds of lime-stone. The well known " Purbeck marble," masses of which you might have noticed forming the font of the village church hard by, is wholly composed of the shells of extinct Paludinæ! The *Planorbis* is a familiar fossil form in the upper Eocene beds of Hampshire, where it may be seen of a size that well suited the sub-tropical conditions of climate which marked the period when it was alive. *Cyclas, Pisidium, Lymnea,* &c., are equally abundant in beds of the same age. Even the existing *species* have a vast antiquity. *Planorbis corneus, P. vortex,* and *Valvata piscinalis,* are found fossil in the Norwich crag, showing they were living in England just before the advent of the long northern winter of the " Glacial epoch," when Europe was swathed in an ice-sheet as Greenland is now ! *

---

* The student desirous of making himself more fully acquainted with our land and fresh-water molluscs, cannot do better than get Tate's work on this subject, published by Hardwicke, Piccadilly

The most familiar objects one comes across have an interest which science is every day intensifying, and which is well worthy the attention of the most cultivated minds.

The other objects to be found in any pond or tarn will occupy many " half-hours " on the part of the young observer. Whilst noting the shells living there, and dredging the weeds and mud to find them, he cannot fail to notice many of the smaller species cemented or matted together, so as to form a rough tube. They are the cases of Caddis-worms— creatures to be met with in abundance in all such spots as these. The objects themselves are the larvæ of a neuropterous fly, whose first start in life is as aquatic animals. They are not alone in this respect, many species of dragon-flies, &c., sharing a watery life with them. How marvellously they are adapted to such conditions may be seen by the special bronchial filaments on each side the body. There are many more species of caddis-flies than are usually supposed, and as this old tarn is just the spot to find them if they are to be found anywhere, we will draw attention to some of the commonest forms.

Fishes, the larvæ of dragon-flies, and water-beetles have a sharp recollection of the juicy sweetness of a caddis-worm deprived of its shell ! You can hardly get a more taking bait for fresh-water fish, than such a denuded larva. Hence the absolute necessity for such a protection as is obtained by forming a case of dead shells, sand, leaves, twigs, &c., which more than compensates for the natural softness of

the body. The head and the first three segments of
the body are hard and horny—a most useful fact
in the economy of these creatures, seeing that these
are the parts necessarily required to be thrust forth
in obtaining food. The rest of the body is soft, and
at the extremity are a series of hooks, by means of
which the caddis-worm can take firm hold of its
dwelling. The swellings or humps, on the body,
which fill the case, help also to prevent the body
being forcibly dragged out. In looking out for
these interesting objects, you will not fail to find

Fig. 25.

Case of *Phryganea grandis.*

one species, the *Phryganea grandis* (Fig. 25), whose
case is invariably formed, not of shells, but of pieces
of leaves and other vegetable matters so cemented
together that they form a cylindrical tube. You will
notice that the pieces are arranged *spirally*, either
from left to right, or from right to left, generally the
former. The tubes are of nearly equal diameter
throughout, and the larva of this species has the
power of turning itself inside, and thus of presenting
its head at either end as it may wish. Not less
common than this species of caddis-fly, are the larvæ
of another genus, named *Limnephilus*, or "pond-
lover." One of them (*L. rhombicus*, Fig. 26) uses
pieces of moss, cut lengths of rushes, grass, &c., and

arranges them in a transverse and oblique direction, so as to form quite bulky masses. Another com-

Fig. 26.

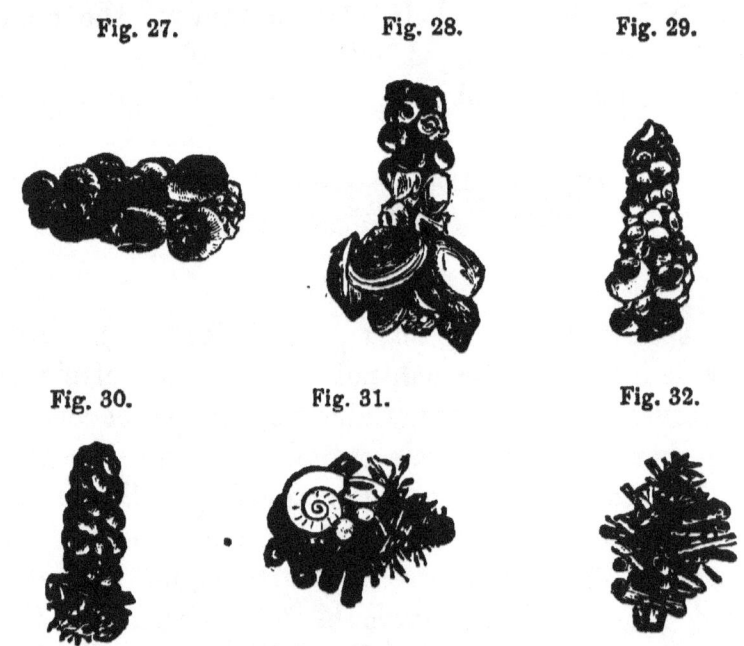

mon species (*L. flavicornis*) is not at all particular as to what materials it uses in forming its cases, as the following sketches will show. Shells are employed very abundantly, and most of the caddis-worm cases to be met with in

Fig. 27.   Fig. 28.   Fig. 29.

Fig. 30.   Fig. 31.   Fig. 32.

Cases of *Limnephilus flavicornis.*

any ditch or tarn, are the work of this particular species. Indeed, the *flavicornis* seems to be exceedingly capricious in its selection of building materials. At one time it will choose only seeds, at

another only shells or grains of sand. The shells
are often fastened together even when their inmates
are yet alive, and the latter have to put up with this
forcible captivity till such time as the larva shall be
transferred to its next or winged stage of existence,
and the cementing material binding the elements of
its former case together, shall be dissolved away.

Another common form of caddis-worm case is

Fig. 33.

Case of *Limnephilus lunatus*.

Fig. 34.

Case of *Anabolia nervosa*.

made by an allied species, *L. lunatus*, which, like the
species of an allied genus, *Anabolia nervosa*, makes its
tube of fine sand, or the equally fine fragments of
fresh-water shells. In both these species, the case
has attached to it small twigs or other pieces of
wood, as balancers. These twigs often extend far
beyond one end of the tube. In hunting for these
" small deer," it is more than probable you may
come across another species of caddis-worm called

Limnephilus pellucidus (Fig. 35), whose case is formed of entire leaves, or large pieces usually of willow or poplar. Sometimes, it is composed of pieces cut out from the stems of bulrushes, &c., and flatly laid over each other, so as to form broadish masses. In the interior of these is the slender tube containing

Fig. 35.

Case of *Limnephilus pellucidus.*

the larva. The leaves, &c., form a capital protection, and you have to pull the pieces quite from each other before you can fully decide that they were formed as worm-tubes. We have also caddis-cases of yet other species, with straight or curved tubes, sometimes gradually tapering to one end. Such are the cases of *Sericostoma, Setodes,* &c. They are formed of sand, or very small stones, neatly cemented together. Some species of *Setodes* make delicate little tubes, entirely formed of silky secretion, without any admixture of extraneous objects. Not uncommon in ditches and tarns, is the caddis-tube of the *Molanna angustata* (Fig. 38). It will be met with most abundantly in ponds

Fig. 36.

Case of *Sericostoma.*

Fig. 37.

Case of *Setodes.*

having a sandy bottom. The tube is long, broad, and rather flattened, and is composed of fine sand grains cemented together. The upper surface, at the front end, projects over the larva, so that it forms an ingenious covering whenever the larva is forced to protrude its head in search of food. These larvæ generally live on vegetable matters, although they have been said to be not indifferent to the ova of fishes, &c. The mechanism of the tubes of caddis-worms is, geologically speaking, very ancient; for similar cases are found in such abundance in the Miocene strata of Central France, that actual rocks are composed almost wholly of their remains.

Fig. 38.

Cases of *Molanna angustata.*

The larvæ of the *Ephemera* and Water-beetle (*Dytiscus*) inhabit the same water, as many small fishes find out to their cost, for these creatures are as ferocious, after their kind, as the greater land carnivora. The latter feeds on tadpoles, and keeps down the tendency to swarm of these reptilian progeny. The *Dytiscus* is especially fierce, and, when kept in an aquarium, will not hesitate to attack the stick that is pointed near it. One grip is generally sufficient to settle a poor tadpole, as the jaws actually meet through its sides. To the microscopist the breathing tubes (*tracheæ*) of this insect are very interesting. The best way to obtain them is to make a careful incision along the centre of the back with a pair of fine scissors. After a prolonged soaking in acetic acid, and repeated washing, the skin may be removed almost entire.

The tracheal or breathing system of the *Ephemera* must be served in the same way, to obtain it as a microscopical specimen. It is, however, much more difficult to manipulate, on account of the fragility of the leaflets.

Space only allows brief reference to the surface insects, the well-known Whirligig Beetles (*Gyrinus*

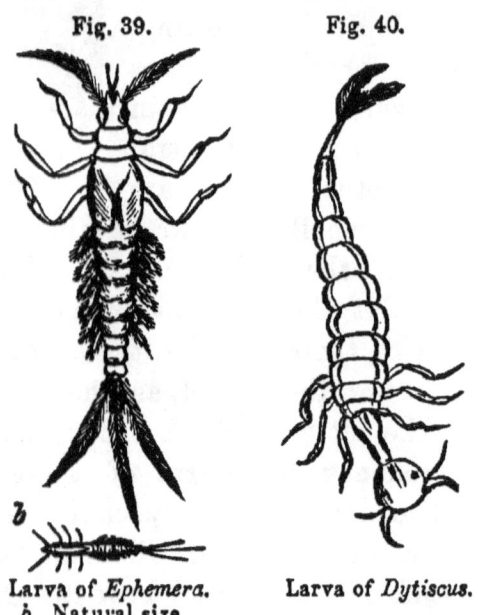

Fig. 39.   Fig. 40.

Larva of *Ephemera*.   Larva of *Dytiscus*.
b. Natural size.

natator), to be seen going through their fantastic quadrilles on the surface of every stagnant pool. But these humble creatures have a fair geological antiquity; for the Forest bed, cropping up from beneath the glacial deposits of the Norfolk coasts, shows that this same species was in existence long before England became an island for the second time, and when the existing German ocean was the site of a lake. The prepared legs of this beetle are good objects for the microscope, either for transmitted or polarised light. Whilst searching for things that can thus be turned to use, do not let us forget the common Water Fleas, whose antiquity is greater than that of any object we have yet mentioned. The shales overlying many of our coal seams are quite fissile, owing to the myriads of fossil cases of these creatures which strew their surfaces, and thus cause them to split up readily. In every fresh-water deposit, of every geo-logical age, you find remains of fossil water-fleas ; and it is surprising how little the general type has altered through the thousands of centuries that must have elapsed since they were called into existence ! The

Fig. 41.

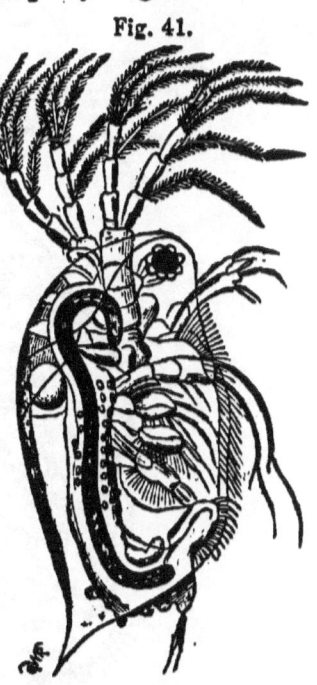

Daphnia pulex (male).

living forms are quite visible to the naked eye, but it requires optical aid to bring out their individual beauties. You may be certain of finding several species in any decent pond or tarn. The commonest, perhaps, is *Daphnia pulex*—the typical water-flea (Figs. 41, 42). The following illustrations show them

as they appear under the microscope, when viewed
by a one-inch objective.   The eye is a very beau-

Fig. 42.

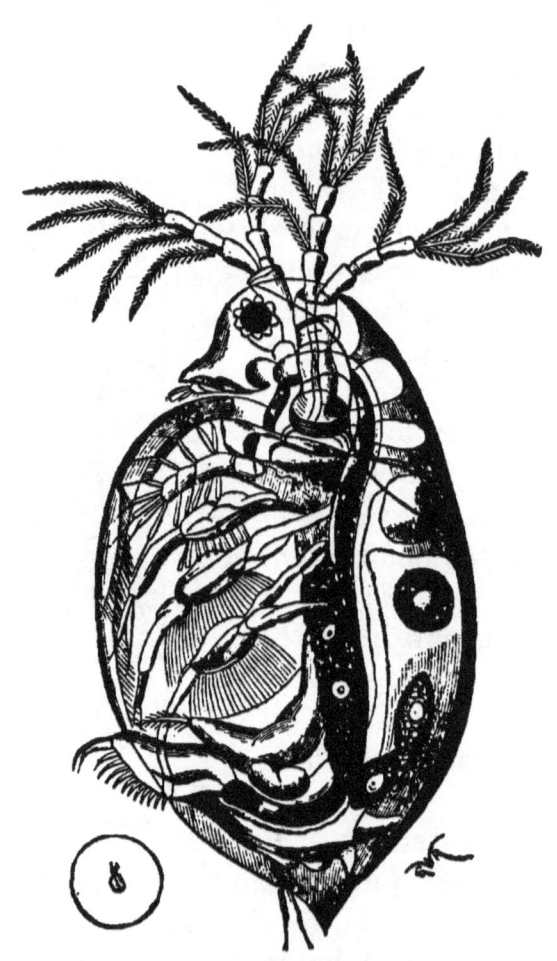

Daphnia pulex (female).

tiful object, having about twenty lenses, whilst
the mouth is seen to possess really a complicated

apparatus. Where there is duck-weed growing on the surface of the water, there you may expect to find this species in particular, in the greatest abundance. The females are much commoner than the males, and may be found throughout the year;

Fig. 43.

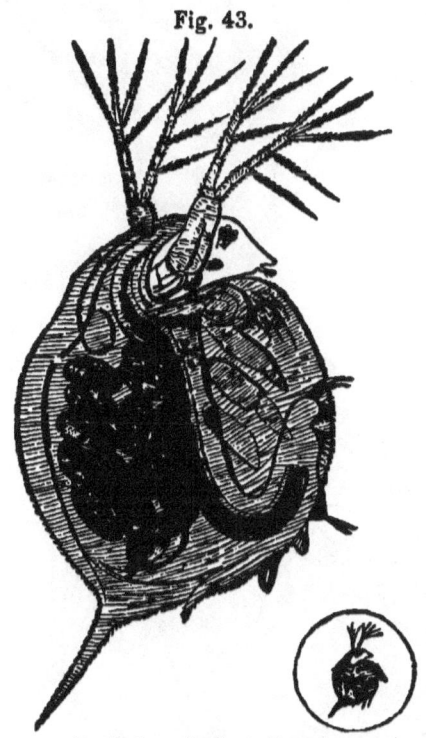

Daphnia schœfferi (female).

whilst the males are generally only to be obtained in the autumn months. Dr. Baird enumerates seven British species of water-fleas, of which *D. schœfferi* is perhaps most common, next to *D. pulex*. It may be readily known from the latter by its

E

greater size, although its eyes are smaller in comparison. Another species, common about London, is *D. vetula* (Fig. 44), or the "spineless" water-flea, so

Fig. 44.

Daphnia vetula (female).

called on account of its not having the spine at the end of the body, which is so distinctly seen in the aforementioned species. Two other species, *D. reti-*

culata and *D. mucronata* (Figs. 45, 46), complete
our present list. The latter has been also found
in the neighbourhood of London, but neither is so
common as those first referred to.

The *Cyclops*, although frequently very abundant
in old tarns, is a very different object to the water-
fleas, though belonging to the same natural history
group. You may find it in such spots as that we
have been investigating, about June or July. When

Fig. 45.   Fig. 46.

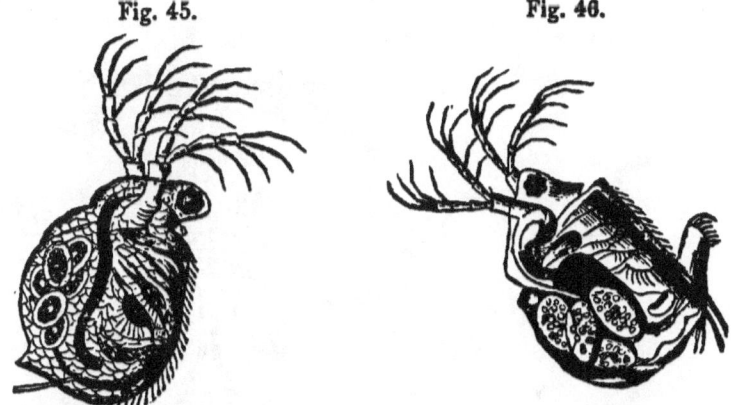

Daphnia reticulata (female).   *Daphnia mucronata* (female).

magnified, you see that its name is not badly obtained, for it is a miniature, as far as its sight is
concerned, of those fabulous one-eyed monsters of
Greek mythology, employed by Vulcan to forge the
thunderbolts of Jove. Its form is elegant, and is
clad in a transparent horny shell, composed of many
pieces dovetailed and jointed together like a piece of
ancient armour. In the common species, *Cyclops
quadricornis*, this covering consists of ten plates or

segments, four of which encase the head and thorax
in such a manner that no division is perceptible
between these two parts of the body.   The re-
mainder of the segments are devoted to the protection of the abdomen, &c.   This horny shell-
covering answers a double purpose.   It protects the
soft and seemingly gelatinous body from injury, and
also serves as an external skeleton for the attachment of the various muscles and articulations.   It is

Fig. 47.   Fig. 48.   Fig. 49.

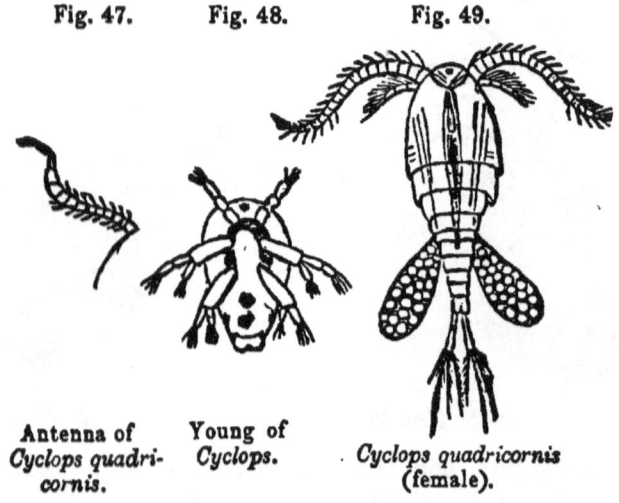

Antenna of   Young of
Cyclops quadri-   Cyclops.   Cyclops quadricornis
cornis.   (female).

in the first and largest of the segments of the
armour that the solitary eye is placed, which has
earned for the creature the name of *Cyclops*.   The
antennæ are double, and are placed on either side
the eye; hence the specific name of *quadricornis*.
In the female, the largest pair of antennæ are longer
and more tapering than in the male, and are as

transparent as if they had been made out of spun glass. Those of the males are thicker and shorter, swelling towards the tips. By means of the antennæ, therefore, the student will not find it difficult to distinguish the sexes (Fig. 47). In its progress through the water, the cyclops moves with a rapid jerking motion, which may be best seen in an aquarium, when it is between the eye and the light. Its principal propelling organs are five pairs of oar-like feet ; each foot consists of a common stem, from which spring two jointed branches, liberally supplied with short, bristly appendages, called *setæ*. The female cyclops may, in July, be further distinguished from the male by its external ovaries, which hang suspended from either side the end of the body like bunches of grapes (Fig. 49). So abundantly do these creatures multiply, if left undisturbed, that it has been calculated one female, in the course of a year, would become the progenitor of nearly four millions and a quarter of young ! Nothing can be more unlike the parent cyclops than the young, as may be seen by Fig. 48; and indeed, for a long time it was classed by naturalists as a distinct genus. It is only by repeated moulting that it eventually attains the parental resemblance. The water-fleas and cyclops are, without doubt, the staple food, not only of fishes, but of other aquatic creatures as well —an end for which their marvellous powers of reproduction remarkably fit them.

In such places as these tarns, it will be next to

Fig. 50.

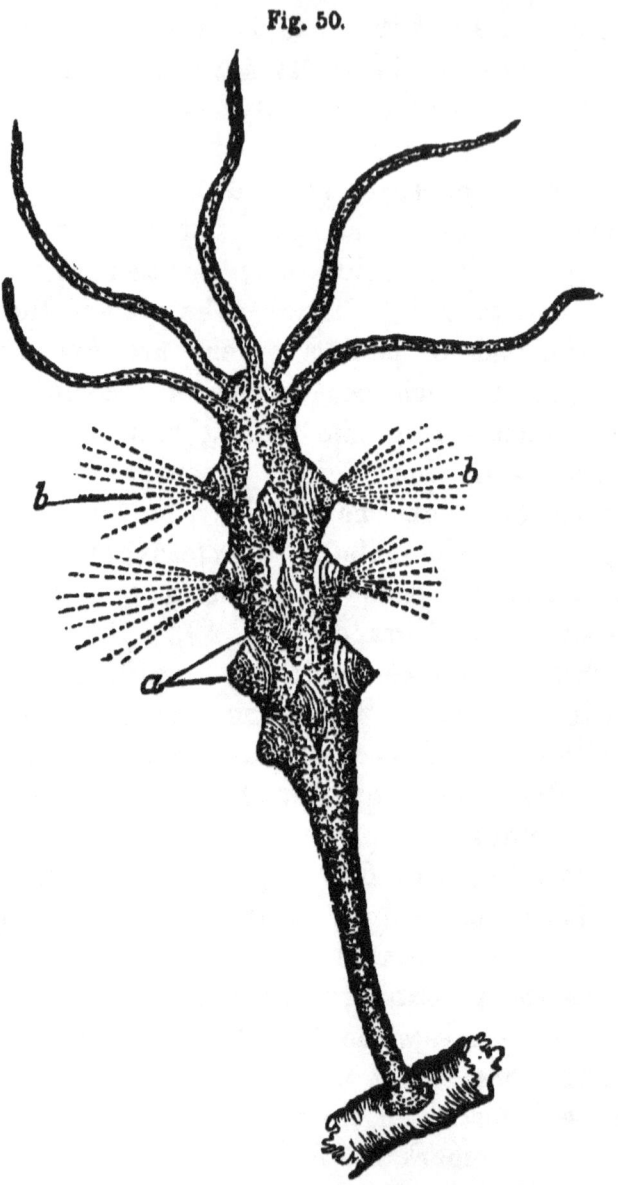

Hydra (magnified), showing prominences *a*, and *b* eruptions, whence Spermatozoa are disseminated.

impossible for you to pull out an aquatic plant without finding one, if not two species of that interesting little zoophyte, the Hydra. As an object for the aquarium it is unequalled, for there you may more distinctly see it, and watch its daily life, which is full of interest. Some of our readers may be

Fig. 51.

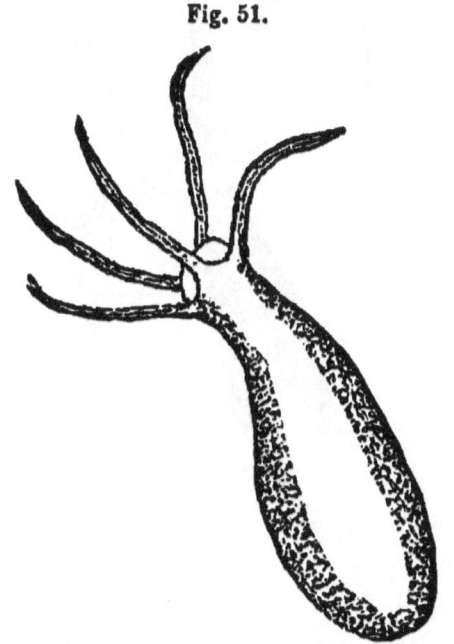

Second stage (magnified) in development of Hydra.

acquainted with the experiments of Trembly on this creature, than which none ever more fully proved the tenacity of its life. He found that by turning the polyp inside out, as you would the finger of a glove, no harm was done, but that the hydra seemed quite as able to digest with its new stomach as with its

old one! Cutting a hydra to pieces not only did it
no injury, but actually conferred a benefit, for each
fragment budded into a distinct animal!   Lately,

Fig. 52.

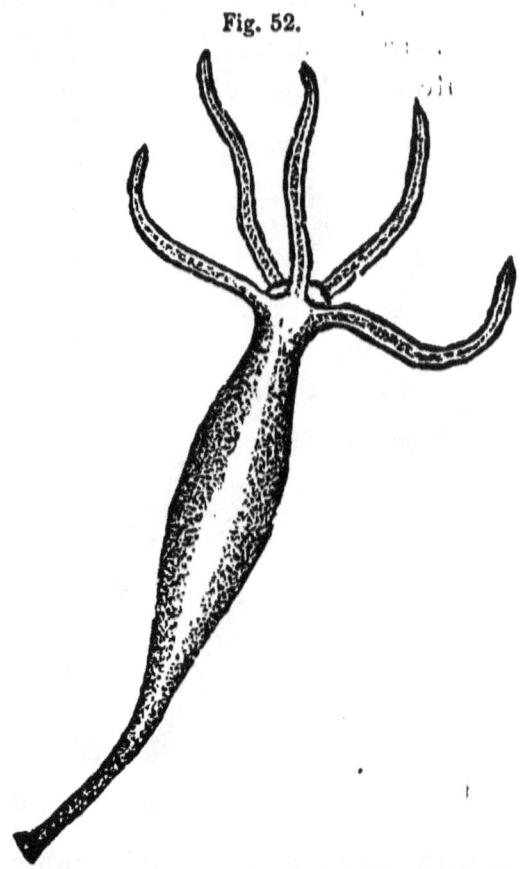

Development of Foot-stalk of Hydra, magnified.

few men have devoted so much attention to our
English hydras as Mr. James Fullagar, of Canter-
bury. That gentleman has kept hydras for years,
and his observations upon them are very interesting.

He noticed that, in winter, many specimens of *Hydra
vulgaris* were studded with little round, white lumps.
These burst, and extruded spermatozoa, as seen in

Fig. 53.

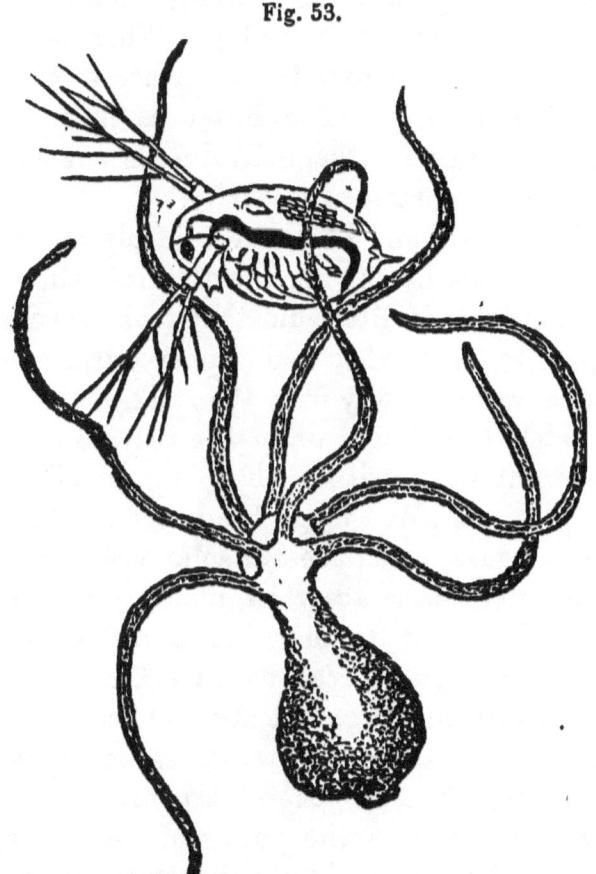

Hydra attacking Water-flea, magnified.

Fig. 50, *b*. The sperm cells and the ovi-sacs are found
in the same polyp, and the ovum sinks to the bottom
of the water and lies hidden in the mud. It is from

this ovum that a new hydra will be evolved in the following spring. The first stage in the development of a new hydra, from an egg, is very curious. When first observed they are mere minute rounded lumps of jelly, with starlike tenacles. When more advanced, the rounded part is lengthened into a small foot-stalk (Fig. 52). The latter is still further lengthened, and now the individual is supposed to have arrived at a state of maturity.

Mr. Fullagar found he could multiply the hydras in his aquarium by cutting them up into slips as he would plants! So little did they seem to suffer by this process that when the upper surface of an individual was cut away from the stalk, the tentacles immediately seized on a water-flea that happened to come incautiously within their reach (Fig. 53). Much more complex though the latter creatures are than the hydra, when the tentacles close over them and the water-flea is absorbed, it has to give up the ghost, and submit to have its animal substances digested. The little green hydra (*H. viridis*), also to be met with, although not always so commonly, in the same places as the *vulgaris*, does not appear to differ in its habits or general organization. Both species seem to have the power of benumbing or paralysing the living objects that come in contact with their tentacles, in a similar manner to that possessed by sea-anemones. Mr. Fullagar discovered that this stinging power was due to the presence of certain fine threads contained in the numerous tubercles with which the tentacles are thickly beset. These are called " urticating threads," and the animal seems to have the power of thrusting them forth at pleasure. By pressing the tentacles of a hydra between two pieces of glass, Mr. Fullagar forced these nettling or "urticating" threads out. The tentacles are rendered very powerful weapons of retention by means of the three recurved hooklets attached to them. Myriads of these arrow-headed stings are crowded on the tentacles, and yet the full grown size of the little hydras rarely exceeds a quarter of an inch !

One can hardly wonder at the revolution which has taken place in natural science within the last fifteen years, when we consider how that wonderful instrument, the microscope, has opened our eyes upon the fulness of the animal kingdom. Even to glance at the multitudinous objects which this tarn could afford—at the Algæ which mantle its shallower surface, or the *Desmids* which might be skimmed off its mud—would occupy a little volume. The latter are among the most elegant of natural forms, and their ornamentations might be studied for the arts with considerable profit. Perhaps on the same leaves or stalks of water plants as those where you secured the hydras, your sharp and trained eyes may detect those even more wonderful, because more highly organized creatures, the Rotifers, or "wheel animalcules." Many of the wheel animalcules, however, are free swimming, active little animals, others being permanently fixed, as the "crown-animalcules." The male and female differ from each other, the males being generally smaller than the females. Indeed the former have a briefer life altogether, as well as a less complex organization. Their chief duty seems to be the fertilization of the females, and that accomplished, their right to existence is gone. All the wheel-animalcules belong to the *annuloida*, and in many of them there is a distinct ringed appearance. Their organization is relatively high. They possess a nervous system, a distinct alimentary canal, mouth, and vent. Their common name is derived from the anterior disk, which is fringed with cilia; when the latter is in rapid motion, it resembles the quick revolution of a wheel. The respiratory apparatus, ovaries, etc., of all these interesting creatures render them very interesting to microscopists. The cilia of the disks are in two or more sets. These wheel-animalcules have the power of stretching themselves out and retracting, like worms. Frequently their tail acts as a claw, and enables them to anchor themselves to aquatic leaves. The so-called "wheels" or ciliated disks, can be drawn in at the animal's pleasure. What renders the Rotifera most interesting to young microscopists, perhaps, is that, owing to the transparency of their bodies, you can see all the complicated arrangement of the digestive and other organs, and witness what is going on. The commonest species, and one which you are almost sure to find in

any standing water, is the *Rotifer vulgaris* (Fig. 54).
Some, of them, as the *Melicerta ringens*, and others,
surround their fixed bodies with a caddis-worm
like tube, made up of small pellets.

Fig. 54.

Rotifer vulgaris.

Perhaps the *Floscularia* is one of
the most beautiful of all the wheel-
animalcules. Like the rest, it is
usually to be found adhering to the
fresh-water plants. It has a gelatinous case, and is exceedingly transparent, so much so that unless the
eyes are sharp and to some degree
trained what to look for, you are apt
to pass it by. Frequently its presence may be known by a number
of minute algæ and other substances
attached to it. Its food consists
of small algæ, or rather of their
spores. When searching for them,
it stretches itself out of its case, and expands its
" wheel," or ciliated disk, which consists of a number
of long and delicate tentacles spread out in fan-like
form from the lobes which surround the mouth. In
the species figured (*F. cornuta*) there are five of these
lobes, as well as the so-called *horn* (*a*), whence the
specific name. You may notice, if you watch the
motions of this creature carefully under the microscope, the currents running into and out of the
mouth. The ova are usually deposited at the base
of the foot.

We have already referred to the Algæ—the green
scum that mantles every standing pool. Space,
however, only permits us to point out that in the
microscopical study of the humble forms of this
group there is a world of interest, engaging the
attention of some of our best men of science. For
it will only be by familiarising ourselves thoroughly
with the nature and organisation of these lowly
forms, both animal and vegetable, that we shall
ever be able to rise to a thorough understanding of
those complex organisations which distinguish the
highest organisms.

The Volvox (Fig. 56) has been, in its time, bandied
about from the animal to the vegetable kingdom,
until its real nature was known. It is now set
down as one of the confervoid algæ, and, although
only just visible to the naked eye, it may be found
in such a tarn as that whose chief contents we have
been endeavouring to describe. In the aquarium, it
may be observed rolling through the water in pretty
much the same manner that a balloon makes its way
across the sky on a still day. Only a low optical
power is required, to convince the young naturalist
that he has in the volvox one of the prettiest objects
it is possible to imagine. It is a globe of the
most delicate green colour formed of a transparent
membrane, which is marked with a net-work of
fine lines, ornamented with darker green spots just
where the lines cross. What is most singular is
the manner in which the volvoces reproduce them-

Fig. 55.

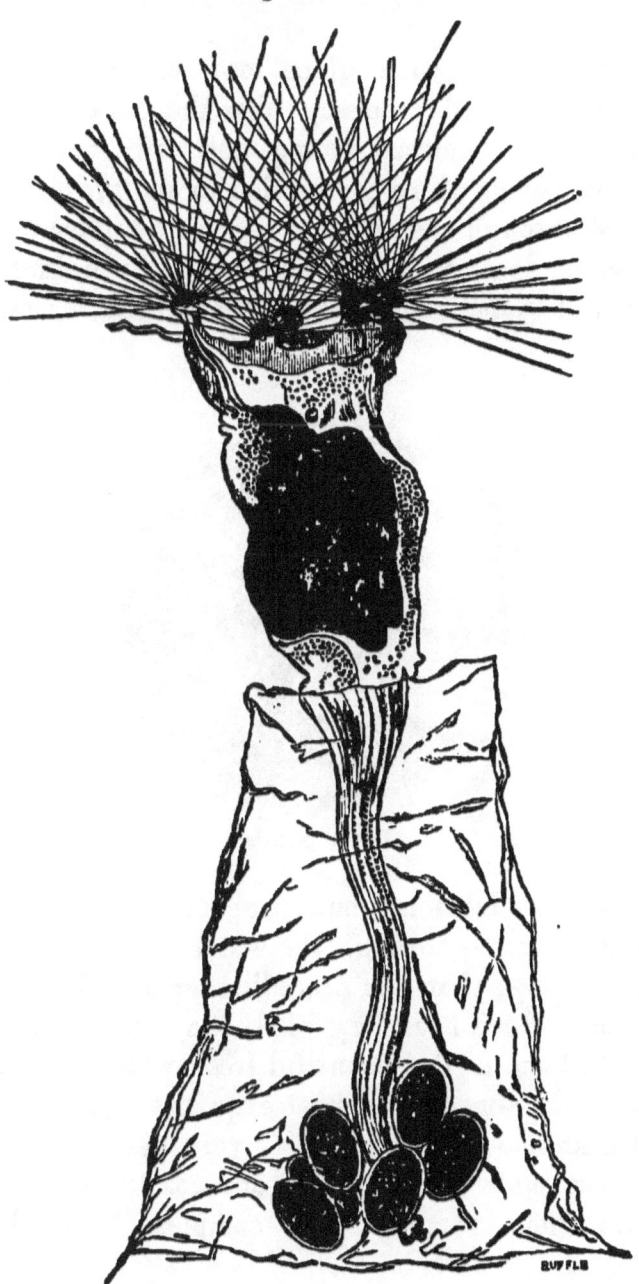

Floscularia cornuta, magnified.

selves. Within each globe may be seen smaller
globes, fashioned precisely like the parent. Even
within these enclosed young, not unfrequently you
may perceive a third generation in embryo! When
viewed through the microscope with a higher power,
the green spots seen at the crossing of the lines, are
made out to be bunches of delicate hairs, by means

Fig. 56.

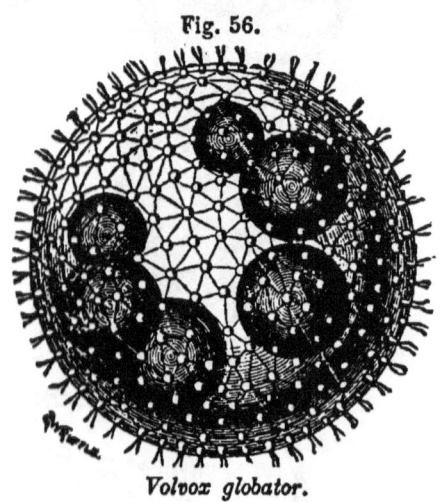

Volvox globator.

of which, it is more than probable, the volvox is
enabled to move through the water.

Much rarer than the preceding aquatic forms, but
a species which it is very likely may be met with in
our old tarn, is the beautiful fresh-water polyzoon,
Plumatella—one of the most exquisite objects in the
entire animal creation. It is very nearly allied to
the "sea mats" (*Flustra*) of our coasts, so that its
organisation is really very complex, being little

lower than that of the mollusca, to which they are in many respects related. In Fig 57 is a colony of these creatures, attached to the stem of the common water crow-foot, as seen by an ordinary pocket-lens. The mouth is surrounded by numerous tentacles, which sweep the water actively in search of food. The organ bearing these is technically called the *lophophore,* or "crest-bearer," and it is generally of a horse-shoe shape. It is difficult to give an adequate idea of this beautiful object by means of a woodcut. The play of the cilia, the whirl of particles towards the mouth, together with the ever - shifting and

Fig. 57.

Group of *Plumatella.*

F

graceful movements of the whole organ, and of each tentacle separately, must be seen to be thoroughly appreciated.

Fig. 58.

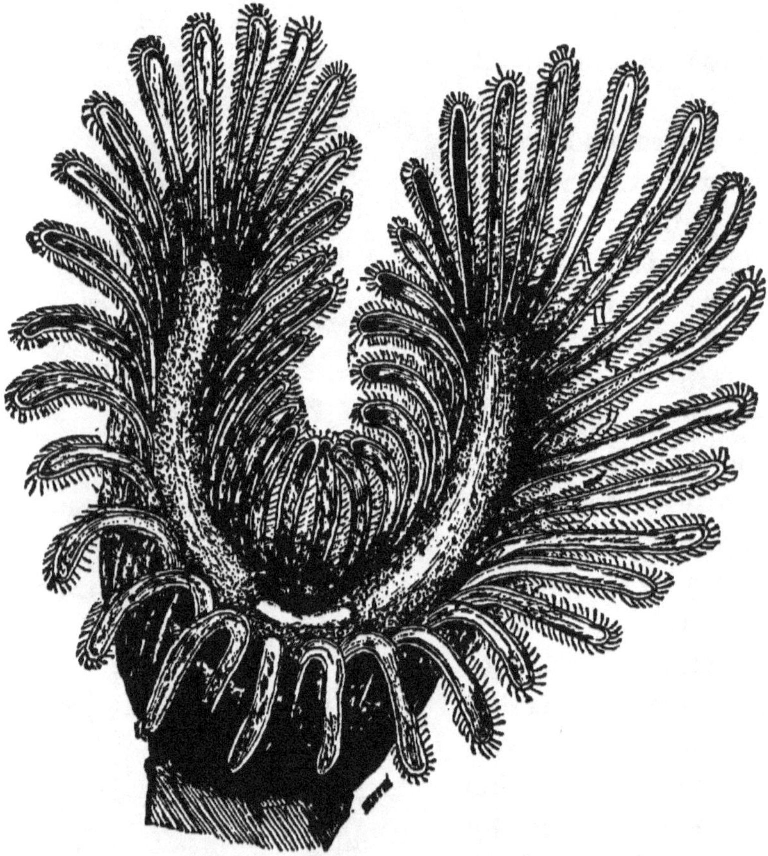

Lophophore of *Plumatella repens*, × 120.

And now we leave our young student, after having directed his attention to the principal objects of the tarn, to make his way for himself. Every new form identified will be to him a fresh source of pleasure; and such intimate knowledge of and acquaintance with the Creator's works cannot but exercise a chastening and subduing effect upon the mind. In after years, too, the naturalist will remember the outings which these studies necessitated as among the sunniest spots of his life, when dull cares fell off his shoulders, as Christian's burden did at the open sepulchre, and his mind was elevated and purified by a more intimate association with God's creatures.

CHAPTER III.

THE REPTILES IN THE TARN AND THE GREEN LANES.

BEFORE leaving the pond, let us devote a few minutes' attention to other of its occupants against which a good deal of foolish prejudice has been long entertained—foolish because ignorant. We allude to the reptiles which find a congenial home amid the aquatic weeds and other plants, and which, perhaps, have amazed you not a little when you were attempting the difficult task of angling in the few square inches of the clear surface. You observed your float bob under water at an angle of forty-five degrees, with a rapidity that caused you to clutch your rod convulsively, thinking that nothing less than a three-pound tench could have produced the commotion. What a feeling of disappointment, nay, of disgust, was yours, when you carefully "struck" your prey, and, on hauling it ashore, saw a poor little eft, that you durst not disengage, fastened on the hook! Many a time have we seen such disappointments revenged, and such captures disengaged, by the cruel process of pounding the latter under the heel.

It was formerly a common and general belief, and we have personally met with not a few instances of it, that many of the diseases incident to cattle resulted from the latter drinking water in ponds where efts were unusually abundant. Ancient superstitions linger longest among our agricultural populations, and, even when these have begun to doubt them, they still "survive" among the children. Hence the tales told by the latter, with feelings of breathless awe, pretty much represent the same narratives as repeated by their elders not many generations ago. We have a lively recollection of the way in which the poor efts or newts were regarded by our childish playmates. The common belief was that the toad could "spit fire," and the convulsive action of the throat, caused by these reptiles being obliged to swallow their air instead of breathing it, was sincerely regarded by us as a sign that the toad "was getting ready to spit!" On the other hand, it was equally an orthodox doctrine with us that the efts or "askers," as they are generally called in the north of England, could emit venom. With what feelings of awe did we regard the boy who was bold enough to handle one of these reptiles! Not even the Maltese looked with greater fear on St. Paul when he handled the viper. Equally, it was an unquestioned belief that the poor, elegant

blind-worm could "sting," and the forked tongue,
both in this reptile and the common snake, was put
down as the sting itself. We may smile at these
childish notions, but in our opinion there is a serious
side to them. These erroneous ideas, as we have
seen ourselves, were the means of inciting children
to stone frogs and toads to death, and to destroy
reptiles of every kind whenever met with. They
were thus the means of introducing innocent childhood to acts of cruelty and destruction, and of
forming habits which, in after life it may be, were
exercised upon other and higher objects than
reptiles.

The water newts occupy the lowest natural history
position among the reptiles. Professor Huxley
groups them along with fishes, under the name of
Ichthyopsida, or "fish-like," on account of their
possessing gills during the earlier periods of their
development and for other structural reasons. They
are generally comprehended under the class name of
Amphibia, in which they appear side by side with
our frogs and toads. The young of this group of
animals are familiar to us under the name of
tadpoles, in which stage they possess true gills,
fitted for breathing the air dissolved in water. In
all cases, however, true lungs are eventually developed, even in those genera where the gills are
retained through life. All the amphibia, too, pass
through some kind of metamorphosis after leaving
the egg. In the great majority of cases, they

commence life as water-breathing larvæ, when they are provided with gills; whilst in the adult state respiration is carried on by means of true lungs. The gills are generally external, and placed on the sides of the neck. Frogs and toads usually possess two sets of gills, one external and the other internal. The former, however, are the soonest lost. The true lungs of the amphibians never reach such a high stage of development as is to be found in the true reptiles.

Let us give precedence to size, and select the

Fig. 59.

The Great Water Newt (*Triton cristatus*).

Great Water Newt (*Triton cristatus*), for our first example. It is almost sure to be found in one of these old tarns, although it is not so common as the Smooth Newt. Its name would lead you, perhaps, to expect a larger-sized creature, for its length rarely exceeds six inches. It is very voracious, feeding on almost anything it can come across, even the smaller smooth newt having to serve as an occasional repast. The aquarium has done a great deal in English families towards familiarising the young with common natural history objects; and there can be little doubt that the knowledge thus

gained has greatly dispelled the ignorant prejudices
against them.   Among others, the newts have come
in for a share of observation, and very pretty, graceful objects do they look when in the aquarium.
The Great Water Newt is not such a favourite in
this respect perhaps, as the Smooth Newt, its rough
warty back having rather a repulsive appearance.
This is relieved, however, by the bright orange
colour of the belly.   The eggs of this species are
generally deposited early in April, and their deposition goes on till July.   Both by this species
and the Smooth Newt, the eggs are carefully and
skilfully enclosed in the leaves of aquatic plants.
Mr. Higginbottom states that if a plant with long
leaves be thrown into a pool where there are Tritons,
for only a single night during the breeding season,
it will be found on the following morning to have a
number of its leaves folded, and within each fold an
egg.   If everything goes on right, in a fortnight
the egg has so developed that it forces the folds of
the leaf open.   In three weeks, the embryo is fully
formed, and the young tadpole swims away, to feed
most voraciously, even on the tadpoles of the smooth
newt.   For three months the young are purely
aquatic, breathing by gills alone, and showing no
signs whatever of any legs sprouting.   After that
period, however, an important change sets in.   The
legs are formed, the fore-limbs first—this being the
reverse of the development of the young of frogs.
In proportion to the rapidity with which the legs

are formed the gills are absorbed, and thus their material so far goes to form the limbs. At length, just at the time when the legs are so far perfected as to enable the triton to leave the water, the gills have been lost altogether, there being no further use for them. No doubt, many of our readers have been puzzled at the various different appearances which the same species of triton presents. These

Figs. 60 and 61.

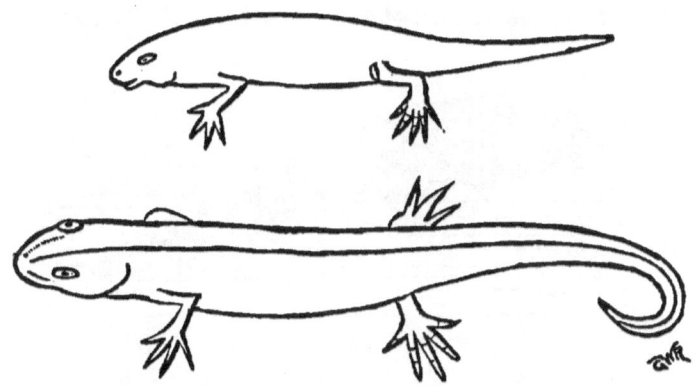

Great Water Newt, at end of first and second years.

are due to the fact that it takes three years to develop the newt to maturity, and the different stages of that period are represented by peculiar external appearances. Thus, at the end of the first year of its life, the triton is only two inches long, at the end of the second year, three inches, at the end of the third four, and at that of the fourth it will be found to have reached its greatest size, which is five or six inches. Not until the *breeding* season of the third year, does the crest along the

back begin to show itself. Then also, the tail
expands, and a permanent silver stripe appears
along each side. Mr. Higginbottom states that the
triton does not return to the water till the end of
the third year, when it begins the work of repro-
ducing its species. It then becomes extremely
voracious, and the male assumes its full crest,
which, however, only lasts three months, as it
disappears when the female has deposited the ova,
and both sexes then return to a terrestrial existence

Fig. 62.

Male of Smooth Newt.

until the following spring. During winter they
hybernate, generally in some damp spot, where
scores may sometimes be found rolled together into
a ball. At this period, respiration is very low, and
is carried on by the external surface of the skin.
No food is taken, as none is required; extra tissue
having been laid up against this emergency.

The common Smooth Newt is that which is
generally known as the "Eft" (*Lissotriton punc-
tatus*), with us it is by far the commonest of its
kind. Its skin is smooth, and thus it may always

be distinguished even from the juvenile stages of
the Great or Warty Newt. Beneath the throat is a
kind of collar, and the male, during the breeding
season, has a beautiful
continuous crest, run-
ning from the top of the
head to the tail. This
crest is regularly fes-
tooned along its edge.
The upper parts of the
smooth eft are of a light-
brownish grey, inclining
to olive ; whilst the under
parts are of a yellow,
and, in the spring, of
an orange colour. Both
sexes are spotted, the
male most. The entire
length of this species,
even at the adult stage,
never exceeds four inches.
Like the great water
newt, this species pre-
sents different appear-
ances during the various
stages of its career from

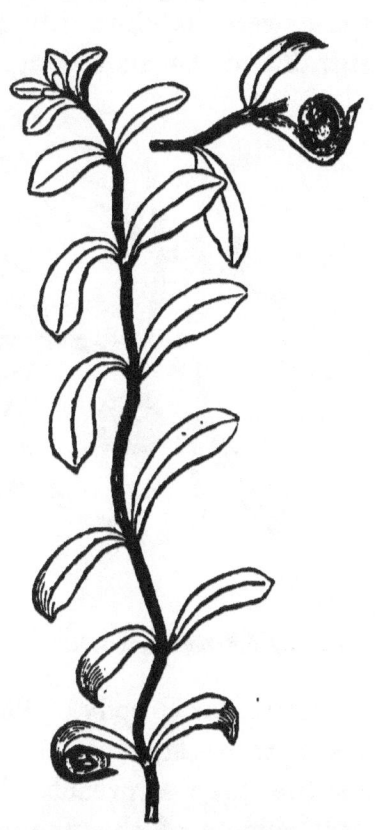

Fig. 63.

Callitriche verna, with leaves containing Ova of Newt.

the ex-tadpole state to that of full maturity. Mr.
Robson of Elswick, has carefully watched the larval
stages of this species, and made the results of
his observations known in two capital papers con-

tributed to 'Science Gossip' in 1872. Its eggs were
deposited in the folds of the *Callitriche verna*,
similar in manner to that already described in the
preceding species. In thirteen or fourteen days,
these were hatched, the larvæ being about three-
eighths of an inch long, with large eyes, and an

Fig. 64.

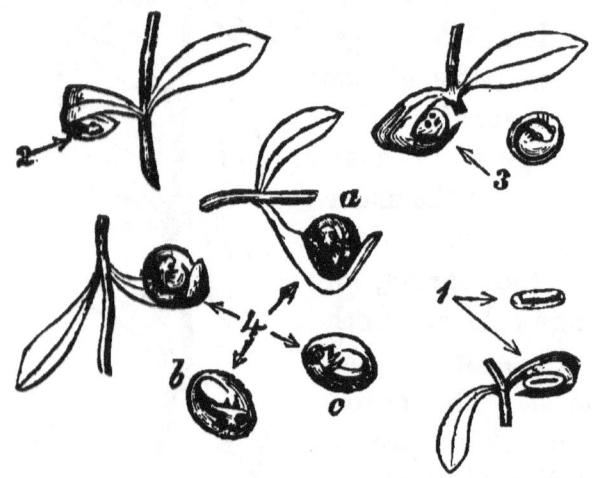

Showing different stages in Development of Ova, from 1 to 4, &c.

amber coloured body. The breathing organs (gills)
are now so transparent as to be scarcely visible.
As the eggs approach the time of hatching, the
development of the young tadpole within is plainly
visible, even to its changing its position, until it
bursts the egg with its minute head.

It is of this species that the tales are so common
regarding its venomous character. We need not
stop to refer to them further, as our readers must

have come across them at one time or another. Still
less need is there to contradict them, or to show the
fallacy of believing that one of the most harmless of
God's creatures can in any way be connected with
evils like those recorded to have been produced by
it. Both male and female newts cast their skins
frequently, and these, in the aquarium, may be seen

Fig. 65.

Female of Smooth Newt.

settling at the bottom. By dint of a little care the
exuvium may be collected, by floating it over a
glass slip, and allowing it to dry. It will then be
seen to be a perfect envelope, having been moulted
from every part.

The Smooth Newt soon gets accustomed to the
aquarium. We have kept
them, and bred from them;
and remember how they
became accustomed to our
tap on the glass front of
the aquarium, which tap

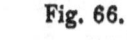

Fig. 66.

Tadpole of Newt.

had became associated in their experience with
small bits of beef or worms, with which we fed them.
The tadpoles of this newt are very bright, cheerful
objects, and the aquarium soon looks lively with
their constant and graceful movements.

In some of our old tarns there is met with yet another species of British newt, called Palmate (*Lophinus palmatus*). Its distribution is isolated, although it appears to be chiefly southern. It has been found in the neighbourhood of Edinburgh, Bridgewater, Dartmoor, Hereford, &c. It is the most beautiful of its kind, having, in the male, a straight crest. The body is beautifully marbled with olive-grey and white. Only the hind feet are palmate—hence the name of the species. The female is usually much paler than the male, and differs from it so much, especially in the spring, that it has been thought another species. It should be stated that, when keeping newts in an aquarium, if the cast-off skin is wanted for preservation, care should be taken to secure it soon after it has been sloughed, otherwise its former possessor will surely make a meal of it!

The frogs and toads resemble the newts, especially in their larval stage, in many particulars. But there is no doubt their general organisation is higher. Like the palmate newt, the hind limbs are generally webbed. In the frogs, the skin is an active agent in the work of respiration, although the lungs are pretty well developed. As there are no ribs by which the cavity of the chest can be expanded, the air is taken into the lungs by a process that very much resembles swallowing. The spawn or ova, both of frogs and toads, is familiar to all country people. It is deposited in masses or strings, the former about March, about the roots of plants, or rotting weeds, and this too in enormous quantities. The geographical distribution of the common frog is as remarkable as its exceeding commonness. It is widely spread over Europe, from north to south, except, perhaps, Ireland, where it does not appear to have been naturalised until about one hundred and fifty years ago. It is now more or less common in that country—a fact this, which

Fig. 67.

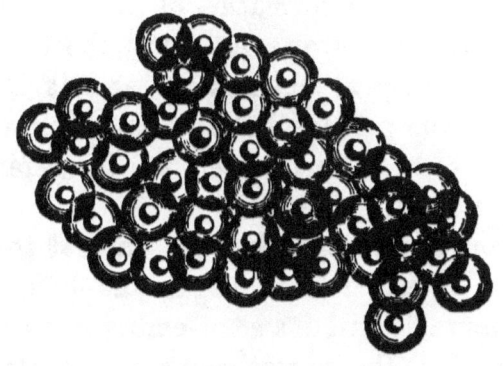

Spawn of Frog.

proves that Ireland is not unadapted to it, and that the reason the frog does not occur there indigenously, is due to certain physical disturbances which took place before it had been dispersed so far to the west. The late Professor Edward Forbes worked out the theory of the distribution of reptiles in the British islands in a most remarkable manner. As every one knows, they are not so abundant in Ireland as they are in England, and popular tradition, in endeavouring to explain such a notable fact, has done so by making Saint Patrick banish them from the Green Isle! But England, in a similiar manner, has not so many indigenous species of reptiles as the adjacent continent. Professor Forbes showed that the cause of this paucity of species in a westerly direction is due to the physical disturbance which separated England from the continent, and Ireland from England, before the thorough distribution had been carried on to the latter country. It is certain that the formation of the German Ocean and the Irish Sea are among the most recent of important geological phenomena, and it is equally certain that the present distribution of animals and plants can only be accounted for by reference to phenomena of this kind.

Professor Quatrefages has shown that the young Frog, after it has left the egg, and before it has become a larva, is still in a semi-embryonic condition. At this period, the digestive tube and its appendages are very rudimentary. The greater portion of the body is filled by a large mass of yolk, enclosed by the skin, and the development of the larval frog proceeds by the absorption of this alimentary matter. The young tadpole of the frog at first exhibits no trace whatever of limbs. It swims about like a fish by the action of its tail, which is a most important and extensive organ, longer and wider than the body, supported by a prolongation of the vertebral column, and moved by powerful muscles. Shortly afterwards, however, two little projections appear beneath the skin and muscles of the front and hind parts. These increase in size, are supplied with nerves and veins, and presently the shoulder and hip-bones are developed. The tail now disappears, being no longer required, but in its gradual disappearance it has not been useless, for it has been absorbed, and thus its substance converted into the now more important organs. With the tail also disappear the gills, for the true lungs have been developed meantime, so that by the period when the legs enable the creature to quit the water, the substitution of lungs for gills also enables it to breathe the atmosphere.

The frog tadpoles are deadfully voracious, and are confirmed cannibals. No sooner does one die than a hundred come to the funeral, and give it a decent interment in their stomachs! Nay, let one appear sickly, and it will be the signal for the rest to worry it into the desirable condition of food! The dense green scum, or confervoid vegetation which mantles the surface of the stagnant tarn, appears to be the legitimate food of the young tadpoles, but the adult frog itself is insectivorous. According to Mr. M. C. Cooke, its favourite food consists of minute insects, such as green plant-lice, other and larger insects, small slugs, &c. He goes on to say, "This habit ought to procure for frogs, not only the protection, but the fostering care of gardeners and all cultivators of the soil. How much less cause would they

G

have to complain of insect enemies, if they would but exercise more care in the preservation and increase of toads and frogs; and establish on their own domains a kind of 'local game law,' instead of winking at the persecution, if not really encouraging the extirpation, of their best friends!" We distinctly remember favouring the frog above the toad, in own boyish days. We knew nothing of its insect-destroying benefits, but it was an article of faith with us that, " frogs made the water clean !"

In the winter time, the frog, like other of our indigenous reptiles, hybernates in holes, &c., to be revived by the warmth of the ensuing spring. Not unfrequently, when the hybernating period is drawing on, they get into queer holes—into crevices of trees or rocks, or down deserted coal shafts. Should they get into some of the crevices which are afterwards filled up, either by infiltration or by the rocks closing, then they may be come across as " frogs in the solid rocks," to furnish wonderful paragraphs for country newspapers! For we may dismiss at once the idea about these or any other reptiles having been preserved *alive* since the rocks were formed. Experiments have proved that hybernating frogs are not able to live in such masses as plaster of Paris more than twenty years. We know that however slowly a fire burns, it *will burn out* in time if no fresh fuel be added. And, as these imprisoned frogs are slowly absorbing their own tissues even when hybernating, and there is no possibility of obtaining fresh food to supply the waste, death must ensue in a greater or less time. Hence when *living* frogs are found in rock fissures, we may safely conclude that they cannot have been there many years, even if they have been there so long.

Our common British frog is not the same species as is eaten in France, although we long believed that it was. The latter is the Edible Frog (*Rana esculenta*), and is rather rare with us; not absent,

Fig. 68.

Head of Edible Frog.

as some naturalists have supposed. Nay, we have actually introduced it into British gastronomy, and frog's legs may be bought in tins whenever the reader should feel inclined to experiment on a new article of food. The edible frog, in its choice of habitat, nearly resembles its commoner relative. It is not difficult to identify by its greater size, its triangular shaped head and prominent eyes. The body, in some respects, partakes of the character of the toad, in being covered with a series of scattered warts. Its colour is generally of a greenish tint, and its length about three inches. The hind legs are the parts selected for food, and these are said, when stewed, to taste like the flesh of young rabbits. The edible frog occurs in Norfolk, but there is reason to believe it has been introduced there. In the fen districts of Cambridgeshire, however, it seems to be indigenous, but rare. During summer evenings, it is almost certain to make its whereabouts known, by its much louder and more musical note than that of the common frog. This louder note is produced by certain vocal sacs or bladders, placed near the angle of the mouth. Out of the nine species of frog found on the Continent, only two are met with in great Britain; whilst out of the three species of European toads, two are natives of this country. It will be seen, therefore, that Professor Edward Forbes' view is not without strong evidence in its favour.

Our Common Toad needs no description. We are sorry that prejudiced ignorance continues to impute to it so much power of inflicting injuries, for this poor reptile is regarded, in consequence, as a sort of zoological pariah, to be shunned, stoned, or killed whenever found. It is the type of the ugly and the foul, and our literature continues to hand down and cherish this ignorant idea about the "bloated toad!" All there is harmful about this poor beast is the secretion of the skin, which is acid, and evidently protective. Many a young and playful puppy that has endeavoured to carry a toad in its mouth has found out the properties of this secretion to its cost, and the foaming at its mouth has plainly indicated its disagreeable nature. But, to the dog's master,

this was only another proof of the venomous character of the reptile, and an additional reason why it
should be destroyed! This "toad's envenom'd
juice" has long been known to the ancients as well
to the moderns.

And yet, this common object is far more intelligent
than many of its congeners. It is easily tamed and
domesticated, as is also the Natterjack (*Bufo
calamita*). We kept a pair of the latter a long time,
and they seemed quite to know their keeper and
their home. By means of its long folded tongue
the toad is very quick at catching insects, and so far
is a most useful aid to a careful gardener. We are
very glad to notice that the custom of keeping tame
toads in gardens and hot houses is increasing, and
we have never inquired as to the result without
finding the gardeners full of praise of the working
qualities of their reptilian assistants, and possessed
of a fund of anecdotal information respecting their
habits. You may always know, when the seemingly impassive toad is on the alert. The sure
sign is a curious twitching movement of the hind
toes. As is well known, toads are in the habit of
moulting their skins, but it may not be so generally
imagined that this cast off coat is turned to practical
use by the toad eating it! Just before moulting,
the toad may be seen rubbing and pressing against
its sides with its feet. The skin then begins to
burst open along the back, the toad meantime
rubbing away until the loose skin is gathered into

folds along the sides and hips. Then, grasping one hind leg with both the front ones, it draws the skin off as if it were a pair of stockings. The skin on the other leg follows in a similar manner, and so, in short, does the rest of the loose skin. When all this is finished the toad makes a hearty meal of it.

As Mr. Cooke remarks ('British Reptiles'), the toad is much more terrestrial in its habits than the frog. Like the latter, its ova are deposited in water, and its larva are tadpoles, and therefore fitted for an aquatic life. "Toad rudd" or "spawn" may be known from the ova of frogs by its being arranged in double chains, and not deposited in a mass. The natterjack toad deposits its spawn in a similar manner, and its young also assume the tadpole form —a common feature of the amphibia. Calculations have been made to show the wondrous fertility of the toads, and it has been computed that the female natterjack does not lay less than nineteen thousand eggs! It is well such is the case, and, as you may see in the shallower parts of the tarn, nothing less than an enormous fertility could develop such hosts of tadpoles, for the water is perfectly thick and black with them! But think of the enemies to which they are subject, and how many of them! The fierce larva of the dragon-fly, of the great water beetle, the boat-flies, newts, fishes, sticklebacks, &c.— the tadpole has all these to withstand; and the chief defence of the species, if not of the individuals, is that it brings forth such a numerous offspring!

The Natterjack, or "yellow-back," as it is sometimes called, is very unlike the common toad in
many respects. Its distribution is not so extensive,
but where it does occur, it often does so plentifully.
The eyes in this species are more projecting, and the
line of bright yellow running down the middle of
the back, is not only a good means of identification,
but shows the origin of its common name. Its
chief peculiarity is the rapid manner with which it
can run, almost like a mouse. Not less surprising is its climbing powers, for it can surmount
anything that comes across its path. When suddenly
found, it has a knack of shamming death—a
trick very common among the lower animals. In
some parts of England, the natterjack is distinguished by the country people from the common
species, by the well-earned name of the "Walking
toad." Mr. Cooke thinks that the name "natterjack," is derived from the Anglo-Saxon *naedre*,
"nether," or "lower," (in allusion to the creeping
habit of reptiles) and "jack," from *jager*, "one
who runs."

The development of the higher amphibia, among
which our frogs and toads rank, furnishes a good
illustration of embryology. It is a known fact that
the early or embryonic stages of the higher members
of the same group of animals is frequently represented by the *permanent* condition of the lower.
This is exemplified among the objects we have been
considering, for the transitory stages of a young

frog or toad, in which, as a tadpole, it breathes by
gills, and has a fishlike tail instead of limbs, is
permanently represented by the perennibranchiate
reptile, the *Proteus*.   Again, in higher order, the
next stage in the life-history of the frog, when the
external gills have disappeared, but when the tail
is still present, is permanently represented by the
adult condition of the various species of newts.
Such, also, seems to have been the rule which re-
gulated this class of reptiles in their appearance on
the stage of existence in the various geological
epochs.   The first reptiles were amphibians, of
marine habits, much resembling the newts, or
possibly the *Proteus*, only much larger.   This, as the
Archægosaurus, swarmed in the early Carboniferous
seas.   Next came the labyrinthodont frog-like animals
(Batrachians), to which all the carboniferous reptiles
even of the later period belong, with the exception,
perhaps, of a species of tree lizard.   During the
Triassic epoch, gigantic Batrachians abounded, and
assumed that external, tailless appearances peculiar
to our frogs and toads.   Lastly, it was later on that
the higher forms of reptiles appeared, and as the
Secondary ages passed away, the principal zoological
feature was their differentiation so as to people the
seas, oceans, rivers, lakes, swamps, the dry land, and
even the air, with their various forms !

Let us now quit for a while the bank of the tarn
on which we have been so long engaged, and seek
for other objects, most of which will be found in

the green lanes. There we may meet with many allied, in some respects, to the newts. In the dry spots we may find the viper, one or two species of lizards, the blind-worm, &c; whilst in the moister places, a careful examination will almost certainly enable us to come across the common snake. These old lanes, unaltered for centuries, with areas leading into adjacent fields, where the manure heaps are lying, are just the places for our indigenous land reptiles. Or, if they be not, a stretch of a few hundred yards to an adjacent heath will enable us there to find them.

The true reptiles and birds have been separately grouped by Professor Huxley under the name of *Sauropsida*, in allusion to the many anatomical and other resemblances reptiles have to birds, in spite of their dissimilar external forms. Among these we may reckon the following : The true reptiles never, at any stage of their existence, possess gills, as do the amphibia. The red corpuscles of their blood are nucleated; the skull is articulated to the vertebral column by a single condyle ; each half of the lower jaw has several pieces, and is attached to the skull by means of a special bone termed the "quadrate bone." When we have got thus far, however, we are obliged in our study of recent forms, to stop. But the geological series supplies us with many intermediate forms between groups so unlike as birds and reptiles. On the one hand, such genera as the *Archaeopteryx* of the Oolitic period, and the *Ichthyornis* of the Creta ceous, afford us illustration of true birds with reptilian affinities. The former had a long tail, like a lizard, feathered to the tip; and other reptilian characters —the latter had bi-concave vertebræ, a reptilian tail, and mandibles in which teeth were implanted. The fossil reptiles, on their side, afford us species having a similar leaning towards birds. The *Pterodactyles*, or flying lizards, of the secondary rocks in many respects present us with ornithic features, The *Campsognathus* was another ornithic reptile that walked on two legs. So that it would seem as if the gulf of separation between the birds and the reptiles was not so wide as we have been in the habit of hastily supposing.

Our British snakes are neither numerous nor very harmful. The very name is a terror to most people, and as Mr. Cooke remarks, "very few possess courage enough to attempt staring one out of countenance." The reason of the peculiar stony glare of snakes' eyes is due to their not possessing eyelids. Eyelids are not required, for the simple reason that the outer layer of the skin is stretched like a film over the eyes. Hence their power of gazing so fixedly, and without winking. When snakes shed their skins, this part over the eyes is shed along with the rest, and that, perhaps, is the only time when a snake really winks. The commonest species with us, and in fact, in Europe, is the Ringed Snake (*Tropidonotus natrix*). It is absent from Ireland, for the geological reasons already adduced. Not only is the common snake perfectly harmless—much as you may have shuddered when you unexpectedly disturbed it, perhaps whilst botanizing —but it is capable of being tamed to a considerable degree. The Rev. J. C. Wood mentions boys at a certain school, each of whom had his pet snake.

Fig. 69.

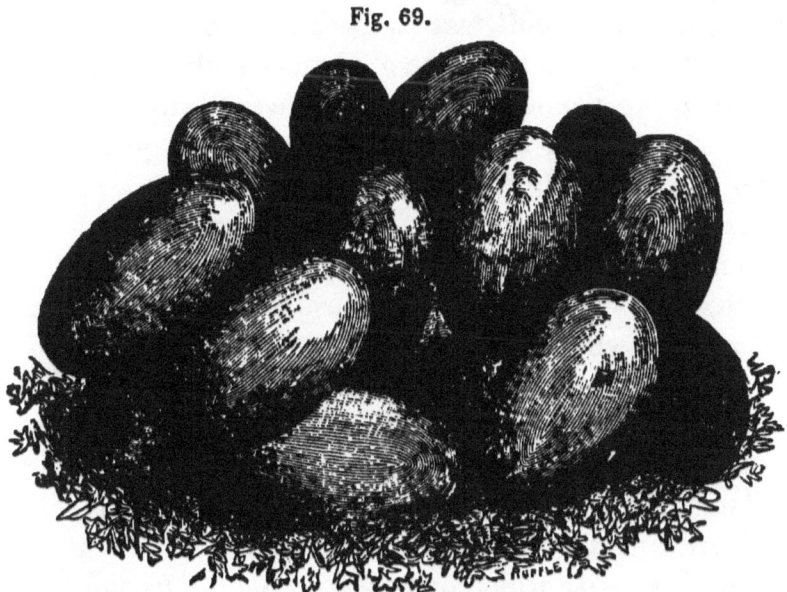

Eggs of Common Snake.

Indeed, anecdotes of the harmless snakes are to be found in plenty. Like nearly all reptiles, this species brings forth its young in the egg. It usually lays from sixteen to twenty, and fastens them together by a glutinous secretion. A dunghill is a favourite spot for their deposition, and we have seen old heaps of stable manure in which hundreds of snakes' eggs

had been laid. After hatching, the female snake
appears as if she had done all she could for her
future progeny, and therefore she does not trouble
herself any further about them. Snakes are not
unfrequently kept in ferneries, and very pretty do
they look under such conditions. . Their food is young
frogs, young birds, eggs, mice, etc., but unless hungry, it is a difficult task to force them to eat. Even
if you cram the frog down a snake's throat, it will
cast it up again, and the unpleasant odour which
all snakes give off when displeased, tells you it is
no good going on with your attempt. When in the
act of swallowing, say a frog, a snake turns it
round much in the same way that a pike does a
fish, until the prey is in the most favourable position
for swallowing.

The Common or Ringed Snake is very fond of the
water, and is, moreover, a graceful swimmer. It is
said to dive after the newts, when hungry, and to bring
them ashore in its mouth to make a meal of them. It
is not difficult to distinguish the common snake from
the Viper, with which ignorant people often confound
it, and perhaps make it suffer for the latter's sins.
In the first place, the snake delights in damp situations, whilst the viper seems to prefer drier spots.
Its colour varies considerably, but it is generally of
a brownish grey, with a greenish tinge, the back
being ornamented by two rows of small black spots,
with blotches along each side. The heads of the
snake and the viper are, however, the best means of

rapidly distinguishing them. That of the former is covered with large plates, and about the neck there is a collar or ring (whence its name of "ringed snake") of a bright yellow colour. The viper's head has a much more "wicked" expression, and the top has a peculiar "Death's head and cross-bones" kind of blotches, which may have been taken—in the old

Fig. 70.   Fig. 71

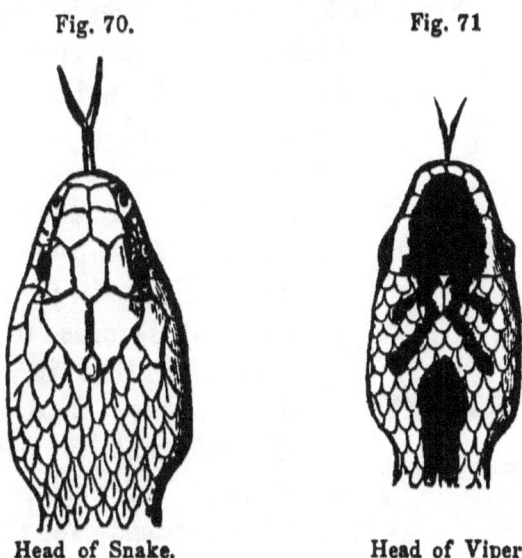

Head of Snake.   Head of Viper.

days, when it was believed that nature ticketed the character of her goods by certain outward signs—as a Cain-like mark of the creature's disposition.

The Smooth Snake (*Coronella lœvis*) is much rarer than the foregoing. Indeed, to come across one is quite a zoological "find." It is common in the south of Europe, and seems to get proportionately rarer as we proceed farther north, with the ex-

ception, perhaps of Sweden. It is much shorter than
the common snake, rarely exceeding two feet, whereas the latter is sometimes four feet in length. In size
and general appearance, it more nearly resembles
the viper, and it is not impossible it may have been
often taken for the latter. Like its congener, the
ringed snake, it is, however, quite harmless.

For some time back the chief places where it has
been found in this country have
been Hampshire and Dorsetshire,
although record is made of its
being also discovered in Scotland. Canon Kingsley records
in 'Science Gossip' for 1872,
several specimens from his own
parish, and records it as his
opinion, also, that it may be
much commoner than is supposed, but that it has been
taken for a red variety of the

Fig. 72.

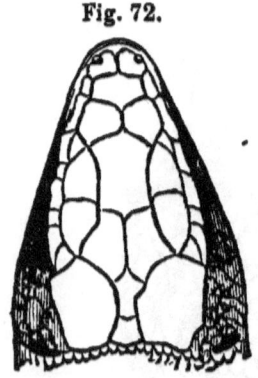

Head of Smooth Snake.

viper. He thinks it may have spread over this part
of England before the geological separation of
England and France.

The viper is a well-known reptile, especially
among country people, although those less used to
the fields and lanes and their inhabitants might
readily confound it with the common snake. This
is the only venomous species inhabiting England.
Like the common snake, it never reached Ireland,
the geological separation occurring before its extreme

westerly extension. It is abundant in Scotland, however, where in numbers it excels the common snake.
All our reptiles, including snakes, hide up during
the winter; and popular belief asserts that during
that season the bite of the viper is harmless. The
following illustration of the anatomy of this interesting creature may prove useful:

The poison apparatus of the viper consists of the

Fig. 73.

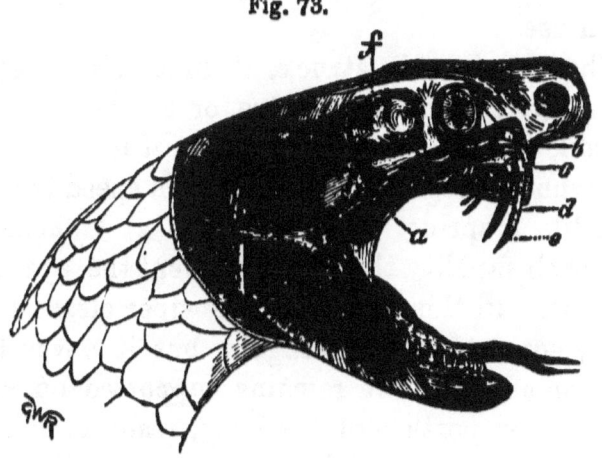

gland in which poison is secreted, the *duct* or canal
which it travels along, and the *fang* by means of which
it is injected. The *gland* is placed at the side of the
head (*a*), and consists of an assemblage of lobes.
The substance is soft and yellow, with a spongy appearance. The *duct* or canal through which the
poison is conveyed to the fang is a narrow cylindrical tube swelling in the centre of its course into a
kind of reservoir, and terminating in the base of the

fang (*b*). This latter is a tooth in the form of a tube, much longer than the other teeth, and curved (*d*). It is placed in the upper jaw, one on each side of the mouth. On the outer surface of the fang, near the apex, is an elongated opening or slit (*e*), from which a canal passes through the hollow in the interior of the tooth, and is united to the duct which communicates with the poison-gland. These fangs fall backwards, and lie concealed in a groove in the gum when not in use.

When a viper is struck, it first coils itself up, leaving its head in the centre, or at the summit of the coil, and drawn a little back, as if for the purpose of reconnoitering. The animal then speedily uncoils itself like a spring. Its body is next launched out with such rapidity that for a moment the eye cannot follow it. In this movement the viper clears a space nearly equal to its own length; but it never leaves the ground, where it remains supported on its tail or posterior portion of the body, ready to coil itself up again and aim afresh a second blow, if the first should fail. To do this the viper distends its mouth, draws back its fangs, arranges them in the right direction, and then plunges them into its enemy by a blow of the head or upper jaw after which the fangs are withdrawn. The lower jaw, which is closed at the same moment, serves as a point of resistance, and favours the entrance of the poison-fangs; but this assistance is very slight, and the reptile acts by striking rather than biting.

A great deal of misconception has arisen respecting the fatality of the viper's bite. Professor Bell states that he had never seen a case that had terminated in death. There can be little doubt, however, that fatalities have arisen, but it has been when the person bitten has been in a low or morbid condition of body. The reader will find the pro and con statements on this part of the subject discussed in Mr. Cooke's 'British Reptiles,' as also the repeated question whether the viper swallows its young.

The manner in which snakes crawl is perhaps not generally known. Popular belief associates the crawling movement with the primal curse, believing that before the Fall, snakes or serpents were not belly-crawlers. This we know to be wrong, for as far back as the Eocene period, huge snakes lived in what is now Great Britain—long before the appearance of man. Moreover, comparative anatomy sees in the structure of snakes an adaptation to their habits of life as perfect as the legs of a mammal or the wings of a bird. An examination of the skeleton of a snake will show that there are an enormous number of ribs, which are extremely movable. There is no breastbone, and the ends of all these ribs are free. It is on the free ends that the snake really crawls, and thus gets along pretty much after the same fashion that a millipede or centipede crawls. Each of the free ends of the ribs is attached by muscular fibres to the large scales which may be seen on the under side of snakes, and which are

H

really folds or plaits of the skin, as any snake-moult will show. This flexible movement of the ribs of a snake and their adaptability for crawling purposes are further assisted by the cup-and-ball mode in which the vertebræ are articulated. The forked tongue of the snake appears to be more of an organ of touch than of taste. It may also be used as a protection, in assisting to terrify animals by its repeated darting in and out of the mouth. The teeth, in like manner, are evidently of no use for mastication, only for prehension.

The Blindworm (*Anguis fragilis*) connects, in some respects, the snakes and the lizards. It has no external evidence of limbs, and hence common tradition assigns it a place among the snakes. An anatomical examination of its structure, however, is sufficient to do away with this notion, and to cause it to be placed with the lizards. Although no limbs are visible externally, the rudiments are to be found concealed beneath the skin. This atrophied condition may be accepted as a proof that some distant ancestor of the blindworm had true lizard-like limbs, and that disuse has caused them to assume this rudimentary condition, just as the American cave animals are found with rudimentary eyes, incapable of vision. Another feature associating the blindworm with the lizards, and disassociating it from the snakes, is that its eyes have moveable eyelids—a feature we have seen the snakes do not possess. There is a further difference in the jaws of the blindworm, which are like those of lizards. Other features they have also refer them to the lizard family; so that, altogether, there can be no mistake as to which group they should be placed in.

We have scarcely a commoner reptile than this pretty little creature, always excepting in Ireland. You are almost sure to find it coiled up in the mossy hollow on the sunny side of one of these lanes. We have frequently found it in deserted birds'-nests, and

Fig. 74.

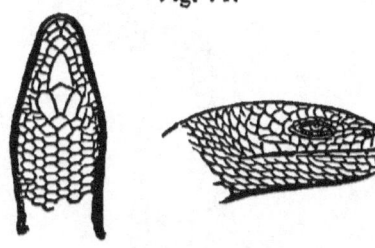

Head of Blindworm.

well remember, when a boy, and when we regarded all the snake kind with equal suspicion, the horror that thrilled through us when we inserted the hand into some nest we knew of, to feel if the eggs were all right, and felt the cold presence of a blindworm instead! Like the viper, the blindworm brings forth its young alive, eight or ten in number. This, however is due to the eggs being kept in the body of the mother until they are hatched. The scientific name of this species (*fragilis*) is not badly earned, for whenever the blindworm is taken hold of or alarmed, it becomes quite rigid, and the end of the tail will then break like a rotten stick. Notwithstanding the vices fathered on this really pretty object, it is perfectly harmless. Its common name is taken from its supposed blindness, but like those of the mole, the eyes are only small, and partially hidden by the scales. It is seldom more than nine or ten inches in length, and looks to perfection when seen gracefully and silently gliding through the grass

Fig. 75.

Tail of Blindworm.

on the hedge-bank. In Lancashire and Cheshire, whilst the blindworm is believed to be eyeless, the viper, or adder, is affirmed to be deaf. An old distich alludes to this belief, and shows us how the poor, harmless blindworm has been made to share the enmity that the viper, perhaps, does deserve. The adder, addressing the blindworm, says:

"If I could hear, and thou could'st see,
  There should nobody live but thee and me."

Let us conclude by noticing the Common Lizard (*Zootoca vivipara*) the female of which, as the name implies, brings forth its young alive, the eggs being kept in her body previously, and hatching at birth. Perhaps the only thing you see of this harmless reptile when you disturb it is its tail, and that is just disappearing. Indeed, you may have taken it for a snake or a viper getting out of your way. This is perhaps the commonest of all our British reptiles, and may be met with abundantly, even in Ireland. If you can steal on it unawares, do so, and watch the celerity with which it catches insects. This lizard forms a good and useful adjunct to a fernery, which it will keep quite free from insects, etc.

Fig. 76.

Head of Common Lizard.

The Sand Lizard (*Lacerta agilis*) was formerly confounded with that just mentioned, but it is quite distinct. In form and colour, however, it varies considerably. The commonest variety is of a sandy-brown, with greenish sides in the male, but brownish in the female. The belly is generally white, and spotted. It is thicker and more clumpy-looking than the common lizard, and

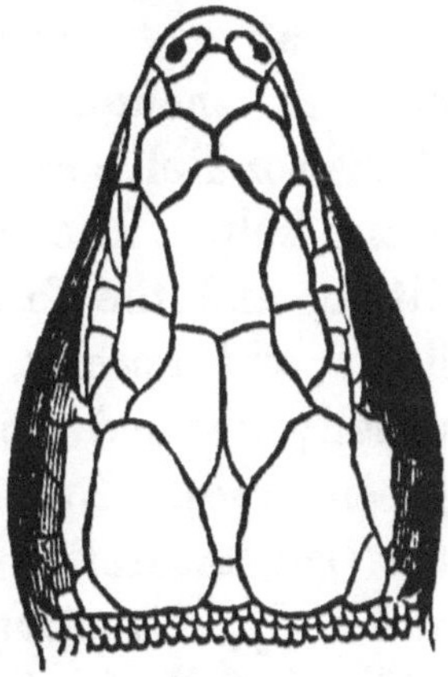

Fig. 77.

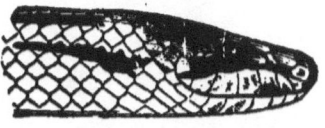

Sand Lizard.

may be found on the adjoining sandy heath, that being the locality most affected by it; whereas the common lizard likes to sun itself on the banks of our green lanes.

Our readers are aware that, as the limits of space allow us only to draw attention to the most familiar objects to be found in a country walk, we cannot dwell at any considerable length upon them, attractive though they may be. Such books as Professor Bell's and 'Cooke's Reptiles' will give all extra help. The latter is rich in folk-lore and tradition, and the former goes into accurate detail of habit and species. Let us now turn to objects usually deemed more attractive—the birds of our green lanes. But it should be remembered that to the true naturalist there is no high or low, beautiful and ugly, attractive and unattractive. Every form of life is full of interest, and equally testifies to the wisdom and goodness which have placed it in the spot where it is most fitted to flourish.

CHAPTER IV.

THE BIRDS OF THE GREEN LANES.

WHATEVER might be the floral beauty of our lanes and fields, more than half their charm would be gone if the birds went. Apart from the music of their songs, which fills the air and engages one's ear, their movements create an animation whose absence we can hardly realize. Even in winter, when the time of the singing birds is gone, the sharp cries of the sparrows, or the plaintive notes of the robin and tit, relieve the lanes of their loneliness. We associate the most pleasing of out-door recollections with birds and flowers, which have served as themes to poets of all ages and climes. It is impossible for the most non-naturalist of pedestrians not to be amused as well as interested by our feathery tribes. Birds-nesting has attracted many a young naturalist, and made him such; and as a rule, we generally find that our most distinguished men in this department of natural science first acquired their tastes in such a manner.

Our native birds may be roughly grouped into the migratory and non-migratory species. Of the former we have two kinds—those that come to us in the early summer, and leave in the late autumn for more southern climes; and those birds which, on the contrary, visit us in the late autumn and remain during the winter, leaving us again on the approach of spring. The origin of these migratory habits has not yet been philosophically discussed. That, some time in the history of the past, it has been developed through changing physical circumstances, few naturalists will doubt. No geological period throws light on the possibility of such a habit being formed, except the Glacial epoch—the last of any extent that affected the northern hemisphere. The slow but sure increase of cold which then affected these latitudes must have largely influenced the habits of British birds. Those incapable of standing against cold would be driven each winter further and further to the south, whilst those habits of attachment to localities which many birds possess, would cause them to return to their original homes whenever circumstances allowed them, that is, in the summer months. It is of the migratory birds principally that so many anecdotes are told of their returning every year to build in the same place as they did the year before, showing how strongly developed is what phrenologists would call their "locality." It is a geological fact that during the long continuance of the Glacial period,

British mollusca migrated to seas further south, to
return to British areas when the cold had departed.
Beds of fossil shells, of the same species as those
now living in our seas, are found on the shores of
the Mediterranean. They no longer live in the
neighbourhood, but we know from the contents of
our English "Crag" formations, that they were
British before the commencement of the Glacial
epoch, just as we know they live in British seas
now. Again, arctic mollusca and arctic animals,
such as the reindeer, glutton, &c., dwelt in this
country during the cold period in question, thus
replacing the original inhabitants which the cold
had driven further to the south. Arctic birds would
doubtless come with the rest of the fauna, to depart
afterwards, when they had become attached to these
latitudes, in order to exchange a rigorous for a
temperate winter. In the case of land animals and
marine mollusca, we have their remains to testify to
the geographical changes. But we cannot expect
any geological deposit to chronicle a similar origin
of migratory habits on the part of birds. Arctic
plants still live on our high mountains, and arctic
mollusca in the deeper and colder parts of our seas,
both to add their testimony to the general weight of
evidence in favour of the forced climatal movements
of organic beings. In this way, therefore, we think
a knowledge of the general physical and vital conditions of the Glacial period will throw light on, if
not thoroughly account for, those singular habits

which induce certain species of birds to leave us on
the approach of winter, and others from the extremer
north to take their places.   Dr. Tristram and others
have shown that our migratory birds which pass the
winter in Africa, are affected by the same love of
locality there as they display here.

The rambler will not see many birds of prey in
our green lanes now. What with gamekeepers and
the previous absence of a gun tax, they have
been pretty well thinned off. The Sparrow-hawk
(*Accipiter nisus*) still keeps its place among us, its
small size, perhaps, having protected it.   Perhaps
its nest may be found in some neighbouring tree,
where it has taken possession of one that formerly
belonged to a crow. The young female sparrow-
hawks seem to be terrible cannibals, for it is
authoritatively reported of them that they will
destroy and devour the young males! The female
bird is one-fourth bigger than the male, and proportionately more powerful. We remember watching
one of these birds strike at a sparrow last summer.
The latter dodged to and fro, and at least reached
the cover of a barn. But long before the Hawk
could get over his disappointment and fly away, it
was literally "mobbed" by a host of angry chirping
sparrows that rushed from the eaves of the building,
and literally made the hawk glad to get away!

The Kestrel (*Falco tinnunculus*) is another of our
commonest birds of prey. Like the preceding
species, it will sometimes make a home of an old

Fig. 78.

The Kestrel, male and female.

crow's nest. Kestrels seem to be most numerous during the late summer, when the hay is stacked and the corn carried; and, as this is the season when the field-mice and meadow-mice would then take up their comfortable quarters for the winter in such store-houses, the kestrels do great good to the farmer by keeping them down. In this efficient work they are ably joined by the Barn Owl. If you are out in the dusky part of the evening you may see the latter bird silently sweeping over the meadows and fields, a foot or two above the ground, mouse-hunting. It flits across the lane like a white ghost, and almost startles you by its sudden nearness. If you examine one of these birds you cannot but admire the soft plumage, which renders their flight almost noiseless. It is singularly in contrast with the stiff feathers of those birds of prey that affect the daytime. But it is not difficult to see that if the owls had a similar plumage to the hawks, it would be in vain for them to go out mousing. Our field mice are amongst the most active, as well as the most timid of mammals, and the slightest sound would cause them to hide up. Possibly, such a ramble as that just supposed may make you acquainted with the short-eared owl (*Strix brachyotus*), especially if your walk is towards the end of September. In the south of England this bird then makes its first appearance to stay for the winter; but there is reason to believe that in some parts of this country it abides the whole year round. It is only in the

Fig. 79

The Short-eared Owl (*Strix brachyotus*).

northerly parts of Britain, however, that such is the
case, and this is a good instance of how a migratory
habit over-laps, so to speak, that of a continuous
stay. It loves the open country, and roosts on the
ground, under the shelter of dry grass or heath.
The keen sight of this bird is proverbial among
naturalist-sportsmen.

The Kite (*Milvus regalis*), is now comparatively
rare in this country, a circumstance that is as much
due to the felling of our woods, where it formerly
bred, as to the wholesale destruction to which all
birds of prey have been subjected by game-keepers
and others. Formerly, it was just as common as it
is now scarce, and it was then much in use for
hawking purposes. All the kites may be distinguished by their long, forked tails. This bird is
still common in Algeria, and the Rev. Dr. Tristram
states that it there readily approaches man, and hangs
about the Arabs' camps, waiting for the offal, and
keeping an eye on the poultry stock. It is a noble-
looking bird, and it is more than doubtful whether
we have not lost more than we have gained by its
comparative extinction. Another rare British bird,
which was also once common, is the Hobby (*Hypo-
triorchis subbuteo*), a closely allied form to the falcons.
It is a summer migrant whenever it does visit us,
departing in the winter months, for southern Russia
and the Crimea, where it is very common. There,
on the smallest group of trees, you may be sure of
finding at least one nest of this bird. It feeds on

small birds, and seems to have a preference for the
larks.   It is also common along both shores of the

Fig. 80.

The Kite (*Milvus regalis*).

Mediterranean, the Sahara being its southern limit,
as it also is of many other birds, both raptorial and
otherwise, which may be called "British."   Geology

Fig. 81.

The Hobby.

shows us that during the Glacial period the Sahara was a sea, so that there has been a good geographical reason, both before and since that era, for our migratory birds reaching their southern limit in that particular latitude.

In our walk along the river side, it may be that we disturbed a stately-looking Heron (*Ardea cinerea*), who had previously been steadily looking at the water as if he contemplated suicide. This bird was once very commonly distributed, and still is in certain localities. It is a pity it should have been so hunted down, for it forms a conspicuous object in river scenery. In Norfolk it is still common in many parts, and pairs may not unfrequently be seen flying over the city of Norwich in the daytime. But perhaps the place where it is actually abundant is on the banks of the Orwell, from Ipswich to Harwich. Here, at low water, you may see scores of these birds fishing. It is quite as abundant in the river Deben, which runs up to Woodbridge; and also in the Stour, which joins the Orwell near Harwich. The extensive mudbanks of these estuarine rivers would look quite solitary were it not for the numerous herons and gulls. It is an unsocial bird, and prefers solitude to company. Still, you may generally expect to see a second heron not far off, if you see one. These birds generally roost in trees, and a collection of their nests forms a "heronry." The fact of a wading bird nesting in a tree is very unusual. Elm trees appear to be the favourites,

I

Fig. 82.

The Heron.

and the nests are generally made right on the top.

In reclining on the banks of the tarn or river, it is possible you were pleasantly surprised by a flash of colour for which you could not at first account. Your eyes followed it as quickly as they were able, until, when the object as suddenly came to a stop, you discovered it was a Kingfisher—certainly the most handsome of our British birds. From the position it has taken up, if you watch it carefully, you soon see it dart rapidly headlong into the shallow water—a movement for which it is well adapted through its short feet being placed so far down the body. Nothing can be more exquisite than the metallic sapphire blue of the wings of this bird. The beak is of course the principal agent in procuring food, and we accordingly find, among the various species of kingfisher, a great modification of this organ. The genus has a wide distribution, and therefore it may also be supposed to possess a comparatively high geological antiquity—these two facts being usually complementary. It is more than likely that you may watch the kingfisher dive five or six times without securing a fish, for this act seems to partake with it very much of the character of a lottery. It has recently been ascertained, however, that on such seemingly fruitless divings it is really hunting for water-beetles. It is exceedingly difficult to tell the sexes of the kingfisher; and almost equally so to discover its nest, which is generally in some hole in the river or tarn bank. The nest is generally constructed of small

Fig. 83.

The Common Kingfisher.

fish vertebræ, &c., with considerable skill. The young do not leave the nest until they are fully fledged, when they may be seen seated together on some bough, and greeting their parents as they pass to and fro, looking after food for them, and probably teaching them the art of fishing. The kingfisher is rather a difficult bird to shoot, but it is a great pity it is not even more so, for its beautiful plumage, comparable with any tropical species, renders it so attractive an object that every gun is pointed at it whenever a chance occurs. The recent rage for showy feathers in ladies' bonnets also has had a great deal to do with its decimation. In this respect, the fair sex are among the greatest destroyers of animal life, the entire kingdom of nature being ransacked to furnish them with furs, feathers, beetle's elytra, &c. The generic name of this bird (*Halcyon*) is derived from the ancient belief that when it was hatching its eggs, the water was always calm and still, and many allusions to this idea are to be found both among ancient and modern poets.

In the same waters as the heron and kingfisher affect, you may see the Moor-hen plashing and swimming, if you are careful to approach noiselessly. These birds always seem to us to be good illustrations of how soon new habits are acquired. It is one of the most timid of all the feathery tribes, and yet you may see it disporting in the dykes which run alongside the railways in the eastern counties, utterly regardless of the passing trains, let them whistle and roar as loud as they will! There cannot be a doubt that a few generations ago, the ancestors of these individuals were startled by the trains, but

their descendants have grown accustomed to them,
and aware that they do not threaten their life or
limb.   Similarly we find that the martins and
swallows, which, when telegraph wires were first
stretched, were often found dead, having killed
themselves by flying against the wires, have now
learned to know them, so that few accidents occur
among them.

The Moor-hen (*Gallinula chloropus*) is too well
known to need description.   Its nest may be
found in the middle of the thick rushes fringing
the tarn, the eggs being of a reddish-white colour,
spotted with orange-brown.   It is a pretty sight to
see the young frolicking in the water with the
mother, and equally worthy of notice to see how
they separate, and squat among the reeds and
plants when disturbed.   The Coot (*Fulica atra*) is a
larger bird, and may at once be identified by the
naked patch in front of the head and the pink-
coloured beak.

Emigrants tell us, there are few sounds they miss
so much in distant lands as the song of the lark and
the cry of the cuckoo.   We can readily understand
this, for both these birds are associated with the
early summer—the most charming season, in our
opinion, of the whole year.   The Cuckoo is one of
the most familiar of all our birds, as regards its call,
not so, however, as regards its appearance, for we
have seen some strange blunders made concerning it.
The cuckoo is a true climbing bird, it and the wood-

pecker forming almost the only native species belonging to this group. The swallow and the cuckoo also form the types of our migratory birds. Their coming and departure are so easily noticed

Fig. 84.

The Cuckoo.

that it cannot be wondered at we should discover their arrival and departure so readily. In our walks in the country there are few cries to which we listen so promptly and with such pleasure as that of the cuckoo. Then again, we have always associated it

in our boyish days with the habit of sucking other
birds' eggs, and of cowardly turning tail when
"mobbed" by a few smaller nest-builders. We
know it builds no nest of its own, but drops its eggs
in that of other birds, nature appearing to have
endowed every hen cuckoo with the power of laying
eggs similar in colour to those of the species in
whose nest she lays, in order that they may not be
detected by the foster-parents. Recently, the apparent carelessness of the female cuckoo for her
young has found an apologist, who declares he has
repeatedly watched the mother occasionally visit the
nest in which she laid eggs, and even the young
cuckoo when hatched. It is very certain that, in
spite of the attention that has been paid to the
cuckoo by ornithologists, there are few of our
native common birds with which we are less
acquainted. The young cuckoo, also, was further
associated in our youthful natural history experience
with its selfish habit of ousting its smaller and
feebler foster brothers and sisters, and of occupying
not only the whole nest, but the active services of
their parents in supplying its voracious appetite with
food.

The common songsters of our lanes and woods are
too well known to need any description. The blackbird, thrush, robin, and wren—who does not know
these objects? They are associated with our earliest
recollections—they are immortalised in the literature of the nursery! Who does not remember the

inexpressible thrill of pleasure on finding his first
bird's nest? How clear seem the blue of the blackbird's eggs, and how marvellous the mottlings on
them! We have carefully kept the secret of their
whereabouts, and been at no small trouble to conceal
our trail in the long summer grass, for fear other
boys should track us! Those days are gone, but
thank Heaven, not the love of nature which was
then manifesting itself after its own fashion! Who
can describe anything more purely elevating than
the chorus of thrush, blackbird, and lark in the
early summer? We cannot bring it to memory without the perfume of the hawthorn seeming to cross
our nostrils, and the bright yellow buttercups
appearing at our feet.

Hardly less common birds are the Tits (*Parus*).
Their pretty confident ways, in the dreary winter,
when we are glad to see any bird at all, win our affec-
tion. You may watch them taking their short hops and
flights at that season, turning their heads towards
you in the most knowing manner. At no other
time do their blue and green colours seem so
pleasing, and the birds appear as though they knew
it, for they allow you to approach nearer to them
then than at any other time. In the summer, you
may revive other of your boyish recollections by
noting how these birds draw you away from their
nests by their tantalising cries. In proportion as
you go further away, they seem more fidgetty, until
when you are far enough away, the tits fly and leave

you in the lurch. You have been annoyed, when you were older, by seeing those daring birds daintily feeding on the young buds whose development you were so anxiously awaiting.

The Bearded Tit (*Panurus biarmicus*) is an allied

Fig. 85.

The Bearded Tit.

species, not near so common as the above. If you are in Norfolk you may see it among the reeds of some tarn or "broad," running up and down with surprising agility. Its habitat, and the long pair of black moustaches which give to it its name cannot fail to help you in its identification. In Cambridgeshire it is tolerably common, and you may also find it haunting the banks of the Thames. Perhaps you may find as the companions of the bearded tit those singular and now rather rare birds the Ruff and Reeve (*Machetes pugnax*); for they are limited to almost the same localities. It is the male bird to which the common name of "ruff" is given, in allusion to the collar of feathers or hackles round the neck, which are generally distended during the breeding season, like those of cocks when fighting. The reeve, therefore, is only the female bird, more sober-looking and devoid of any ornaments of this kind. As both the Greek and Latin names of this bird signify, the ruff is exceedingly quarrelsome, and fighting appears to be with it a real pleasure. In the Fen districts, they will collect on little mounds for the purpose of having a "round," until the ground

Fig. 86

The Ruff and Reeve (*Machetes pugnax*).

is quite worn by the stamping of their feet! The immediate object of such a fight is the possession of one of the fair sex. Their manner of fighting, with head lowered, frill distended, and wings trailing the ground, rushing at one another, leaping and striking with the bill, is very similar to that of gamecocks. You will find the variety in the colour of the ruffs, however, very similar—no two being found completely alike. The frill round the neck of the male only lasts about three months, from April to July. These birds were once so common that they were sold in the markets—now they are among the rarest of our native species. Let us hope that the Act for the preservation of small birds, now in force, will protect those forms, which appear to be hunted down in proportion as they are getting scarcer. The ruff is a migratory bird, and makes its way southerly at the approach of winter.

Let us next notice a bird conspicuous for its absence, in the summer, from our green lanes; but which more than atones for this, in the opinion of the sportsman, for its abundance in the winter. It is a migratory bird, but one that comes to us in the dark months, preferring our mild winter to the more frigid one of its summer habitat. The Fieldfare (*Turdus pilaris*) is, as its natural history name indicates, nearly allied to our common song thrush and blackbirds. It differs from these familiar birds, however, in its habits being gregarious. Mr. Hewitson tells us that, in Norway, he has noticed two hundred nests of this species within a very small space. In that country, it is the commonest of all summer birds, so that it does not make such a long migratory journey as, for instance, the swallow.

The fieldfare generally arrives in England about the middle of October, but sometimes even earlier. Then you may see it collected in great numbers on the meadows, or "marshes," as they are called in

Fig. 87

The Fieldfare (*Turdus pilaris*).

Norfolk, where it feeds greedily on the slugs, worms, and beetles. By-and-by, as the weather grows colder, it shows the omnivorous character of its dietary, by resorting to the hedgerows, there to feed on the hips and haws. They are not particular to an occasional turnip, in lieu of any other food; whilst the berries of the ivy and mountain-ash are also included in their bill of fare.

On the heath where you found the common lizard basking in the sun, your attention must have been drawn by the circling overhead of a pair of birds, whose plaintive cry was most miserable, and which led you to imagine the nest could not be far off. Perhaps it was not, but you may depend upon it the hubbub grew louder in proportion as the birds drew you away from it. This is a common trick with various species of the feathered tribe. Occasionally the birds in question approached so near that you could see their glossy green backs, black breasts, and white underparts, relieved by chestnut tail coverts, and having the head ornamented by a pretty curved crest. It is the Peewit, or Lapwing (*Vanellus cristatus*), still better known as the "green plover," and its eggs as "plover's eggs." The latter articles, however, in spite of the high price they fetch in the London markets, are very heterogeneous! You may find the eggs of nearly half a dozen species of birds sold as "plovas"—the most common being those of the black-headed gull. At Scoulton, about ten miles from Norwich, there is a "gullery" which pays well enough to have it protected and cared for, where these gulls annually assemble, and where an average of thirty thousand

Fig. 88.

The Lapwing.

eggs are collected and sent to the London market.
The practice of selling them as " plover's eggs " is
as old as the time of Sir Thomas Brown, who refers
to it.   The peewit may be called a resident species,
and few will deny that it is an ornament to our
open spaces, and always seems to give to them by
its cries, in our opinion, an additional wildness and
charm.   As a rule, however, great numbers of the
peewits move southward on the approach of winter;
these and other birds, by their semi-migratory
habits, connecting the actually migratory and non-
migratory species.   As a rule, you will find them
returning to the same spot, year after year, for
nesting purposes, beginning to pair towards the end
of March, and forming their slight nests (on the
ground) in April.   Every one is acquainted with the
olive-brown eggs, spotted and dashed at the larger
end with a darkish umber colour.   How soon the
young learn their best policy is concealment!   They
are active as soon as they are hatched, and whenever
a supposed enemy approaches, cower down close to
the ground, so that their mottled brown backs render
it difficult to identify them.   Beetles, land-snails,
and, when the peewits get to the shore, crustaceans,
such as sandhoppers, shrimps, &c., form their food.
The reason for the many names given to this bird is
not difficult to find.   That of " peewit " denotes its
cry, that of " lapwing " is a good allusion to its
limping flight; its metallic green back has earned for
it the title of " green plover," whilst the change to

a darker and duller hue in winter then obtains for
it the name of " black plover."

The woods and hedges of our lanes are, however,
the hiding and nesting places of most of our common
British birds. Along the " backings," as they are
termed in Lancashire, you have the artistically
woven nests of the Whitethroat, Blackcap-Warbler,
Robin, &c. The nests are always highly finished
by those birds possessing slender delicate feet
and beaks. You cannot expect such a result from
aquatic birds, for their webbed feet and broad beaks
are not the proper tools with which to make a highly
finished nest. Hence the latter is generally characteristic only of such birds as the water-wagtail,
redpole, blackcap, &c. Another fact we may draw
attention to here, as it is connected with our
songsters. As a rule, the young of the latter, when
hatched, are in a very helpless condition. They are,
in consequence, exposed to additional dangers.
Compare this state with the perfect condition in
which young chicks and ducks emerge from the egg.
The contrast is as decided as it is possible for it to
be. May not the time necessary for young songsters
to develop their plumage have a relation to their
habits of singing? They have a chance of *learning*
at that time, for the parent birds, especially the
males, pipe to them. And Mr. Wallace has shown
that young birds neither build nests so well nor
sing as well, as those of two summers—proving that
they are capable of being taught by experience. It

K

has always seemed to us that the naked and helpless
condition of the young of our singing birds, had
something to do with their learning their characteristic notes during the period of their fledging.

There are few prettier birds than the Yellow
Bunting, or Yellow Hammer, notwithstanding its
commonness; which has the advantage, however, of
animating our country lanes. Birds with striking
plumage are not necessarily confined to the tropics,
for we should go far and fare worse than find such
elegant and daintily ornamental forms as the
redstart, goldfinch, bullfinch, or the pied wagtail.
Every physical geographical condition of the British
islands has its peculiar species—our aquatic and
wading birds in tarns, rivers, estuaries, and by the
sea-shore; our heaths and moors peopled with stone-
chats, whin-chats, golden plover, &c.; and our
woods and hedges by the finches, thrushes, common
creeper, and the majority of the hard-billed birds,
Of these, we may take the Hawfinch (*Coccothraustes
vulgaris*) as an extreme type of the adaptation, in
strength of the beak, to the kind of food affected by
its owner. If you come across a bird having a beak
more conical and larger than usual, you may almost
rest assured it is the hawfinch. It is not so common
now as it formerly was—indeed in most localities it
may be called "rare." But we have seen it in small
flocks frequently in the plantations in Norfolk and
Suffolk. As its name implies, a part of its food is
obtained from the kernel of haws, although the

berries of the ivy, hornbeam, &c., are not passed by. Its beak is evidently in its way as regards

Fig. 89.

The Hawfinch.

nest-building, for it does not construct anything like so elegant an abode as those birds not so distin-

guished.   This bird is said to have the largest
geographical distribution of any of our native species,

Fig. 90.

The Bullfinch.

ranging from Siberia to Palestine.   In the Bullfinch
(*Pyrrhula vulgaris*) we have a common and some-

times (at least in the opinion of gardeners and fruit rearers) a too familiar species. But you see it to advantage only in the month of May, in the most secluded and lovely of our green lanes, with the chiff-chaff, chaffinch, willow wren, and tom-tit for its neighbours, and where the wild flowers and ferns are growing most thickly. There you may expect to find its nest, loosely but symmetrically made, but so cleverly woven together and lined with fine material, that its apparent lightness is thus more than atoned for. In this you see the five or six eggs, of a pale-blue ground colour, ornamented at the larger end with spots and blotches of purplish brown. Should you find the nest after the young have been hatched, you cannot fail to be amused by the clamour of the young fledglings for food, and the concern manifested by the parents at your too near approach to the family circle. Equally common with the bullfinch, and quite as pretty a bird, is the Siskin (*Fringilla spinas*), which you may see, perhaps, in company with its acquaintance the Lesser Redpole. November, however, is the month when this bird may be seen most commonly, and if you are still, you will see it clinging gracefully to the withered stems of hawkweed, or quickly hopping over the twigs of clover or alder, in hopes of finding unscattered seeds. The siskin is, however, only a winter visitor among us, coming from northerly regions, but coming at very irregular times and seasons, evidently according to the cold. In many of its ways, the manner with which it

twitches its head, hops about, and clings to branches,
it will remind you of the tits. When you meet

Fig. 91.

The Siskin.

with a flock of siskins it is worth your while to
watch their antics—you cannot fail to be interested,

as well as amused. They seem the most restless
beings in creation, and hop about and cling to tiny
twigs, pleasantly and even merrily chirping all the
time, so that you would think they were simply
amusing themselves, and not engaged in the arduous
duty of seeking for "daily bread." Both the nest
and eggs of the siskin very much resemble those of
the goldfinch, only on a smaller scale. For, although
a winter visitor, this bird frequently remains to nest
with us, and therefore to stay the whole year.

Not far from the spot where the bullfinch nests,
in some of the old woods close by, where perhaps the
Great Green Woodpecker is to be seen, you may
watch the Common Creeper make its spiral curves
round the trunk of some old tree, diligently searching
for insects. It is not easy to follow its rapid motion,
for apart from its smallness, the back is so like the
ground-work of the tree trunk that it is a capital
protection for it. The small legs and comparatively
long beak of the common creeper (well does it
deserve its name, for no other word so well expresses
its movements) are admirably adapted to its habits
and food. It is possible that whilst you are watching
it you may catch sight of another bird, which, had
Solomon known of it, might have taken the
distinguished place the wise man has given to the
ant. The Nuthatch (*Sitta europæa*) is a good
provider against the winter months, laying up store
of provender in the shape of nuts and acorns, which
it will bury in the earth. Now you may have your

attention drawn to it by its loud and distinct " tap."
Approaching quietly to the spot whence the sound
proceeds, you see this grey-coated bird with a

Fig. 92.

The Nuthatch (*Sitta Europæa*).

hazel-nut (depend upon it, the finest of the bunch!)
wedged in the bark of a tree. It is standing
head downwards over the nut, hammering away
with its comparatively powerful, wedge-shaped bill,

aiding each stroke by the clapping of its wings.
Presently the hard shell gives way, and the juicy
kernel is the reward of perseverance. It will,
perhaps, go to the same tree time after time, until
you find quite a litter of empty nut-shells at the
base. But it is not so thoughtful about its present
appetite as to forget the demands of December and
January, for it is in those months that you may see
it disinterring the buried spoils of the late summer.
In the winter-time, when the leaves are gone, you
may watch the nuthatch with greater ease. Whilst
you are then doing so, you cannot fail to be attracted
by a noisy chattering of certain other birds. This
noise you had, perhaps, noticed in the summer, and
endeavoured to discover what it was, but the thick
foliage and the birds' too rapid disappearance forbade
you. In the winter months, you have, so far, an
advantage. It is the Jay (*Garrulus glandarius*),
certainly one of the prettiest in plumage of all our
native birds, as the demand made by ladies for the
wing-feathers only too fatally indicates. It feeds on
pretty much the same kind of diet as the Nuthatch,
acorns, beech-masts, hazel-nuts, &c., although it is
not indifferent to the charms of a flesh diet, consisting of grubs, worms, mice, eggs, and small birds;
varied, in the proper season, with a desert of cherries
or plums. If you are in an old oak-wood you are
pretty sure to see this bird, for that is the spot it
most affects. The young will follow their parents
like chickens, and chatter terrifically when hungry

Fig. 93.

The Jay (*Garrulus glandarius*).

or disturbed. The jay, like the Starling—which will stay with us the winter through if the season be not too severe—is remarkable for its powers of

Fig. 94.

The Sedge Warbler (*Sylvia salicaria*).

mimicry, and therefore is capable of being made into a household pet. In Sussex especially, you may frequently see tame jays at the cottage doors.

We omitted, when drawing attention to the birds frequenting the marshes, to mention the Sedge Warbler (*Sylvia salicaria*). It is a most remarkable species, and like the American mocking bird, famous for its powers of imitation. It mimics the song or cry of the swallow, sparrow, thrush, lark, &c., so perfectly that you can hardly tell the difference; and has the knack of concealing itself so that you cannot tell whence the sound comes, and so are bewildered to hear the song of a bird which you never before knew affect such a habitat. It is a graceful little object, and its nest is no less attractive. Not far off perhaps, you may hear the Reed Warbler, and see it clinging to the tall sedges of bullrushes with its delicate little feet.

One cannot but be struck with the fact that there is quite as much adaptation of birds to the various circumstances of life they affect, and that without any broad variation from the bird-like type, as we meet with in mammals. The feet and bill are of course the organs most modified. But we see in the divers and ducks, how the feet, when placed behind the centre of gravity of the body, must assist in diving and swimming. The modification in the bills, even of our British birds, is very remarkable, and it is impossible for an attentive student to go through a museum without noticing it. How different is the contrast between the soft bill and wide gape of the Goat-sucker (Fig. 95) and those of the Wood-cock and Snipe! The latter is long and pointed, and supplied with a remarkably sensitive tip, which must be admirably adapted for searching far below the surface in boggy and marshy ground for various larvæ and worms. Indeed, there is not a single department of natural science that, by the marvellous adjustment of life-forms to all the possibilities of physical conditions,

Fig. 95.

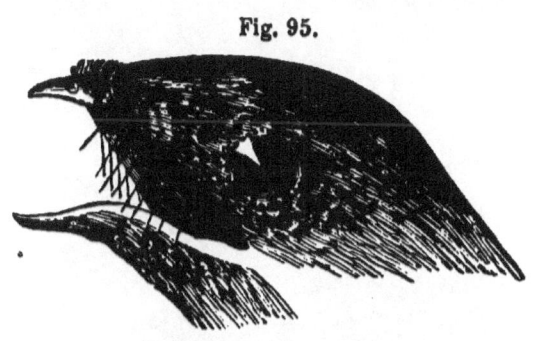

Goatsucker (*Caprimulgus*).

Fig. 96.

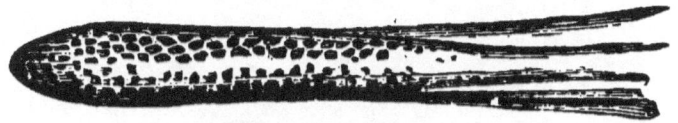

Bill of Snipe (Yarrell).

does not silently but emphatically tell us of the antiquity of existing species, and of the parallel modifications in generic types which have been made to keep pace with geological changes. In this way the inorganic world, as represented by the necessary alterations of physical geography, has always been directly related to those vital changes which were necessitated in consequence. Therefore, the history of the wonderful adaptation of means to an end, as exemplified by all organic forms, can only be properly and philosophically understood when related to the past inorganic changes and evolutions of the earth's history.

CHAPTER V.

HERE are few objects more generally noticed than the butterflies and moths which give such animation to a country stroll. Of various colours and patterns, they seem fit associates for the flowers and blossoms on which they love to dwell for a few seconds. The most careless observer has been amused by their fantastic flutterings, and many a boy has been educated into a naturalist through following them with his cap. The well-known metamorphoses through which they pass, also, are better known than the vital economy of any other forms of creature life. For a long time they were believed peculiar to the butterflies and moths, but naturalists now know that such a change is not peculiar to them—nay, that it is repeated and varied in many ways among the invertebrate animals. Let the three stages of caterpillar, chrysalis, and imago be undergone by three distinct creatures, instead of in the lifetime of

one, and we should have a strong analogy in the
hydrozoa and jelly-fish. Structural investigation
has shown that the immature organs of wings, &c,
may be traced in the caterpillar of a butterfly when
it is only a few days old, and before it has attained
anything like the bulk of body which its voracious
appetite presently obtains for it. Let any one who
wishes to trace the gradual perfection of the organs
from this immature stage to their perfection, carefully study Professor Duncan's lecture, on 'Insect
Metamorphoses,' delivered before the British Association in 1872.

If you care to sacrifice one of the commonest
butterflies you may meet with in a country walk to
your new-found love for science, you will not be
without food for wonder for many a day to come,
especially if you possess two things—a microscope
and patience! In its eyes you may perceive com-
pound lenses, thousands in number, each one of
which is capable of refracting a ray of light proceeding from any object. In its coiled-up proboscis
you discover an ingeniously-jointed and flexible tube;
and in the antennæ marvellous and mysterious
organs of a sense with which we mortals are
unacquainted. For it is a well-known fact among
entomologists, that if the young virgin female of
many species of moths and butterflies be enclosed
in a perforated box, it will draw numbers of the
males from all parts of the horizon to it. The sense
that can be operated upon so refinedly must transcend

anything with which we are acquainted. For, immediately one such male insect has paired with the female, the charm is broken—no longer are the ardent cavaliers attracted!

The internal structure of the *Lepidoptera*—a name well given to butterflies and moths, as we shall presently see—is also of great interest to the microscopist. The mouth-tube is not formed for breathing, but for *suction* only. Aëration is carried on by a series of tubes ramifying through the body, and receiving the air through openings in the sides of the abdomen, which resemble, to compare small things with great, the port-holes of a ship. These are called the *trachea*, and when you dissect and examine such portion of an air-tube through the microscope, you see it is formed of a spiral thread of chitine so closely wound on itself as to be impervious. The nervous system runs through the body from head to tail, and is gathered into knots, from which radiate threads of nerves, where the legs and wings are situated. Just as we find our towns and cities best supplied with lines of converging rails and telegraph wires, to administer to the more active commercial and social life, so do we always find in the invertebrate animals the nervous ganglia gathering thickest in those parts whence motion or other active functions have to proceed.

To the young student of microscopy, we can recommend no objects which are so readily obtainable, or that can be better studied by him, than the

L

scales of a butterfly's or moth's wing. He may
never have heard of such scales, but when we tell
him we simply mean the coloured dust that powders
his fingers after handling a butterfly, and that this

Fig. 97.   Fig. 98.

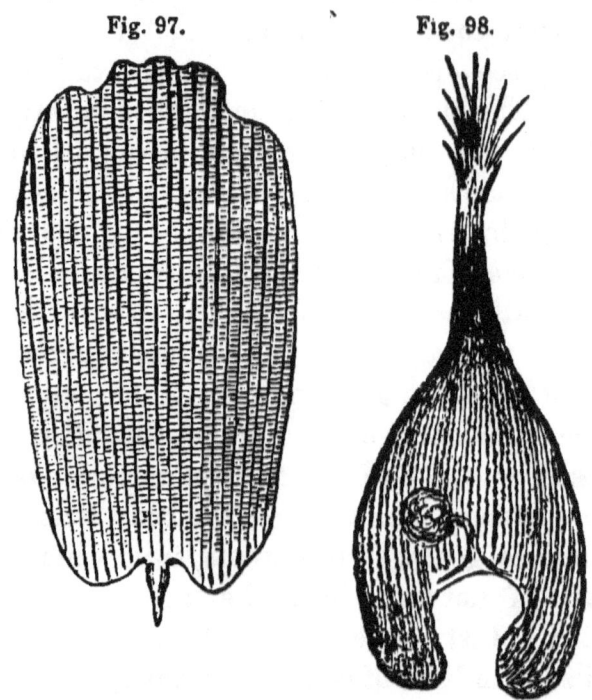

Scales of *Pieris brassicæ*, × 450.

dust when placed under the microscope assumes a
distinct form or shape, which varies according to the
species of butterfly from whose wings it has been
taken—he may feel inclined to experiment. Indeed,
as regards their wings, butterflies and moths differ
from dragon-flies, beetles, &c., chiefly in having these

dusty scales completely covering the membrane. Rub them off, and you will see the clear, transparent membrane, resembling, to the naked eye, that of the insects just mentioned. Under the microscope, however, even this transparent membrane differs, for you now see it punctured with myriads of minute holes, in each of which a distinct scale, or atom of dust, had been implanted. These butterfly scales may often be seen terminating in a little peg, which is the part that is implanted in the membrane of the wing (Fig. 97). In the Common White or Cabbage butterfly (*Pieris brassicæ*) there are found two kinds of these scales. Those of the Meadow-Brown butterfly (*Hipparchia janira*) terminate in a peg. The scales of this species furnish a good test for the microscope, in determining the fine lines (Fig. 99) which striate the thicker and lower portion. Catch one of the common blue butterflies, that you are sure to see plentifully on a sunny day, and its scales will furnish you with a battledore-shaped object, beautifully marked on the broad surface (Fig 100). Every species of butterfly, no matter how near may be the external resemblance in size, colour, or marking—and many of our native species are nearly related in this respect—differs

Fig. 99.

Scale of *Hipparchia janira*, × 450.

microscopically in the shape of its scales. This alone, therefore, is a good method of determining a species.

Not less beautiful objects, and requiring a much lower optical power to perceive them, are the eggs of butterflies and moths. Like the scales, they differ with each species, both in form and arrange-

Fig. 100.   Fig. 101.

   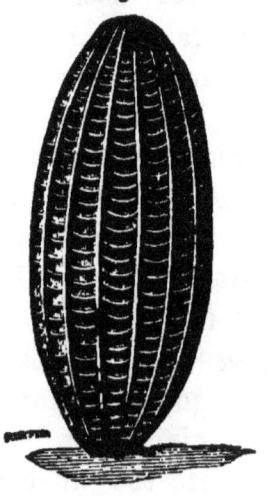

Battledore Scale of   Egg of *Pieris brassiœ.*
Polyommatus Alexis,
× 450.

ment. Some of them are so common and yet so attractive that they have obtained popular names. Among these are the eggs of the Lackey moth, which are found encircling twigs like the broad glass bead rings often made by children. These eggs go by the name of "fairy bracelets." With a one-inch objective, the eggs of butterflies and moths stand

forth beautifully. Indeed, we know of no object
that can compete with them for this low power.
Take those of the white cabbage butterfly (*Pieris
brassicæ*), for instance. They are common enough,
and when placed under a low magnifying power,
not only do the longitudinal and cross markings
stand strongly out, but there appears a beautiful
rainbow-tint as well. The eggs of the common
meadow-brown butterfly (*Hipparchia janira*) are of

Fig. 102.   Fig. 103.

Egg of the Meadow Brown.   Egg of *Vanessa atalanta*.

a different shape, blunted at the ends, and fluted in
their longer direction. Still prettier are the eggs
of the well-known Red Admiral butterfly (*Vanessa
atalanta*) (Fig. 103). In them, the upper part is
depressed, and the sides are fluted, the ridges
standing forth strongly in relief, and beautifully
ornamented.

We have a group of rarer butterflies which go by
the popular name of Hair Streaks, whose eggs are

very singularly marked.   In general appearance
they are not unlike the round dried cones of the
larch, and they have a dull white colour (Fig. 104).
The eggs of that much commoner butterfly, the
Little Copper, in some respects, are not unlike the
former, although they perhaps have a more general
resemblance to a poppy-seed (Fig 105).   Those of
the Blue butterflies, again (*Polyommatus corydon*).
(Fig. 106), are worth notice.   These, it will be seen,.

Fig. 104.

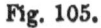

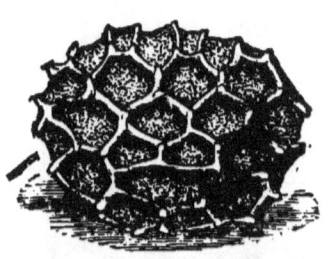

Egg of Brown Hair Streak.   Egg of the Small Copper.

still more nearly resemble the eggs of the Brown
Hair Streak.   The eggs of moths partake of pretty
much the same style of shape and ornamentation as
those of butterflies, although there is, perhaps, a
greater range in form.   The eggs of the common
Buff Tip moth (Fig. 107), for instance, are roundish,
with a flattened base, the surface being ornamented
with a very delicate tracery.   The eggs of the
Cabbage moth (*Mamestra brassicæ*, Fig. 108) are
very common, and, as will be seen, assume quite a

different shape and ornamentation. Those of the common Magpie moth (*Abraxas grossulariata*, Fig. 109)—an insect that obtains its name from its *pied* or black and white wings, by which, and its yellow body, it may readily be identified in any garden— are also worthy of study. The necessary minute observation required to discover the places where the lepidoptera deposit their eggs cannot fail to develop in the young student those habits of minute research

Fig. 106.

Fig. 107.

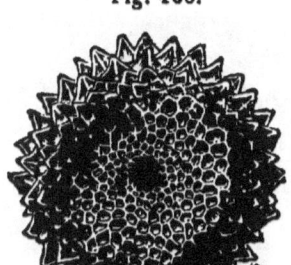

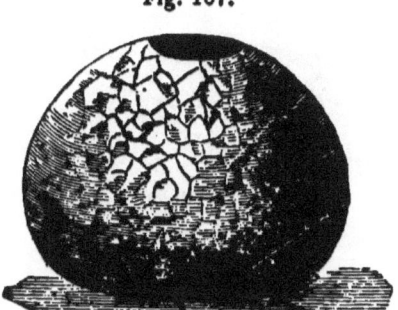

Egg of *Polyommatus corydon*.   Egg of the Buff Tip Moth.

and patience without which no man can ever become a good naturalist. And in studying them he cannot fail to be struck with the wonderful instinct that has caused such eggs to assume the colour or tint of the object to which they are attached, or admire the wisdom which, in the person of a little butterfly or moth, has contrived to place these future broods where they have the best chance of development! Nowhere in the entire animal kingdom, perhaps, is the law of *mimicry* so well exemplified as with the lepidoptera. Not only have many of the larvæ or caterpillars the power of varying their external colour to those of the plants on which they feed, but even the fully developed insect is similarly protected. Many of those little moths, the Tineidæ, when settled on a leaf, look like the droppings of birds. Others, when their wings are folded, have that prolongation which has given some of them their names, as our "Swallow-tail," so leaning

Fig. 108.   Fig. 109.

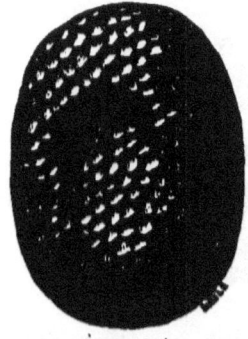

Egg of the Cabbage Moth.   Egg of the Common Magpie Moth.

against the plant on which the insect is resting, that they look like a leaf with its footstalk. The colours of the wings, also, and the mottlings, have in many cases a similar protective function. None have better shown this wonderful adaptation of butterflies and moths to the circumstances of their existence than Messrs. Wallace and Bates. In Fig. 110 is an illustration of the common Orange-Tip butterfly (*Anthocharis cardamines*) at rest on an umbelliferous plant. The student can now see the meaning of the delicate green mottling on the exterior

Fig. 110.

The Orange-Tip Butterfly at rest.

of its wings, and how, when the wings are closed at rest, they must protect the insect from its numerous foes. Looking at the illustration, even, it is a bit of a puzzle to tell which is the butterfly and which the umbel of the flower. Some of our common moths exhibit this peculiarity quite as strongly, and among them none more decidedly than the buff-tip (*Pygæra bucephala*). Well do we remember, when a boy,

Fig. 111.

The Buff Tip Moth at rest.

mistaking this moth at rest for a bit of dried twig, which the yellow end that has given to it its name causes it greatly to resemble. This moth you may find on most dry banks, or on the trunks of trees, especially the lime and elm, coupled in pairs. The Lappet moth (*Lasiocampa quercifolia*) is another " mimetic "

species, its specific name implying its resemblance
to the leaf of a tree, long before the new doctrine of
"mimicry" had arisen. Its mode of spreading out
its wings still further carries out the resemblance to
a dried leaf. The caterpillar of this insect feeds
on the blackthorn and willow, and spins a long,
blackish, and coarse cocoon among the lower twigs,

Fig. 112.

The Lappet Moth at rest

the moth itself generally appearing in June. It
has been imagined that our local fauna produced few
insects of this kind. The well-known " stick " and
"leaf" insects of tropical countries have been long
known, and furnished matter for curiosity, not
scientific investigation. Now, however, a truly
scientific basis has been found for this resemblance,
and the insect fauna of every country is yielding

examples showing the operation of the general law. Even the caterpillars take advantage of it, and by their minute resemblance to twigs and thorns are enabled to elude their enemies.

Few entomologists have popularised the attractive study of entomology more than Mr. Edward Newman, whose works on British butterflies and British moths we would recommend our young readers to procure. His distinctions between butterflies and moths we give, as a model of simple and forcible description : " A butterfly always flies in the day-time. In the second place, it always rests by night, and almost always in rainy or cloudy weather. In the third place, when it is resting, it raises its wings, pressing them together back to back ; but a moth turns its wings downwards, folding them round its body. Again, the hind wings of a butter-fly are stiff, and you cannot fold them up ; but the hind wings of a moth are almost invariably neatly folded up lengthwise, and quite hidden beneath the fore wings. Then, again, both butterflies and moths have two feelers attached to the head, just in front of the eyes ; we call these antennæ. These in different insects are of different shapes ; but in butterflies they generally have a little knob at the end. The owner cannot stow them away or hide them ; whether the butterfly is asleep or awake, its antennæ are always stretched out in front, or held quite upright. Now a moth, when going to sleep, turns its antennæ under its wing, or conceals them

in some similar manner, both from observation
and injury. Again, the eyes of a butterfly are very
much larger than those of a moth, because the
butterfly flies by day. The waist of a butterfly
is nipped in, making the division into thorax and
body very distinct; but there is no such distinct
division in a moth."

Let us notice a few of the commoner forms, both
of moths and butterflies, that literally intrude
themselves on our notice during a country walk.
You have not to hunt them, they are so common.
The rarer species we leave to the regular entomologist, who knows their habits, and the places where
they will be found, if they are to be met with at all.
Perhaps we have no British butterfly better known
than the Large White Cabbage (*Pieris brassicæ*),
whose eggs and scales we have already noticed. In
this as in nearly all species, both of butterflies and
moths, the female is the larger insect. The Smaller
white butterfly (*P. rapæ*) is a diminutive copy of the
former, but with the blotches at the tips of the
wings less dark. The green-veined White (*P. napi*)
has its own pithy description in its common name.
It is, however, a rarer species. The two former
species are double-brooded, the eggs being usually
laid on cruciferous plants. Both species also have
strong migratory habits, and frequently collect in
large flocks, even crossing the sea. A more elegant
and attractive insect, and one you are sure to meet
with in your walk along the roads or lanes, especially

in the more southern or eastern parts of England, is
the Brimstone (*Rhodocera rhamni*). It is a largish
butterfly of a darkish primrose or sulphur colour,
and with both front and hind wings drawn out into
a point. The hind wings, in this respect, approach
that form which distinguishes and gives its name
to the Swallow-tail. The eggs of the Brimstone
butterfly you may find about the middle of April
on the twigs of the blackthorn, the only shrub
on which the caterpillar feeds. The butterfly
emerges from the chrysalis in July or August, and
may be seen abundantly after then. It will even
hybernate, or lay up, during the winter, and on some
warmer day than usual will turn out for a few hour's
sun, perhaps at the expense of a paragraph in the
county newspaper. Indeed, the sexes usually keep
apart from the time of their leaving the chrysalis
state until the following spring, when they begin
to couple. Hence you may see them in March,
among the earliest butterflies, animating the yet
dull lanes in company with the Tortoiseshell and the
Peacock. We have several species of butterfly
besides those just named, that hide up during the
winter, and turn out in the early spring, up to which
time they have foresworn the married state. After
entering matrimony they still linger on; but their
work is over, and their faded wings tell of their
speedy dissolution. Sometimes they will even live
to see their young broods on the wing—a rare occurrence with insects. The best time of the year,

therefore, to obtain such species for the cabinet is as
soon after they have assumed the winged condition
as possible.

In exactly the same places where the Brimstone
was most abundant, and far away where it never
wanders, you may find the little "Blues" (*Polyommatus*). Surely these are among the prettiest of
all our indigenous species. Perhaps in company
with them may be seen the equally abundant little
"Copper," one of our few native butterflies possessing
that genuine metallic lustre which is seen to such
admirable perfection in some large species of tropical
lepidoptera. The Blues and little Copper are about
the same size, and they are usually found in the
same places, just flying above the grass of the lanes,
or flitting from shrub to shrub on the adjacent heath.
No wonder the latter species is so abundant, for it
has two or three broods every year, which, as they
emerge from the chrysalis, keep up a constant supply
of individuals on the wing. If you examine any
kind of dock you are almost sure to meet with the
eggs of this pretty insect. The large and small
Tortoise-shells (*Vanessa polychloros* and *V. urticæ*)
are also common, but not the less attractive species.
The wings of these two are angled, and the markings
pretty nearly resemble the semi-transparent blotch-
ings on a tortoise-shell comb. Indeed, many of the
popular names of our British butterflies are very
expressive of their leading features. The small
Tortoise-shell is especially common, and it will be

strange indeed if you don't find its eggs on almost
every cluster of nettles, and, later on in the summer,
its angled chrysalis dangling from beneath the ledge
of every wall or paling.   Mr. Newman tells us that
the eggs of this species are so much the colour of
the nettle leaves that it is difficult to detect them—
another instance of this protective power so largely
employed by the insect tribes.   It is in the spring
of the year that the larger Tortoise-shell is most
common, and on fine days you may then see pairs
flirting and coquetting, for it is not until now their
sexual instincts begin to manifest themselves, and
they have passed the winter, indeed, the whole
period since they left their chrysalides, in bachelor-
hood and spinsterhood.   In the latter end of April
or beginning of May our lanes are quite lively with
their gambols, for they love places removed from
human dwellings and on the outskirts of woods.
The wild cherry tree seems to be the favourite spot
for the eggs to be laid upon, as well as the aspen,
poplar, elm, and different species of willow.

Last year British entomologists were on the look
out for specimens of the Camberwell Beauty (*Vanessa
antiopa*)—an insect that is very eccentric in its
appearance, in this country at least, but whose
handsome appearance would be apology enough for
admiring it, even if it were much more common.
Our true British specimens, although rare, seem to
have obtained a varietal distinction.   The border is
of a pearly or French grey, whereas in the con-

tinental specimens it is usually of a cream colour. This is not the only species of British butterfly that plainly proves how, since the geographical separation of England from the continent, decided and perpetual local variations have set in. The Camberwell Beauty selects the white willow as the favourite spot whereon to lay its eggs, and many of the specimens caught during the summer of 1872 were obtained near these willows trees.

We doubt whether even the tropics, with all its marvellous wealth of colours and patterns, can produce butterflies more attractive than our common Peacock and Red Admiral. The former (*Vanessa io*) a popular name, taken from the eye-like spot on the tail feathers of Juno's bird, is quite a sufficient description by which any boy can recognise this butterfly. The interior of both wings is ornamented with similar large eye-like spots, and as the insect loves to settle on the ground, and to open and close its wings as if to show off its beauties to the utmost, you cannot fail to soon identify the species. The late Isaac Taylor, in his 'World of Mind,' alludes to this habit of the peacock butterfly opening its wings, and suggests that it does so because it has a sense of colour and form, and therefore delights in its own adornment. Here again the common stinging-nettle is resorted to—as it is by nearly all the species of *Vanessa*—for egg-laying purposes. The nettle seems to be a great favourite, in spite of its stinging properties, for the larvæ of no fewer

M

than fifty species of insects feed on it! Like some
other of our common butterflies we have mentioned,
the peacock hybernates during the winter, having
quitted the chrysalis state the previous July or
August, and continued single till the coming
spring. Hence you may see full-grown individuals
nearly all the year round. The Red Admiral (*Pyrameis atalanta*) frisks about in its fresh beauty
during September and October, settling on sunny
banks, gravel heaps, and roads, and opening and
shutting its bright marbled white and red wings,
like the peacock. This butterfly also lays up during
the winter, and is turned out by the warmer days
of spring to the great and important task of per-
petuating its kind. Not unfrequently, you may take
the red admiral by night, when "sugaring" for
moths. Allied to it is a less common butterfly, the
Painted Lady (*Pyrameis cardui*), with colours less
vivid, but richer and softer in combination. The
common field thistle is resorted to for egg-laying,
and it may be that this obnoxious plant, as well as
the nettle, are selected on account of their prick-
ing or stinging properties being a protection to
caterpillars, that would undoubtedly suffer if they
fed on a less offensive weed.

In those parts of our lanes that are greenest,
where the turf presses under one's feet like velvet,
we may see another tolerably common butterfly, the
Orange Tip (*Anthocaris cardamines*). We have
already alluded to its markings in Fig. 110. If you

watch its low but irregular flight you will not fail to express some word of admiration. When it is laying its eggs on some yellow cruciferous plant, we see the benefit of the deep reddish-yellow tip at the upper portion of the wings, which has given to this butterfly its popular name. That ornamentation, therefore, is nearly as effective as the mottled green of the sides, when the insect is laying up during cloudy or rainy weather on the flowers of some umbelliferous plant. May and early June are the times when the orange tip is most abundant, and then our green lanes and daisy-decked meadows are quite animated by it. As you passed along the very dustiest parts of the road, you noticed a dull brown butterfly that seems so tame, it allows you almost to take it before making an effort to get away. And when it did rise, it was to drift away a few inches above the level of the road, as if it were some brown leaf that was going before the wind. This was the common Meadow Brown (*Epinephele janira*), whose dusty colour, taken into consideration with its habits, must be a capital protection, and a reason, perhaps, why the species is so common. It is especially abundant in June and July, as well as August. The females select several species of grasses on which to deposit their eggs, and it is on grass of almost any kind that the caterpillars feed. Away on the dry grass of the heath you may find a kindred species, which is not quite so large, although as abundant in such a place as the meadow brown

was in the dusty roads. This is the large Heath-
(*Epinephele tithonus*), a lighter and prettier insect
than the foregoing, but affecting similar habits of life.

And now let us turn to the nocturnal representa-
tives of our butterflies: as a rule they are not so
gaudily coloured, and when they are, it will be the
hind wing that is adorned. Some of our British
species of moths, however, equal in brilliancy of
colouring any of the butterflies. Such is the common
Meadow Tiger (*Chelonia caja*). A careful search on
the grassy bank in July will discover this insect,
and then you cannot fail to admire its rich, velvety-
brown fore wings, with cream-coloured markings;
and the hind wings, with bluish-black spots on a
brilliant red ground. Still more conspicuous is the
caterpillar in June or July, covered with long
hairs that give it the appearance of a miniature
bear. It coils up and shows death when you touch
it. The hind wings of the *Catocala fraxini*—a rare
species—and indeed of most species belonging to
this genus, are very beautiful, consisting generally
of a broad, ivory black border on a Venetian-red
ground. In graceful shape, as well as colour, also,
although the latter is not so showy, the hawk-moths
will compare well. The caterpillar as well as the
imago of the Privet hawk-moth (*Sphinx ligustri*)
are beautifully ornamented. The former may be
commonly found in the shrub whence it derives its
name. It is of a delicate green colour, with seven
purple oblique stripes down the body, which ter-

minates in a horn, black at the tip. The hind wings of the moth are pinkish, with three black bands on them. You may see by the comparative length of the wings, and their swallow-like shape, that all the hawk-moths are capable of rapid and long-sustained flight. Some of them, as the Con-

Figs. 113, 114, 115.

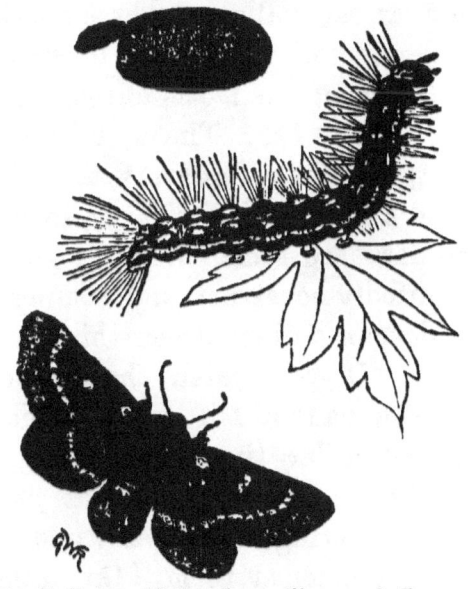

Small Eggar Moth, Caterpillar, and Cocoon.

volvulus hawk-moth (*Sphinx convolvuli*), and the Silver-striped hawk-moth, are especially so. Both the latter carry their long proboscis coiled up like that of a butterfly.

Let us turn to less beautiful, but not less interesting species of this family. As you walk along the lanes, especially during a very hot summer, you

cannot fail to see the hedges often stripped of their
leaves for a considerable distance, and just about
the centre, whence the destruction seems to have
proceeded, you behold a large cobweb-like structure,
on the outside of which are creeping several blackish
and repulsive-looking caterpillars. You poke at the
nest with your stick, and immediately there issue
scores of similar caterpillars. These are the brood of
the small Eggar-moth (*Eriogaster lanestris*) of which
we give a figure of the moth, chrysalis, and caterpillar in Figs. 113 to 115. The moth itself is rather a
pretty insect, of a dingy brown, with white spots on
the wing, and a good deal of soft fur about the head.
The caterpillars are social, living together in the
web they unitedly construct, and issuing forth like
locusts to devour " every green thing " that comes
in their way. If you watch their proceedings a
short time you cannot fail to be amused. They
seem to have regular times for feeding, and issue
forth in single file, crowding on each other's heels,
and leaving off eating as suddenly and unitedly as
if a bell had summoned them. On examining the
nest or web, you will see that the holes leading into
the interior only allow one caterpillar at a time to
go in or come out. When all the caterpillars are
housed, slumbering away their heavy meal—for
they are among the most voracious of feeders—one
caterpillar is left in each hole, as if on guard. This
social condition is limited to the caterpillar stage,
for each afterwards forms a cocoon. Another cater-

pillar that does a deal of harm to hedges is that known to entomologists as *Hyponomeuta padella,* one of the little *tinea* moths. It swarms on the hawthorn and other trees, and, on account of its immense numbers, which more than make up for its diminutive size, it creates sad havoc. Figs. 116, 117, 118 show this common species in its three stages of caterpillar, pupa, and imago.

In the eastern counties, and indeed generally where pollarded trees grow in any great abundance,

Figs. 116, 117, 118.

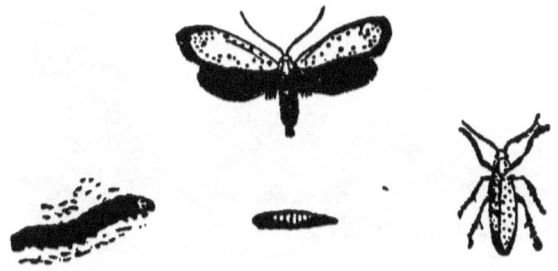

Caterpillar, Pupa, and Imago of *Hyponomeuta padella.*

you may find a large and rather handsome insect, although not gaudily coloured, known as the Goat-moth (*Cossus ligniperda*). It is more than likely that its caterpillar, with its red, shining appearance, will be the first to attract your attention. Fortunately it is not so common with us as it is on the continent, or we should not have such grand old trees enduring in our midst. For the caterpillar of the goat-moth acts the part, in our temperate latitudes, assigned to the termites, or white ants, in the tropics. It is a terrible borer into wood, and if

you examine the trunks of trees in your walk, it is
more than likely you will see them bored and drilled
as if a carpenter had been at work, the only
difference being that the hole is rather oval than
round.   Within the tree in which this hole exists
the larva lives, often at the expense of the tree
itself.   Not unfrequently, when the bark of a tree
is removed, you may see the genuine surface of the
wood literally honeycombed by these caterpillars.
At the base of such trees you will see fine sawdust

Fig. 119.

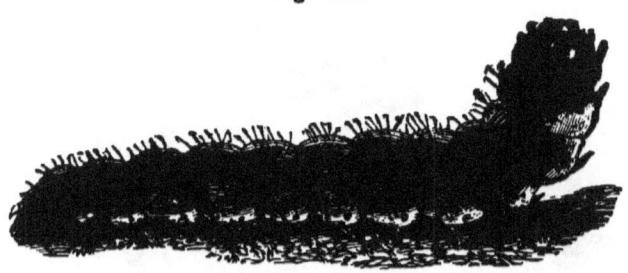

Larva of Goat-moth.

strewn, as if carpenters of a higher zoological
structure had been there.   Whilst you are noting
these holes, a strong rank smell greets your nostrils,
as though you had got a whiff of some passing
menagerie.   That is a sure sign the caterpillars are
still present, for it is this rank smell that has given
to the insect the name of the " goat-moth."   The
goat-moth is one of the largest of our native species.
The willow appears to be the favourite tree for the
caterpillar to practise upon, and the early summer
the time.   Those strangely gustative people, the

Romans, who seem to have tried every living thing to find out whether or not it was good to eat, considered the large, fat, and rank caterpillar of the goat-moth quite a delicacy—having a naturally "high" flavour about it that we cannot at all approach in our "game!" Pliny alludes to it, and mentions how it was the custom to fatten the caterpillar on flour for some time before cooking. In May, the larva forms a large, tough, oval cocoon, composed of fragments of wood and spun silk, about

Fig. 120.

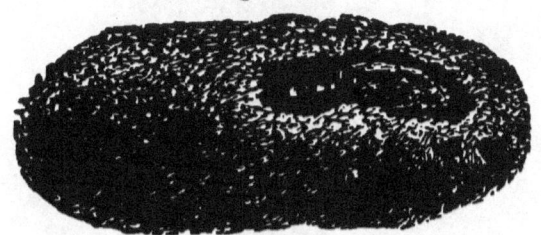

Pupa of Goat-moth.

two inches long. By-and-by this cracks, and the moth emerges, generally in the after-part of the day. It crawls out of the case and cocoon, and waits a short time for its wings to expand and dry —a process of only a few minutes. Then is the time for the young collector to secure it, in all its undiminished beauty.

Even more interesting than the goat-moth is the economy of a still commoner species known among entomologists as the Vapourer-moth (*Orgyia antiqua*). The act of *mimicry* to which we have already alluded is carried on so far that the females

of some species of moth never assume the winged
state, or assume it only partially. Nay, in one case
at least, owing to the absence of wings, the peculiar
rounded shape and markings of the body and the
much longer legs, you would certainly never take
the female fully developed insect for a moth, but
for a *spider!* This is the female of the Mottled
Umber (*Hybernia defoliaria*). On the oak or hazel

Fig. 121.

Goat-moth (*Cossus ligniperda*).

and many other plants, you may find the caterpillars
of the Vapourer moth—which derives its name from
the habit of the winged males rising and falling simul-
taneously in their flight. Not only do these insects
abound in the country, but you may see them in
groups even in the midst of our towns and cities,
where gardens or *boulevards* are planted. The
female never rises to the winged state, the process
of larval development, so common to the lepidoptera,

in her as well as in several allied species, seems to be " arrested " at the pupal stage. Hence it is that, to compensate for her want of wings, whereby she would have a chance of finding a mate, she is able in some peculiar way to draw the males to her, wingless though she be, and that too in crowds! So effective is this power of attracting the opposite sex that, in most cases, the female vapourer moth does not move, through her life, many inches from

Figs. 122, 123.

Vapourer Moth (*Orgyia antiqua*), Male and Female.

the place whence she escaped from the chrysalis condition.

The Lackey moth we have already alluded to, in the beautiful bracelets of eggs laid by the female. The common name is believed to be due to the mode of varnishing or " lacquering " adopted to hold these eggs together. Perhaps your country walk may have so interested you that it is evening before you return, and the dews are settling on the meadows. In the early summer, this is the time and place for you to see the Ghost moth, or Ghost Swift as it is also called (*Hepialus humuli*), so named after the *white* colour of the male. The female is larger,

and has the wings of a *yellow* colour adorned with
orange markings. Many a time, when a boy, have
we turned out, cap in hand, to chase this moth
among the long grass and clover, careless of wet
feet, or of the anger of the farmer whose meadow
grass we were not improving! The moth flies with
a buzzing, humble-bee kind of flight, hovering over
certain spots for some time, so as to form ready
captures. The Brimstone moth (*Rumia cratægata*)
comes out in the early part of the evening, and even
flies in the day-time. You cannot mistake it, for it
is one of our commonest and yet handsomest species,
and a blow with a stick at a hawthorn bush will
almost be sure to start more than one individual.
In the day-time, you will find it resting among the
long grass or the hedge bank. Its name conveys
to you some idea of its appearance. The wings are
of a bright canary yellow, the margins of the fore-
wings being of a brick-red colour. The white- and
black-thorns are the shrubs on which the caterpillars
feed; hence the scientific name. Equally common
is the white Ermine moth (*Arctia menthastri*) which,
as a boy, we remember finding on the grass of the
hedge backings, and used to place in the hollow
of our hands whilst we roused it by blowing with
our breath, to wake it from its sleep! Here, again,
we find the popular name conveying a good idea of
the insect, for nothing could be more like conven-
tional ermine than the pure white of the fore-wings,
speckled with black spots. In June and the early

part of July, this moth is very common in our lanes and byroads. The Water Ermine (*Arctia urticæ*) is not quite so abundant, although common; you may readily distinguish it from the foregoing species, for, although about the same size and shape, the wings, though white, are *unspeckled*. The Buff Ermine again (*Arctia lubricipeda*)—a very handsome and common object in our evening rambles down the green lanes—is nearly allied to the foregoing, and will be certainly seen by eyes on the look-out for it in such places, about midsummer. The popular name pretty well conveys a good idea of its appearance, especially if you remember that the generic term tells you that in shape and size it resembles those moths just referred to. The Yellow-tail moth (*Liparis auriflua*) is also a common insect, whose white wings and yellow tuft spread out like a fan, lead to its ready identification. The Fox moth (*Bombyx rubi*) is of a reddish, foxy-brown, and with a good deal of the same colour of fine furry hair about the body—hence its common name. In June you can hardly fail to meet with this insect, and its caterpillars are very common on the bramble and the heath in August and September. The Emperor moth (*Saturnia carpini*) is rarer, and is a gorgeous insect indeed, the wings—of brown, red, and grey shades—being ornamented with eye-like spots, similar to those of the peacock butterfly. The caterpillar makes its appearance about August, and is of a delicate green colour, ornamented with pink-

Fig. 124.

Emperor Moth.

Fig. 125.

Caterpillar of Emperor Moth.

Fig. 126.

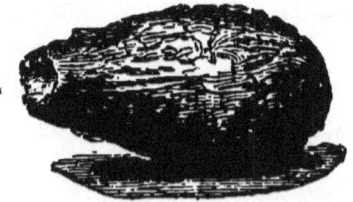

Cocoon of Emperor Moth.

coloured tubercles surrounded by a black ring. April and early May are the times when the moth makes its appearance. But to detail every species of moth that may be met with in a summer evening's ramble would require a separate volume, and that a bulky one. Besides, the student may find in Mr. Newman's ' British Moths ' both figures and descriptions of all he meets with; whilst Mr. Stainton has treated on those much smaller yet not less beautifully-marked insects commonly known as the *Tineidæ*. All that we have attempted has been to notice such forms as obtruded themselves in our notice during a stroll, rather than to follow a regular insect hunt. Many wonderful and interesting lessons may be learnt from the insects of our green lanes— lessons that, thus acquired in early life, will never be forgotten when older years have brought additional cares!

CHAPTER VI.

THE BEETLES AND OTHER INSECTS OF THE GREEN LANES.

HE most indifferent observer must have had his attention occasionally called to other objects than those described in previous chapters. Forms of creature-life abound at every step, and obtrude themselves upon his notice, look which way he may. With most of these, perhaps with all, he is quite unacquainted; and our desire, therefore, is now to introduce the most prominent of them to his notice as fully as our limits will allow.

Beetles are proverbially repulsive objects, although we have a few species whose brilliant metallic colouring relieves them from the general dislike. Some of these are not rare, especially the green Tiger beetle (*Cicindela campestris*). You may see it actively engaged on some sandy bank, its golden-green wing-cases and copper-green belly making it look like a living gem. It rises on the wing with

considerable ease, and flashes past you in the sun-
shine before you are aware what it is. Perhaps you
endeavour to take a specimen as it creeps over the
warm sand, and have found a " tartar." Well does
the insect deserve its popular name, for it is one of
the pluckiest of its kind. A low magnifying power
applied to the golden-green wing-cases, or *elytra*,
causes it to appear so magnificent that an expression
of admiration escapes one's lips when it is thus seen
for the first time. Its perfume, too, is as unlike
that of most of our native beetles as its gorgeous
colours : it is faint, but not unlike the smell of
sweet-briar. In this respect it resembles another of
our native species, which you will most probably
meet with near or among the willow-trees of any
stream side. On account of its perfume, it goes
by the common name of Musk beetle (*Cerambyx
moschata*). In the breeding season especially, the
musky odour omitted by the female is very powerful,
so that it will not be difficult to track its whereabouts. This insect, like some others, emits a
peculiar sound, not unlike the squeak of a bat, from
which circumstance it has acquired the name of
" squeaker." The musk beetle is as lovely an object
as the preceding species, being of a soft metallic
green colour, tinged with blue, gold, and bronze.
You may readily distinguish it from the tiger beetle
by its larger size, deeper tint, and very long
antennæ. The Sun beetles again, are very attractive insects, not much unlike in size and shape the

N

tiger beetles, but without the few spots that occur on the wing-cases of the latter. These you may see running rapidly about on the gravelly path as you walk along. Beetles belong to the order *Coleoptera* (wing-sheathed), signifying that they are adapted for burrowing purposes. Their front wings, instead of being transparent, have some of the same material deposited in them as that which makes the body so crisp and hard. This material is termed *chitine*, and by its deposition in the front wings, they form admirable protective covers to the hind-wings, which remain membranaceous, especially when burrowing in manure and other garbage, as is the habit of the majority of beetles. The larval stages of beetles pass through metamorphoses very similar to those of the butterflies and moths. The grub, however, is perhaps of a lower specialised character, sometimes being quite footless, and re-sembling a worm. In Fig. 127 is given a sketch of the larva of the *Calosoma*, together with the adult insect. This is a species rare with us, although very common on the continent. It is of a greenish colour, and elegant shape, and noted for the manner in which it preys upon the caterpillars of a certain moth which, from their mode of marching two and two as if in a procession, have obtained the name of " processionary moths." The nervous system of a beetle is most interesting, in the way that the smaller nerves are given off by the knots or " ganglia " to the organs requiring stimulation.

Not long ago, we saw a splendid preparation of this nervous system, which had been carefully dissected out of a common beetle, and afterwards mounted on glass as a microscopical object. In Fig. 128, we give an illustration of the manner in which the nervous system ramifies throughout the body of these insects. The beetle here shown is one of our

Fig. 127.

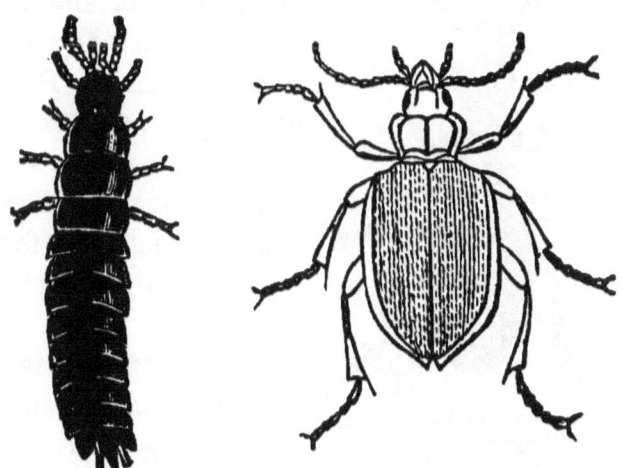

Calosoma sycophanta and its Larva.

commonest species, known as the Ground or Garden beetle. Generally speaking, its metallic colouring, although not attractive, is very pretty. All the *Carabi* are intensely carnivorous, and devour the eggs and larva of other species of insects with great gusto, whenever they can get them. The Rose beetle (*Cetonia aurata*) is another very common form, with short antennæ and a broadish body. It is a very handsome species, the upper surface being of a

N 2

beautiful shiny green, glossed with gold, and the wing-cases, or *elytra*, being further adorned with a number of various dottings and markings scattered over them. The belly is a bright copper colour. If you examine the full-blown roses of some neighbouring garden, you will be almost certain to come

Fig. 128.

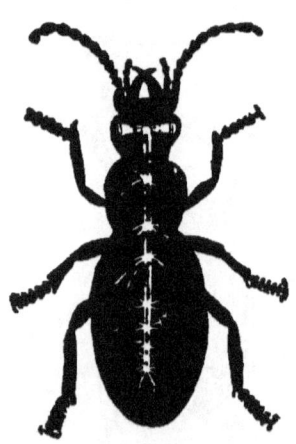

Distribution of the Cerebrospinal System in a Beetle—*Carabus nemoralis*.

across some of these pretty little beetles, for it is from their habit of affecting those flowers that they take their popular name. Privet-blossoms are another favourite haunt of theirs, in some parts of the country. The larva of the rose beetle are fond of old rotten wood, decaying trees, &c. The Tortoise beetle (*Cassida viridis*) is another of our common species, its name being derived from its rounded, flattened, bug-like shape. It is of a dullish green colour, and its thorax is so large that the head is almost hidden—a circumstance which considerably adds to its roundish appearance. The larva of this species is a very singular object, flat and covered with spines, and having a peculiar forked apparatus proceeding from the tail and passing over the back. On this fork, a kind of umbrella is supported, formed of the remains of the leaves on which the larva has been feeding.

All our common British beetles have not the same claim to attention, as regards colour and perfume, as many of the species we have just noticed. Indeed, some of them appear to obtain one chief source of their defence from the noisome odours· they can throw forth at will. Others again are very fierce, and of these none more so than the well-known Cocktail beetle, which derives its name from its habit of curling the end of its long body over its back. The wing-cases are very short in the group to which this beetle belongs. At the end of the body are two glands, whence the stencl proceeds that is so very offensive. The commones. species, perhaps, is that known as the "Devil's Coach-horse" (*Ocypus oleus*), a formidable looking object, a great carnivore, and possessing consider-able powers of endurance. We once cut off the head of one of these beetles, for the purpose of preparing the eyes for the microscope. It was placed in a pill-box, and more than two hours afterwards the separated head retained strength and vitality sufficient to bite through a piece of paper! It well deserves its diabolical name, for we know no other insect which comprehends such a number of repelling traits. And yet it has consider-able courage, for if you point your stick at it, it will seize it, cocking its tail the while, and emitting its noisome stench. It is a very swift walker, perhaps the quickest of all our native species; and you may see it rattling across the path and sticking up its

tail as if defying all sorts of passers-by, human or
otherwise.   The power of emitting noisome stenches
which characterises so many beetles, seems to reach
its maximum in the Bombardier beetle (*Brachinus
explodens*).   It is a rather gracefully-shaped, sober-
coloured and smallish insect, and derives its popular
name from being able to explode a quantity of the
volatile noisome odour, so that it looks like a jet
of vapour or smoke.   This is used solely for defensive
purposes, and is emitted when chased by some larger
carnivorous neighbour.   How offensive it is may be
judged of by the fact that, though the large beetles
can stand a good deal in the way of stench, having
been pretty well brought up to it, they always
recoil at the discharge from the tail of the bombardier, and not unfrequently retreat even faster
than they commenced the attack!   Indeed, even
among the numerous species of beetles with which
we are haunted in this country, it is wonderful to
see the variety of means put into use by them for
self-defence.   Sometimes it is difficult to tell the
benefit accruing from these "dodges," but that
they are useful in the economy of the insect there
can be little doubt.   A common object in one's
country walks is the Oil beetle (*Meloë cicatricosus*).
It is of a dark indigo blue colour, slow in its motion,
and wingless.   Here, therefore, we can see the use
of the offensive oil which it distils from every joint
when frightened.   The larva manages to attach
itself to bees when the latter are seeking pollen or

honey, and is carried by them to their nest, where it lives on "bee-food."

The Sexton or Burying beetles cannot fail to be obtruded on your notice in country lanes, for it is there they abound. Their common name is derived from their habit of burying the carcases of dead reptiles, birds, &c., which they do very neatly, having laid their eggs in them previously, and thus prepared for the wants of an offspring they will never see. Their generic name is *Necrophorus*, and we have many native species common in this country. Like those already named, they have the power of emitting a repelling stench which, in their case, is exuded from the mouth instead of the tail. Any quantity of these beetles may be obtained near where the carcases of moles are suspended, or where gamekeepers have nailed up, as trophies, the supposed enemies of their charge.

Before we proceed to notice other common insects of our lanes, it will be well to glance at a beetle known as the "Skip-jack," from its being able to jerk itself on its legs after being turned over on its back, which is often the case, as it is liable to a capsize on account of its short legs. It springs to its proper position by arching its body, and driving the base of its elytra against the ground, much after the fashion of the old wooden frog-shaped toys, which are made to jump by means of the detachment of a piece of wood placed underneath, from a waxed surface. Compared with their size, these insects will jump to a sur-

prising height, although they have to repeat the
process sometimes, before they can manage to get
on their legs. Several species have this peculiar
habit. Some of them are more interesting to the
general reader on account of their larvæ being the
notorious "wire-worms," which commit such dreadful
ravages among crops. Well do they deserve this
name, not only on account of their attenuated
shapes, but their toughness as well, which is so great
that a garden roller passing over them cannot hurt
them, but only squeeze them further into the soil!
In the destruction of this terrible pest, the crows
are the greatest friends and assistants the farmers
have, as is also the much despised mole, which,
although it may create a good deal of "hummocky"
ground, at any rate, destroys these pests as a
compensation. The harm done by the wire-worms
is increased by the fact that it is said to remain five
years in the ground, before it assumes the pupal stage.

The Stag beetle (*Lucanus cervus*), from its great
size, and the development of the jaws until they
resemble the antlers of a deer, cannot fail to be easily
recognised. You may possibly obtain your first acquaintance with this insect by its flying in your face,
in which case the enormous mandibles will surely
leave their mark. This is one of the largest, if not
the largest, of our English beetles. It is only the
male, however, that possesses these formidable-look-
ing jaws, those of the female not being one-tenth the
size. Judging from these weapons, and the class to

which it belongs, one would take the stag beetle to be dreadfully carnivorous. This is not the case. On the contrary, it feeds chiefly on the juices of plants, which it sweeps up by a peculiar organ that may be seen in the centre of the jaws. The larva of the Stag beetle may be found, like a small, animated tallow candle, in old wooden floors. It has even then a tremendous jaw, indeed, most of the larvæ of beetles have powerful jaws, a feature which is shared to a great extent, by the larvæ of butterflies and moths. The latter drop this apparatus on entering the pupa state, and when they assume the full imago condition, have an apparatus of quite a different character, although answering piece for piece with that of their earlier career.

And now let us turn to a different group of beetles —the *Coccinellidæ*, or Lady-birds, as they are better known by. You cannot help observing these pretty little insects, with their shiny, russet-red wing-cases and flat bellies. The various species have a different number of black spots on the back by which they may be readily known, the commonest perhaps being the Seven-spotted lady-bird (Fig. 129). Not unfrequently, these insects collect in immense swarms. They are exceedingly useful to the gardener and the hop grower, in destroying the still greater quantities of "plant lice" (*aphides*) which collect so thickly on fruit- and rose-trees, and on the foot-stalks of hop-leaves. They deposit their eggs among the "plant-lice," so that the larvæ as soon as born, are in the midst of their most congenial food. The grub has a very flattened appearance, with three large leading segments. When full grown it attaches itself to a leaf by the extremity of its body, and enters the pupal state, in which it is protected by its previously cast-off skin. The full-grown lady-birds frequently hybernate during the winter, so that they may make their appearance on any fine, warm day in winter or early spring.

Fig. 129

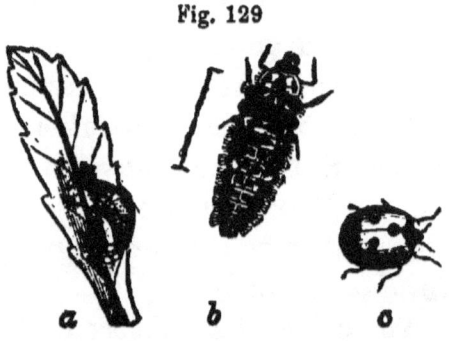

The Ladybird (*Coccinella 7-punctata*). *a*, Larva ; *b*, Pupa ;
c, Perfect insect.

Whilst half-carelessly, half seriously, amusing yourself during a walk by turning over all kinds of objects, more for amusement than anything else, you must have noticed leaves, especially of the bramble or blackberry, which were streaked over with sinuous markings. These are due to the work of minute larvæ of various insects, eating away the green matter between the upper and under sides of the leaf. No fewer than four orders of insects have members which indulge in this mode of getting a living. The two orders most largely represented in this respect are the *Lepidoptera* (by the grubs of the little *Tineina*) and the *Diptera*, or two-winged flies. Not unfrequently you may see a leaf that has been thus mined into by two or three different species of larvæ, each of which has left its individual

Fig. 130.

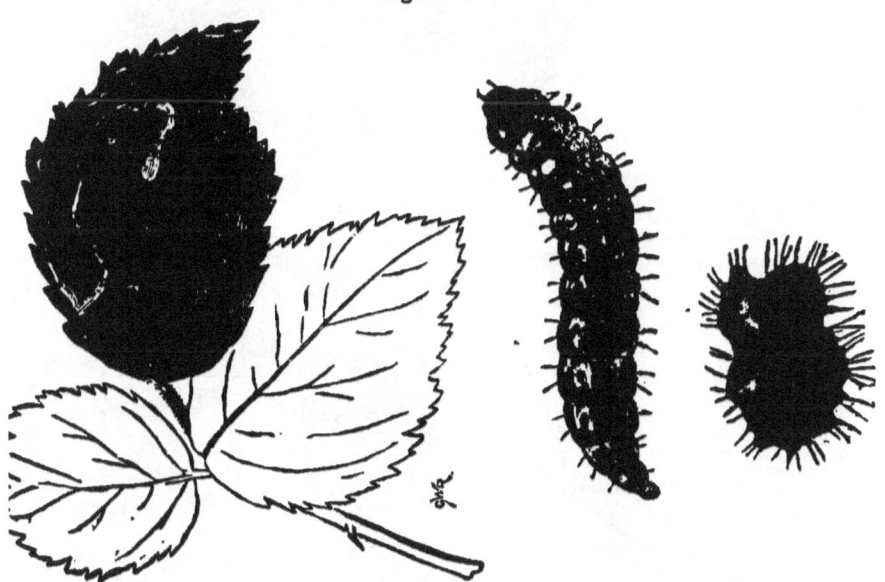

Mined Bramble Leaf, and Larva of *Nepticula aurella*, magnified.

mark upon the surface. One of the commonest of these is on the bramble (Fig. 130) and is the work of a little tinea, called *Nepticula aurella*. This, it will be perceived, mines in quite a different way to another common insect (*Tischeria marginea*, Fig. 131) which eats away extensive patches. The larva forming this mine is of a green colour, and rather

Fig. 131.

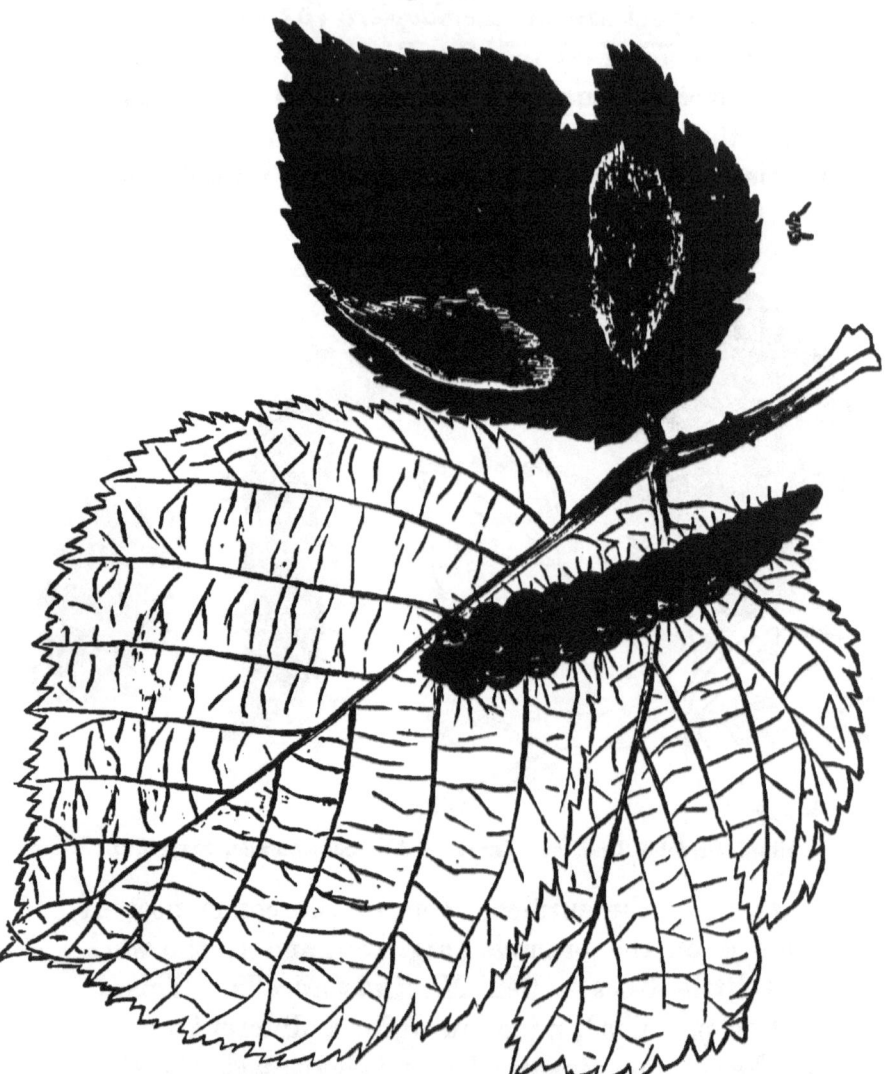

Mined Bramble Leaf, and Larva of *Tischeria marginea*, enlarged.

rigid, with a black head. It changes within the
place it has excavated, to the pupa state, and in
about three weeks afterwards, makes its appearance
in the world as a minute moth, whose utmost

Fig. 132.

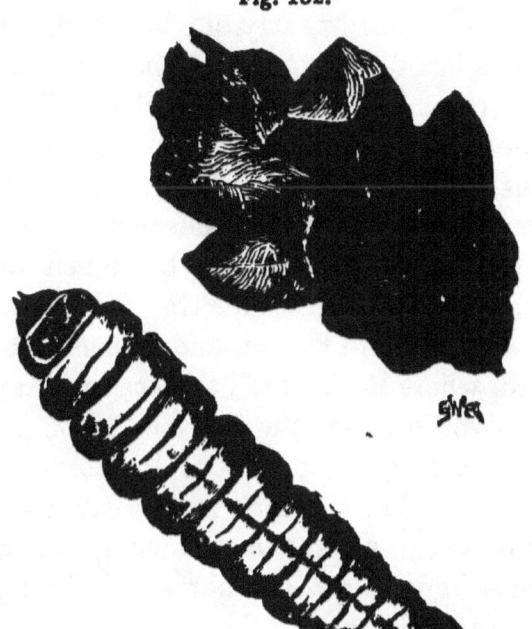

Mined Oak Leaf, and Larva of *Micropteryx subpurpurella*, enlarged.

expanse of wings is not more than the third of an
inch! Some of the larvæ of beetles also are leaf-
miners, especially that group which, on account of
their prolonged snout, are commonly called "weevils."
One cannot be surprised at the number of outward

markings thus left on leaves when we know that in this country we have several hundred species of the larva of tiny moths alone that are engaged in this operation! Look at the leaves of any young oak-tree in June, and you will find that some of them have been mined nearly one half their area, so that nothing has been left except the two thin skins of the upper and lower sides of the leaf. The larva that has done this has no legs. Its whole specialisation seems to have been concentrated in its jaws, which are constantly at work devouring the green parts of the leaf—the chlorophyl. When full fed this species of larva descends to the ground by means of a spider-like thread, and forms a cocoon in the ground, where it stays till the coming May. In that month you may see the tiny moths, of which it forms one, sporting on and about the leaves of the oak. It is about half an inch in the expanse of its wings, which are of a pale golden green colour. This species goes by the name of *Micropteryx subpurpurella*. We have other English species of this genus that are similarly devoted to leaf-mining, some of them in the leaves of the birch. July, however, is the month when oak leaves are most discoloured and marked by the insect leaf-miners. One species of insect whose larva is then at work (*Coriscium brogniardellum*, Fig. 133) is an elegant little moth, about a third of an inch across its wings. The fore-wings are of a glossy brown, ornamented with four oblique spots running from the edges.

Fig. 133.

Mined Oak Leaf, and Larva of *Coriscium brogniardellum,* enlarged

From July to September, these ravages go on, each
species leaving its mark so characteristically that
the entomologist can immediately recognise its
presence.   One of the little moths whose larva
may be thus traced is the *Lithocolletis* (Fig. 134), an
exceedingly small, but very delicately marked insect.
Its larva is of a whitish colour, and many of them
pass their pupa state within the mined-out skins

Fig. 134.

Oak Leaf mined by *Lithocolletis*, showing Larva inside.

of the dried leaf. In October, another species of
larva is at work, which commences its gallery along
the mid-rib of the leaf, and then, after proceeding a
short distance in one direction, turns sharply round,
and works away by one of the radiating veins.
This species is the *Nepticula bimaculella*.   Like a
species just mentioned, it lowers itself to the ground
when it has reached its mature larval condition, and
forms a cocoon in the soil, where it remains, in the
pupal state, until the following June.   During that

month it may be found squatting on the trunks of
oak-trees—a tiny moth, not the quarter of an inch

Fig. 135.

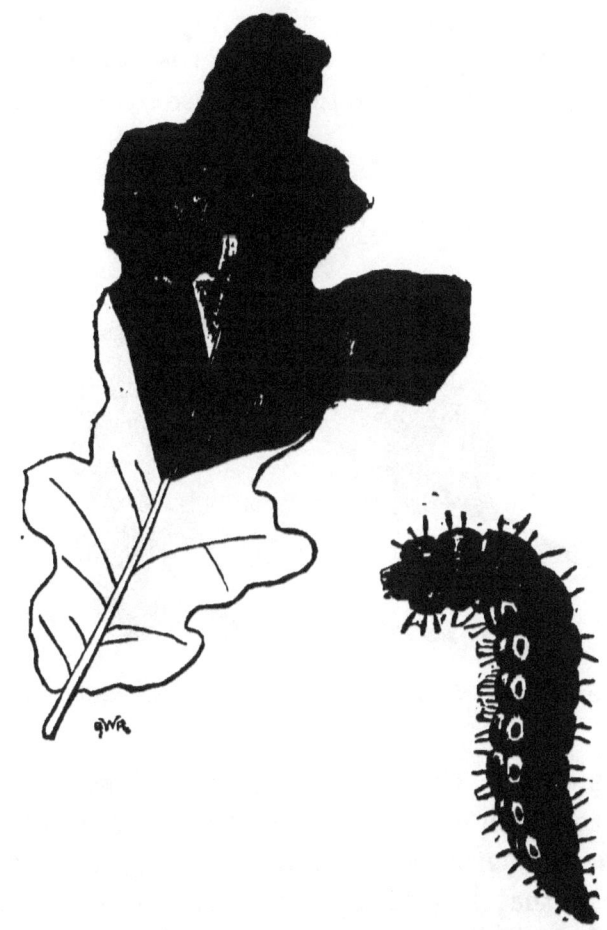

Mined Oak Leaf, and Larva of *Nepticula sub-bimaculella*, enlarged.

across expanse of wings, the fore wings of which are
blackish, with two triangular whitish spots nearly in

o

the middle. Lastly, let us draw attention to the common markings on the leaves of the hawthorn, which are similarly caused by the larvæ of another species of tinea, called *Coleophora nigricella*. In May and June you may see the leaves of the hawthorn disfigured by large brown blotches, caused by the voracity

Fig. 136.

Mined Hawthorn Leaf, and Larva of *Coleophora nigricella*, natural size and magnified.

of this species. On some leaves you may see a small brown, roundish object, about half an inch in length. This is the portable habitation, or case, formed by the larva that has mined the leaf. It is not constructed until the larvæ is nearly full grown, and it is then used for purposes of retreat when alarmed.

Whilst speaking of the hieroglyphic markings on leaves, one is naturally led to inquire concerning another class of objects, which occur as parasites or as malformations. The galls clustering so thickly on pollarded oaks, and the "spangles" or "buttons" which may often be seen almost covering the backs of leaves, are both the work of certain insects which rupture the epidermis, and cause the cellular vege- table matter to assume these monstrous shapes. The same cause is assignable to the "bedeguar," the

Fig. 137.

Gall Insect (*Cynips Kollari*), × 10.

rough red, furry knots so often to be seen on the wild rose. The common gall of the oak is produced by the female of a little fly known to entomologists by the name of *Cynips Kollari*. Hitherto the male insect has escaped detection, and is therefore at present unknown. Recently another species of cynips has been at work in the same direction, and many of our young oaks have suffered in consequence. Until lately this species remained

o 2

unnamed, and the general idea was that it had been
recently introduced.   As is the case with the species
already mentioned, only the female insect has been
observed.   The two kinds of disc-shaped galls common
on the under surface of oak-leaves are frequently a
puzzle to people ignorant of natural history.   In
Fig. 139 the upper portion of the leaf represents
those commonly known as " oak spangles," whilst

Fig. 138.

Gall Insect (*Cynips sp*).

the lower portion is seen bearing those which go by
the name of " button galls."   The former are due
to an insect called by entomologists *Cynips longipennis*, of which we give a magnified figure.   The
" button galls " are caused by another insect known
as *Neurobius Reaumuri*.   Besides these two, there
are at least half a score other species of nearly allied
insects whose attacks produce similar malformations
of the cuticles of leaves of various kinds of oaks.
The sections of these " spangles " and " buttons "

are interesting microscopical objects, as are also the hairs of the latter.

The "Saw-flies" are objects less known to the general public, although the farmer is obliged to own a far nearer acquaintance with them than he cares about. One species, commonly known as the "Turnip saw-fly," or "Black-jack" (*Athalia spinarium*) is exceedingly destructive to the turnip crops. It is the caterpillar that goes by the name of "Black-jack" from its appearance. In the Eastern counties, this creature often lays waste hundreds of acres of turnips in one season. Nothing, except a hard winter, seems able to arrest its ravages. Some years have been marked as the "canker" year through the extraordinary appearance of these costly pests. The insect

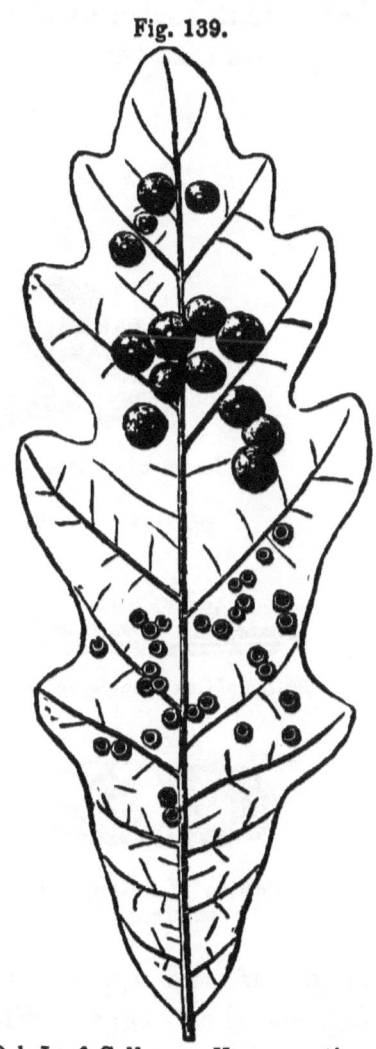

Fig. 139.

Oak Leaf Galls. *a*, Upper portion, with Oak Spangles; *b*, lower portion, with Button Galls.

into which the caterpillar

passes belongs to the same order as our wasps and bees—that known as the *Hymenoptera*. It and its congeners take their popular name from the peculiar

Fig. 140.

Insect of Button Gall (*Cynips longipennis*).

Fig. 141.

Section of Oak spangle, enlarged.

Fig. 142.

Fig. 143.

Section of Button Gall, enlarged.

Tufts of hair from the same, more highly magnified.

shape of the apparatus with which the females deposit their eggs. When properly prepared, it forms a beautiful object for the microscope. It consists of two saws, the teeth of which are again serrated. These saws work alternately, and are strengthened by a back similar to that of the carpenter's well-known "tenon" saw — the saws working in a groove at the back. The illustration (Fig. 145), shows the appearance of these ingenious instruments when seen under a microscope. There

Fig. 144.

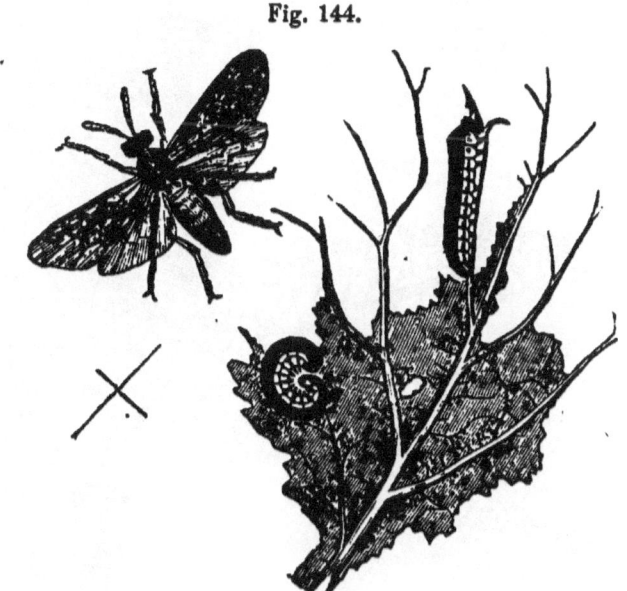

Larva and mature Male Turnip Saw Fly. The latter enlarged to 2 diameters.

are several species of saw-flies, the largest of which is that known as the Great Saw Fly (*Urocerus gigas*), which is a very fine insect. It may be seen on some tree trunk, with its body hunched up, trying for a place where it can deposit its eggs. The body is then so bent that the point of the sheath and the ovipositor can make the first impression at the

desired spot, which has been previously selected by
the antennæ. When the operation of boring has
commenced, the "saw-blades" are worked to and
fro and from side to side, just as a carpenter would

Fig. 145.

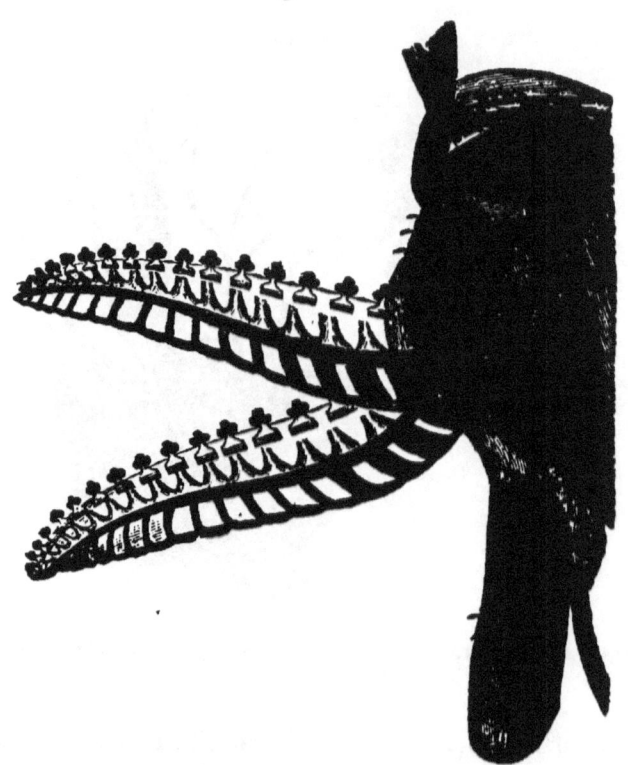

Saws of *Allantus aterrimus*, × 40.

carefully use a slender awl. Meantime, for half an
hour, the insect will remain perfectly motionless, all
its force being utilised in the important duty of
boring a hole for the deposition of its eggs.

Should you ramble down one of our green lanes before breakfast, it is more than likely you may come across an object worthy of your regard, in the person of the Great Green Grasshopper (*Gryllus viridissimus*). Here, the popular name is in error, for the insect is more nearly allied to the crickets

Fig. 146.

Great Saw-Fly.

than to the grasshoppers. Anyhow, it is an interesting insect, although its bright fresh green colour, when it is settled on a long blade of grass, renders it difficult of detection. This, too, has a formidable, sword-blade-like ovipositor, which is often a source of alarm to people who know nothing of its habits. You may hear the calls of this insect

all the summer night through, but its agility and
colour render it difficult to be caught at any other
time than the morning, when it appears to be
resting from its labours. The great green grasshopper is capable of being to a great extent tamed,
but the legs have a curious way of rotting at the

Fig. 147.

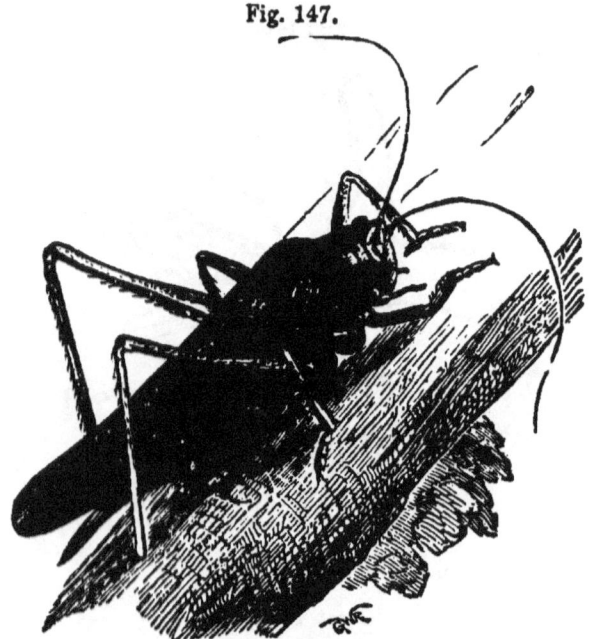

Gryllus viridissima.

joints, and of falling off, unless care be taken with
it. It is a sad enemy to the plant-lice, which it
will devour by hundreds. It is also very pugnacious
and cannibal, and if you place half a dozen together
under the same glass it will not be long before they
make "Kilkenny cats" of each other! The eggs
still further carry out the "mimicry" which is so

useful to the mother, for they are of a brownish
green, and look to all the world like certain grass
seeds.

For the habits of hosts of other objects, the various
species of wasps, bees, gnats, dragon-flies, &c., we
refer our readers to the Rev. J. G. Wood's 'Insects
at Home,' one of the best written and most popular
works of its kind. We only pretend to select just
such objects as we think offer themselves most
prominently, and which no intelligent pedestrian
can do otherwise than notice. There is no lack of
works in each department, ready to the hands of the
young entomologist. Among these, Mr. E. C. Rye's
illustrated book on 'British Beetles' stands foremost. This we can say, in commencing the study
of entomology, a youth will lay up many hours of
pure unalloyed happiness, and have his thoughts
drawn out into fuller communion with the life that
fills land and air and sea with its presence, and
which is thus the best assurance of the Love that
evolved and the Care that supports its manifold
forms!

CHAPTER VII.

THE SNAILS AND SLUGS OF OUR GREEN LANES.

E have already alluded to the numerous fresh-water snails to be found in every standing pool or tarn, and now proceed to describe objects allied to them which are no less common. Nay, many of them are, in the opinion of horticulturists, only too abundant, and without doubt, these gentlemen would express no sigh of regret at their extinction. Here, however, we have not to do with the utility of natural objects. Our task is simply to draw attention to them, and if some of them are injurious to man, possibly we may extract some compensation by turning snails and slugs into objects of scientific interest.

Well do these creatures deserve their scientific name. Many people who call them "nasty soft things" little imagine that in the latter adjective they are applying to them the same epithet as is conveyed under the Greek word *mollusca*, which naturalists employ to include them and their kind. Our marine shells, especially the larger and brighter coloured species from tropical countries, have long been objects of interest ; whilst the thinner but similarly formed shells of our land snails have come in for all the contempt and dislike. But we have many species that construct really pretty shells, and we know of no collection of natural objects which looks better in the cabinet than one of snail shells. Any beginner wishing to have information how to commence collecting these common objects should procure the number of 'Science Gossip' for 1872, which contains an article on 'Collecting and Preserving Land and Fresh-water Shells,' by Mr. R. Tate. The work by the same well-known naturalist, with coloured illustrations, on 'British Mollusca,' will readily enable the student to acquire a good knowledge of our native species.

Let us take the more objectionable kinds of land *mollusca* first—the "slugs." You meet with them, black and white, in all your country strolls, especially in the early morning, or after a shower of summer rain. They need little or no description, as every one is familiar with their elongated and naked black and yellow bodies, with their "horns" or tentacles in front, curiously peering into and feeling everything the animal comes across. They belong to the family *Limacidæ*, and are air-breathing, although, perhaps, you would not think so at first. We have met with people who imagine that slugs are only snails that have left their shells, and that they have the power of returning to them whenever they please. So far from this being the case, slugs make no shells at all, whilst the true snail cannot leave its shell, being attached to it by certain muscles. The Large Spotted slug (*Limax maximus*) is exceedingly common, and this may serve as an example of the general structure of the rest. Over what would be its shoulders if it had feet, is the oval-shaped mantle. Beneath this, you may find a thin shelly plate, so that the chief difference between snails and slugs is that the mantle of the former deposits shelly matter on the *outside*, and the latter *inside*. In both cases, the object is to protect the visceral organs. The shelly plates of the slugs were formerly called "snail stones," and were believed to possess a medicinal virtue when taken for the disease called "gravel." Like the fresh-water snails already referred to, the mouth of the slug is armed with rows of curved teeth, placed on a moveable ribbon. The mucus which slugs secrete so abundantly, and which is one reason for their being so generally disliked, is formed by glands which are situated in the skin. Our native slugs are divided into four genera, according to the relative position of the mantle, the shell, and the breathing orifice. The shell often exists in a very rudimentary state, as in the Black slug (*Arion ater*), where it is represented merely by granules of shelly matter diffused through the mantle. The latter species is perhaps the most abundant of any, and the breathing orifice is situated at the hind part of the shield-like mantle over the shoulders.   It is a very omnivorous feeder, is fond of garden produce, but does not object to devouring earth-worms, or even to making a meal of one of its own species.   Its colour is a brownish-black when adult, but the young are of a whitish or yellowish colour.   Its eggs, which are usually deposited in May, among the roots of plants, are globular and partly transparent.   Singularly enough, on the

Fig. 148.

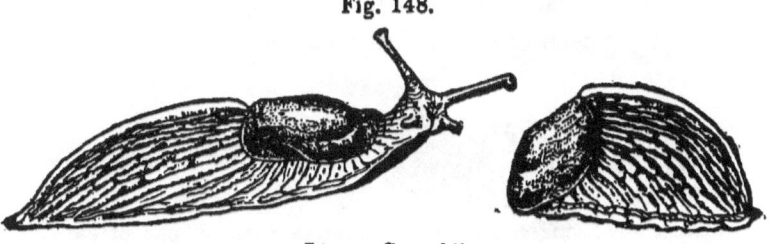

Limax Sowerbii.

principle of the well-known lines that "Greater fleas have little fleas upon their backs to bite 'em," the black slug is infested with a peculiar mite, which may frequently be seen running over the animal's body, the slimy mucus apparently having no influence in retarding their speed.   These mites, which form good microscopic objects, take up their abode in the interior of the slug, getting inside through the breathing aperture.   The slug, however, does not seem at all incommoded by its parasites, but lets them wander to and fro of their own sweet will.   The Garden slug (*Arion hortensis*) is nearly as well known as the species just mentioned, but it is much smaller and slenderer, and is marked with longitudinal grey stripes, the foot (as the base of the body on which snails and slugs crawl, is called) being bordered with orange. The jaw is very interesting (Fig. 151). The eggs of this species of slug are phosphorescent for a fortnight after they have been laid, and the student may see them in the evening on the moist banks of the lanes, giving out a pale light.

The *Limaces*, or true slugs, chiefly differ from the above by possessing an internal shell or plate, the

Fig. 149.

Testacella haliotidea, showing diminutive Shell on end of body.

exterior of the mantle-shield being marked with concentric lines. The jaw is evidently framed for a good purpose, and one cannot be surprised, on seeing it, at the capacity for feeding possessed by slugs. The largest of the limaces (*Limax maximus*) is often five or six inches in length. Everybody knows it, for it is very fond of frequenting our cellars and damp corners, whence it issues during the night on foraging expeditions, leaving its trail, how-ever, behind it, in a silvery, iridescent slime, which often leads to its detection and destruction. It hyber-nates in the mossy crevices of trees, or in decaying wood, and, in the spring, issues forth and deposits its eggs under stones. Like the species already mentioned, it is infested with mites. The Yellow slug (*L. flavus*) often grows to the length of four or five inches, but it may be identified from the foregoing species by the end of its tail, which is keeled, as well as by its yellowish body, covered with blackish-brown spots. Usually its slime is of a yellowish colour, but when irritated, the animal has the power of secreting a bluish-white mucus. Unlike some slugs, this species usually associates in numbers, especially in damp cellars, night being the time when they sally forth on predatory expeditions. You may find it in plenty in damp woods, or under stones; but it may there be distinguished from the Field slug (*L. agrestis*) by the much smaller size of the latter, which is also of a yellowish-grey colour, mottled—the colour, however, varying considerably in individuals. The length of this species rarely exceed an inch and a half. The farmer and gardener are well acquainted with it, as one of their worst enemies; but it is possible to decoy it away from more valuable vegetation by greased cabbage leaves, of which it is specially fond. These leaves may be laid where ducks can devour the slugs, as that dainty bird regards the slug much as we do the "Whitstable Native." One great cause of the destructive powers of this species is its immense fertility, for an individual has been found to lay as many as three hundred and eighty eggs.

The Tree slug (*L. arboreus*) takes its name from

P

its living on trees, particularly on the beech, from which it can let itself down like certain caterpillars, by means of its tenacious slime. This feat, however, is one that most slugs can perform, although they do not practise it to such a degree as the Tree slug. The latter can also climb up its suspended thread. A search under the fallen trees of a damp wood will discover this species, but it is not near so common as those just described. When adult, it is three inches long. Its tentacles are much shorter than those of *L. maximus*, and its colour is greyish, spotted with yellowish-white, with a central dusky stripe, and a dark band running down each side.

Fig. 150.

Jaw of Black Slug.

In the neighbourhood of Norwich, and most cities and towns in the southerly parts of England, another species (*L. Sowerbii*, Fig. 148) is common. It may readily be known by its back being ridged or "keeled" along its entire length. When at its greatest extension it is about three inches in length, the colour being yellowish-brown, and that of the ridge amber. Hence it is one of our prettiest species, and its shape being gracefuller than any other slug, renders it easily recognisable. It lays its eggs in the soil towards the end of the year. Like other species of slugs, it is infested with mites. The Jet Black slug (*L. gagates*) is another local species with a ridged back. It is of a lead grey black, and sometimes even of a dark red colour. When it is at rest, its back is arched in a graceful form, and it then looks rounder than any other species. It is generally found in the neighbourhood of the sea, not far from the coast.

The *Testacella haliotidea* (Fig. 149) is a creature which connects the naked slugs with the land snails possessing shells, in a very remarkable manner. Its Latin name is derived from a little shell that is situated at the extreme or tail-end of the body, which shell is a diminutive resemblance of the " Venus' ears," whose iridiscence recommends them as such general ornaments. The body of the slug is of a dirty yellow colour, about three inches long, when stretched out in the act of crawl-ing. We may almost regard this species as a modified snail, with aborted shell, or as a slug with an embryonic one. It is the terror of the common earthworm, which it will follow up into its burrow—a habit for which its attenuated body admirably fits it. The worms, when caught, are generally swallowed whole. The teeth of this species have already been referred to (page 34).

Fig. 151.

Jaw of Garden Slug.

Our land snails are better known by their shells than anything else, as it is not long since their classification was based on nothing else. Even now, it is often surprising how little collectors know of them beyond the form, &c. of the shells. As boys, we all remember the "luck" which was supposed to be attached to the successful plucker of a snail by the "horns." Whoever invented this joke—and it was very likely the ancient naturalist

who discovered the art of catching a bird by putting
salt on its tail—knew very well that, if you could
get a boy to devote much time to the attempt, it
would keep him out of mischief if it did nothing
else.   The ease and rapidity with which such
sluggish creatures as snails can withdraw their
tentacles on the approach of danger, is very remarkable.   This movement is effected simply by intro-
version, much as an old woman draws her stocking
feet into the leg, after mending them.   Like the
slugs and fresh-water snails, the land snails have
lingual ribbons, armed with teeth, besides their
tolerably powerful horny jaws.   Their breathing
orifice may be seen on the right side, beneath the
margin of the shell, when the creature is in motion.
The reproductive orifice is situated near the base
of the *right* upper tentacle.   During the breeding
season, certain species have a peculiar habit of
shooting "love darts" at each other.

As might have been expected from the nature of
their shelly covering, land snails are very largely
influenced in their distribution by the geological
character of rocks.   Wherever limestone or chalk is
the underlying stratum, there they are sure to
abound, both in individuals and species.   Perhaps
the commonest, and certainly the *largest*, of the
more abundant kind is *Helix aspersa* (Fig. 152).
This species, according to Professor Edward Forbes,
is largely eaten in many parts of Greece; and
even in this country we have known country

"quack" doctors to recommend it, boiled in milk, as a cure for consumption! In the south of France, on Ash Wednesday, both this species and the common Garden snail (*Helix nemoralis*) are sold and eaten. In the winter time you may see groups of five or six of the former shells clustered together, the mouths closed with a tolerably tough and waterproof diaphragm, to protect the molluscs hybernating within. The Apple snail (*Helix pomatia*)

Fig. 152.

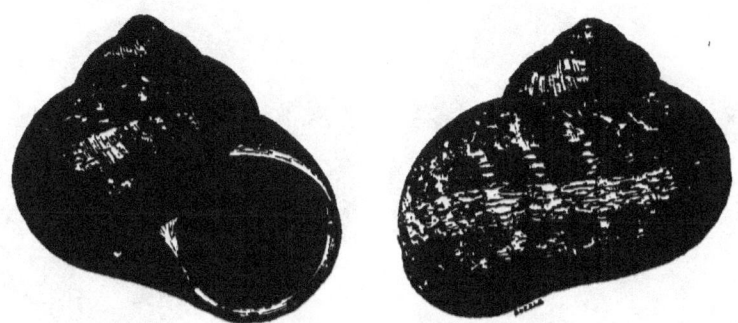

Spotted Snail (*H. aspersa*).

is the largest of our indigenous species, but it is only to be met with in the south of England, under hedges, in woods, and on chalky soils. It seems to have been introduced there about the middle of the sixteenth century, and to have spread since then over most of the southern counties. It was evidently introduced for medicinal purposes, the larger species of British snails formerly figuring importantly in the pharmacopæia—a use which has been left to the "quacks," as a kind of "survival" of a pseudo-

scientific custom. This species was considered a
delicacy by the ancient Romans, who seem to have
ransacked river and land and sea for something
"fresh" in the eating line. Indeed, the use of
snails, not so much as food, although we have seen
they are often employed in Catholic countries
during Lent for this purpose, but for medicine, is
more extensive than is commonly supposed. Large

Fig. 153.

Apple Snail (*H. pomatia*).

quantities are exported alive in barrels to America
for this purpose, and even our London markets
create a demand for them, for the cure of chest
complaints !

The Spotted snail (*Helix aspersa*) is sadly destructive, and anything but a favourite with farmers
and gardeners. It evidently dislikes clayey soils,
however; although this is no particular gain, for
another common species, *Helix hortensis*, the Garden

snail " (Fig. 154) seems to prefer them, and therefore takes its place. Notwithstanding the destructive
habits of *H. aspersa*, if it can get primroses, or
nettles, it will not trouble the farmer for any other
food—the deduction from which fact is that it would
pay to allow a few of these common plants to
remain, in order to draw off and pacify the snails.
The shell of *Helix hortensis* is more globular than
another abundant species, the Wood snail (*Helix
nemoralis*, Fig. 155) which it resembles in many
respects. It is also about one-third smaller in

Fig. 154.

Garden Snail (*H. hortensis*).

size. The eggs of the Garden snail look not much
unlike small peas—and a bad kind they would be for
any gardener to sow! Like most common and
abundant species, it is noted for the varieties into
which its members can be grouped. Of these there
are three very distinct forms, called by Macgillivray
the common banded, the unicolour (not banded) and
the sand-inhabiting kind (Arenicola). The garden
snail is further noticeable for the smell of onions it
can emit—a character shared by several other rarer
species of snails. The normal condition of the shell
of the garden snail is five thin brown bands running

up the whorls, the ground being a pretty yellow.
You cannot fail to notice this species, and its most
marked varieties, when taking a country stroll.
The single and broader brown band running up
the middle of the body-whorl of the wood snail
(Fig. 155) and the black rim round the mouth, will
readily enable any one to identify it.   Like the
species last mentioned, however, it comprises a good
many varieties, all of which are exceedingly pretty.
On it you may find the species of mite to which we

Fig. 155.

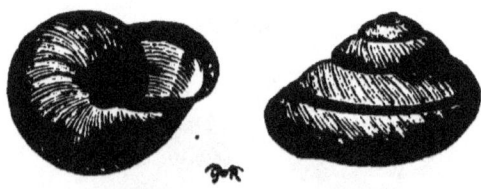

Wood Snail (*H. nemoralis*).

have already alluded as infesting certain slugs.
This species seems to appear in thousands all on a
sudden, whenever a warm shower has fallen; but
you will hardly see a specimen during a continued
drought, as it seems to have the power of *æstivation*,
like the tropical landshells.   The Orchard snail
(*H. arbustorum*, Fig. 156) resembles the wood snail
in its general appearance, but its distribution is far
more local.   The markings, also, are not so definite,
but frequently look as if they were mottled.   On
limestone soils the student will undoubtedly find
the Wrinkled snail (*Helix caperata*, Fig. 157).   The

common name is derived from the numerous, concentric and rib-like striations on the whorls. Its
colour is a dullish yellow-white, relieved by narrow
brown bands. A much commoner species is the
Bristly snail (*Helix hispida*, Fig. 158) which may be
found among the moss and herbage in damp woods
or shady places. It is only about a quarter of an inch
in breadth, and we have known young naturalists to
fall into the error of supposing that this, and other
similar small species, were the *young* of the larger

Fig. 156.

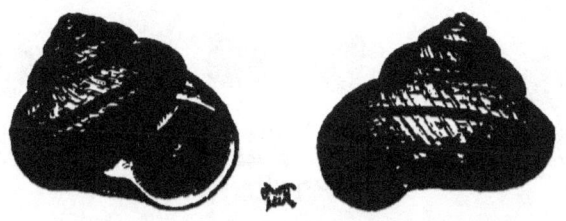

Orchard Snail (*H. arbustorum*).

kinds. The Prickly snail (*H. aculeata*, Fig. 159) is
similarly covered with hairs, but it may readily be
distinguished by its more elongated form. It is
smaller as well, and as it frequents dead leaves
which it much resembles in colour, it is rather
difficult to be distinguished, except by a practised eye.
The Plated or Scaly snail (*H. lamellata*, Fig. 161)
is a northern species, only about the tenth of an
inch in height. The Little White snail (*H. pulchella*,
Fig. 160) is milk-white in colour, having a diameter
of the tenth of an inch. Its striated horny jaw

(Fig. 163) is a good microscopic object. This shell is common among the short herbage of the Downs, and it has been suggested that the fine flavour of Down mutton may be due to the profusion of such small shells consumed by the sheep when

Fig. 157.

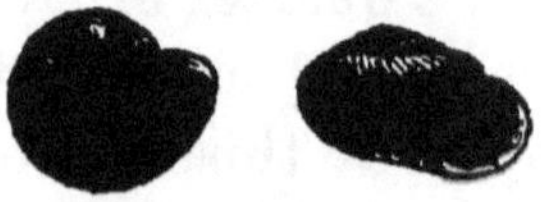

Wrinkled Snail (*H. caperata*).

Fig. 158.

Bristly Snail (*H. hispida*) enlarged.

Fig. 159.

Prickly Snail (*H. aculeata*), enlarged.

Fig. 160.

Little White Snail (*H. pulchella*), enlarged.

Fig. 161.

Scaly Snail (*H. lamellata*).

Fig. 162.

Carthusian Snail (*H. carthusiana*).

Fig. 163.

Jaw of Little White Snail (magnified).

feeding! The Carthusian shell (*H. Cartusiana*, Fig. 162) takes its name from having been first discovered near a Carthusian monastery. It is common on the Kentish and Sussex Downs, and is evidently fond of the neighbourhood of the sea. In many respects this species is allied to the Kentish snail (*H. Cantiana*, Fig. 164), which is a very pretty species, about three-quarters of an inch in diameter, and of a yellowish-white colour. It is abundant on nettles and in moist places in the south-eastern counties, especially in Kent and Sussex. The Zoned snail (*H. virgata*, Fig. 165) is very singular in its departure from the usual habits of ordinary snails. It may be found on dry heaths and the Downs,

Fig. 164.

Kentish Snail (*H. Cantiana*.)

Fig. 165.

Zoned Snail (*H. virgata*).

especially near the sea, where it will be found in clusters on the stems of various plants. This species also disappears during hot and dry weather, to re-appear in such numbers after a shower that some people believe it has been raining snails. It will feed on insects, especially on the lady-birds, but is itself cropped by sheep along with the short grass where it abounds. The Heath snail (*H. ~icetorum*, Fig. 166) is of a circular, flattened form, and has a large umbilicus, or hollow in the centre underneath. The mouth is nearly circular. The animal is very sensitive and sluggish, and it appears to be especially harmed by excessive showers of rain. The Lapidary snail (*H. lapicida*, Fig. 167), or "Stonecutter," obtained its name because Linnæus thought it had the power of excavating into lime-

Fig. 166.

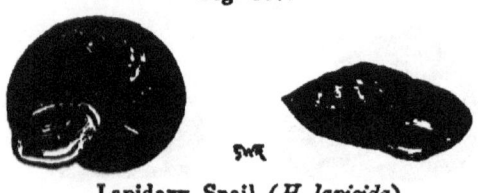

Heath Snail (*H. ericetorum*).

Fig. 167.

Lapidary Snail (*H. lapicida*).

stone. The shell is lens-shaped, and the edge of the diameter is sharp and keeled. The colour is a yellowish-red. It is very abundant in the Peak of Derbyshire, and may also be found in woodland districts. The shell grows to the diameter of one inch. The Rounded snail (*H. rotundata*, Fig. 168) is also one of our commonest land snails, and may be found under stones in damp woods, among fallen leaves, on rocks, and in many other places; but most abun-

dantly in the neighbourhood of decaying wood. The
Ruddy or Rufous snail (*H. rufescens*, Fig. 169), notwithstanding its name, assumes several tints and
shades, and may even be found white. It is
abundant on hedge-banks, especially in limestone
districts. The young shells are covered with hairs,

Fig. 168. Fig. 169.

 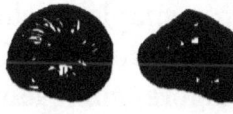

Rounded Snail (*H. rotundata*). Ruddy Snail (*H. rufescens*).

and then very much resemble *Helix hispida*, from
which, however, they may be known by the keel on
the margin of the outer whorl. The Pigmy snail
(*H. pygmæa*, Fig. 170) is a pretty little object, not
bigger than a pin's head, and therefore
difficult to find, although it has a wide
distribution. It must be sought for
under stones, and at the roots of grass;
and especially on dead leaves in moist
woods.

Fig. 170.

Pigmy Snail
(*H. pygmæa*),
enlarged.

Space forbids us to do other than call attention
to various small species of land snails outside the
genus *Helix*. Among these are the *Bulimus,
Clausilia, Pupa*, &c., and a quiet, careful search
among moss or on limestone soils will discover some
of them. The clausilia will be found on calcareous
soils, and is well worth examination, on account of

its peculiar structure. This consists of an elastic appendage which can be used to close the aperture. If you break off the outer part of the last whorl, you will see a spoon-shaped, shelly plate, attached to the column of the spire by the elastic filament or spring. When the animal creeps out of its shell, this is thrust aside, and when it withdraws, it springs the door to: so we see the principle of having a simple mechanism to close the door when we have passed out of or into a room, was in practice long before man adopted it! The pupas may be abundantly found in damp moss everywhere, their brown, horny-looking shells being of an elegant shape, but looking as if the stuff had run short before the spire had been completed, so that it had suddenly come to a conclusion. Notwithstanding the apparent insignificance of land snails, they have a wonderful antiquity. Species of pupa have been found fossilised inside the trunks of ancient Carboniferous club-mosses. They are also abundant, together with fossil bulimi, in the early Tertiary strata of the Isle of Wight and elsewhere. Scarcely less ancient is the family of *Helix*, for they form beds in the Upper Eocene deposits. As far back as the period of the Norwich and Red Crags, the *same* species lived that are still existing in these latitudes. Thus, *Helix hispida* is a not uncommon fossil in the former deposit, and a comparison with modern forms shows that it has not altered in the meantime. An interesting circumstance occurs with regard to an abundant species of fossil helix (*H. labyrinthica*) met with in the Eocene strata of the Isle of Wight. It is extinct in this country now, but it is still living in the United States: a singular piece of testimony, this, to the geological changes which have rendered it extinct in its parent country, but have driven it westerly before those events ensued which now separate the Old World from the New!

CHAPTER VIII.

THE FLOWERING PLANTS OF THE GREEN LANES.

NONE will deny that the flowering plants of our lanes and meadows form the central point in any country stroll taken for the purpose of studying natural history. To leave them out would be a greater omission than that of the character of Hamlet from Shakespeare's celebrated play. Even if we were inclined to neglect plants, we cannot do so and study other branches of natural science. The entomologist must know the leading species, seeing that on them many of the larvæ of the insect he seeks find their proper food. Our wild flowers are distributed everywhere, and are adapted to well nigh every condition of physical existence. They are the delight of childhood, the objects of investigation to mature science, and those of contemplation to the philosopher and poet. Take them out of existence, and we should lose the finest passages and references in the best writers of all ages and all countries.

But the difficulty is to know which to select in the short space we can devote to their consideration. The pretty Daisy "vermeil-tipped and white," abounds everywhere, and with its English look cheers the heart of many a far-off emigrant with its recollection. The grassy margins of the lanes are relieved by its pure white and yellow disks, and, over the hedge, the neighbouring meadows are a perfect sheet of white and yellow, owing to the abundance of this plant and the buttercups. The first-comer of the genus *Ranunculus* is the little Pile-wort (*R. ficaria*), whose star-shaped, shiny yellow blossoms, and glossy dark green leaves, tell us of the approaching summer. It is on these leaves that the microscopic botanist finds one of the most beautiful of diminutive fungi, in the dusty yellow "cluster-cups" which parasitically affect the plant. Succeeding the pile-wort, and taking its place in the meadows and in the green lanes, is the Bulbous Crowfoot (*Ranunculus bulbosus*). Notwithstanding the resemblance of one species of buttercup to another, you will have no difficulty in identifying this species, for the sepals of the calyx are always turned right back; and if this is not a sufficient guide, dig up a plant, and you will find a fleshy bulb-like swelling at the base of the stem which gives to the flower its specific name. By-and-by, as the summer advances, the study of the *Ranunculaceæ* will afford the young student some busy work. He will find species growing on the margins of tarns or pools with lance-shaped leaves and yellow flowers

Q

(*R. flammula*), and others growing in the water, with leaves like those of the chamomile below and resembling those of the ivy above, the flower being a pure delicate white. This is the Aquatic Crowfoot (*R. aquatilis*). Already, in the early summer, he may find the Goldilocks (*R. auricomus*) in the shady places of the woods and hedges. It is a pretty plant, with small yellow flowers, and may be identified at once by the striking difference between the leaves at its base and those higher up the stem, which are very much divided or cleft in comparison. Later in the summer, the bulbous crowfoot will have decayed, but you will hardly have missed it, for its place has been gradually supplied by the Upright Crowfoot (*R. acris*) and the Creeping Crowfoot (*R. repens*), both of which, in their names, carry about them the means whereby the young botanist may distinguish them.

As March approaches its end, and April sets in, our hedge-banks begin to look quite cheerful and attractive. Foremost among the early comers, and almost claiming attention by its large, glossy green leaves, is the plant commonly known as "Lords and Ladies" (*Arum maculatum*, Fig. 171); other names for this plant are "Cuckoo Pint," "Wake Robin," &c., It is singular how the cuckoo has given its name to several early summer flowers that usually flower about the time of its appearance, such as the Cuckoo Flower (*Cardamine pratensis*), &c., and even to the insect enveloped in froth called "cuckoo-spit." The

Arum is in many respects a very peculiar plant. The

corm (a), or root as we should call it, is really an underground stem, which contains a large quantity of starch that has been *misused* in commerce for the purpose of adulterating arrowroot. In the early history of the plant there appears a convolute leaf (b), which eventually opens after having sufficiently protected the spadix and its remarkable cluster of flowers. For some hours after the opening of the spathe, the heat evolved may be felt by the hand, or tested with an ordinary thermometer. The leaves are very acrid, and are sometimes mistaken by children

Fig. 171.

Cuckoo Pint (*Arum maculatum*) ⅓ nat. size.

for those of sorrel. If a portion is placed in the mouth, and chewed a little, the tongue becomes

Fig. 172.

Fig. 173.

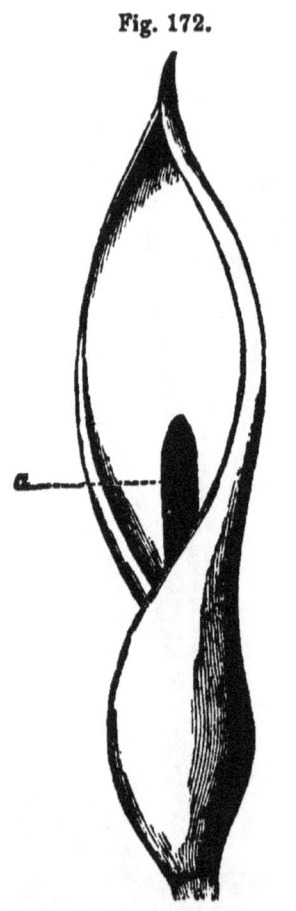

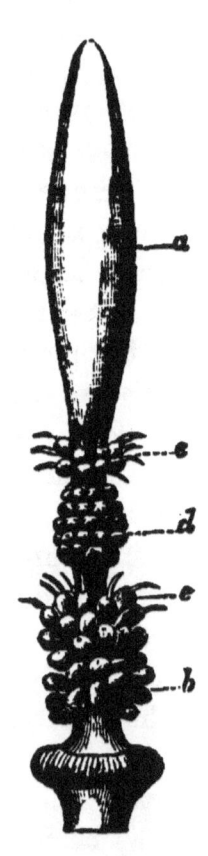

Spathe of *Arum maculatum,* after Lindley, nat. size.

Spadix of *Arum maculatum,* × 3.

speedily blistered, and it is a long time before the painful sensation is removed. The spadix (*a*) (Fig. 172) is a spike with a succulent axis. It is a kind of flower stalk bearing two sorts of flowers of the simplest form, both destitute of corolla and calyx. At the base of this central stalk is a cluster of fertile pistils (b, Fig. 173) surmounted by a frill of one or two rows of rudimentary organs of the same kind (c)

Fig. 174.

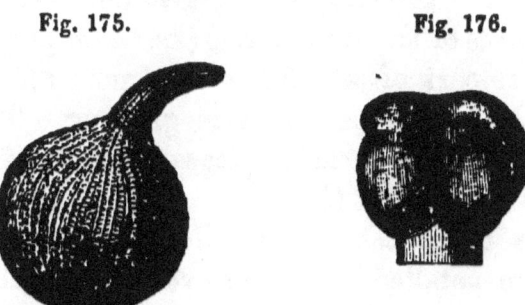

Fertile Pistils, × 25.

Fig. 175.   Fig. 176.

Aborted Pistil.   Perfect Stamen.

Above the latter is a group of perfect sessile or stalkless stamens (d), and still higher another ring of aborted stamens. These parts form very interesting microscopic objects, viewed with a low power. Thus, the perfect female organs are represented in Fig. 174, and the aborted or rudimentary ones in Fig. 175. Up to a certain stage in the life-history of the plant

both these forms are alike. Presently the growth of
the aborted organs is arrested, whilst that of the
perfect form progresses. This is really the main
difference between them. Fig. 176 represents one
of the perfect stamens.

What is that plant growing just at the base of
the hawthorn bushes, and creeping down the hedge-
banks in festoons, its elegant green leaves dark-
ened with a dash of red in them which sets off
wonderfully the azure blue of the flowers? It is
the Ground Ivy (*Glechoma hederacea*) which, in the
north of England, where " yarb doctors " abound, is
credited with a fair share of medicinal properties.
Close by, but growing in clusters more erect, are the
paler leaves of the Red Nettle (*Lamium purpureum*),
the upper part of which has even more red in them,
especially when the plant is growing. The rose-
coloured flowers form a pleasant contrast to and
combination with the blue of the ground ivy.
Clusters of Stitchwort (*Stellaria holostea*), whose
white ten-petalled flowers are very beautiful objects,
dignified by children with the names of " birds'-
eyes," " milk-cans," &c., cannot fail to strike the
eye of the rambler. The seeds of this plant, when
examined with a low magnifying power, are very
beautiful objects. But even more delicately beautiful than any of our early summer plants, in our
opinion, is the little Germander Speedwell (*Veronica
chamædrys*), whose sky-blue petals, four-cleft, will
come off together, bringing the two stamens with them.

The leaves are nettle-shaped, and by-and-by will cover the hedge banks with their clusters. Many people mistake this pretty plant for the Forget-me-not, which is a species in nowise related to it. In old herbals you will find many curative properties ascribed to the speedwell, amongst others as a remedy for gout and cancer. About the same time of year when this species is in flower you may haply meet with another, the Thyme-leaved Veronica (*V. serpyllifolia*), with smaller and lighter blue blossoms, and having narrow leaves not a great deal unlike those of the plant whose name it has borrowed.

Our hedge banks and lane sides are the habitat of another genuinely English plant, the Self-heal (*Prunella vulgaris*). Its scientific name is a corruption of *Brunella*, derived doubtless from its being considered a certain cure for quinsy, the German name of which complaint is "bräune." In Cheshire it goes by the name of "carpenter's grass," whilst in Gloucestershire it is known as "carpenter's herb." Both these names allude to the belief that if a carpenter happened to cut himself, the applied leaves would stanch the blood and heal the cut. The same belief led to this plant being formerly called "hooke-heal," and "sickle-wort," in allusion to its curing the wounds caused by sickles and bill-hooks. In Essex, it is favoured with the appellation of "pick-pocket," but as that name is there given to weeds in general, it is invidious to signal out the present species. Its commoner and more general

Fig. 177.

Self-heal (*Prunella vulgaris*).

name of " self-heal," expresses all that is implied in
" carpenter's herb " and " sickle-wort. A herb for
which it is frequently mistaken is the Bugle (*Ajuga
reptans*), often to be met with in the same situation.
The latter plant, however, flowers earlier in the year,
and, as its specific name implies, is not erect like
the self-heal, but of a creeping character.

The month of June is the time for the more shady
parts of the lanes to be literally aglow with the
showy flowers of the Red Campion (*Lychnis diurna*).
There is no mistaking its oblong, hairy, palish-green
leaves, or the rosy petals of the flower, supported by
their dark-coloured calyx. From June to October,
and even into the winter months, you are sure to
find it in flower somewhere. Associated with it is
the White Campion (*Lychnis vespertina*) that loves to
climb among the bushes and brambles, especially on
the borders of corn-fields. In the summer evenings,
its delicate perfume scents the air, for that is the
time of day when its flowers are expanded the most,
a fact which has procured for it its other name of the
" Night-flowering Campion." A few specimens of the
Ragged Robin (*Lychnis Flos-cuculi*) grow near the
Red Campion, but in the moister meadows or marshes
a few yards off it occurs in such abundance as to
give a tinge to the vegetation. Its colour is a
delicate rose, but you will observe that its petals are
so deeply cleft that the slightest puff of air sets them
a fluttering, a circumstance which has earned for
the flower its name of " ragged."

In our rapid glance at the more prominent of the early summer flowers, let us not forget to notice the more unobtrusive species. They will well repay the observation bestowed upon them. Among these is the little Moschatel (*Adoxa moschatellina*), whose four pale green flowers are arranged in a square cluster at the summit of the stalk, which is surmounted by a fifth. You will be certain to discover this plant in the moist and shady parts of the lanes, right at the base of the hawthorn hedges. Below it, and where the numerous plants of the Dog's Mercury (*Mercurialis perennis*)—a peculiar plant, with large, rough leaves, and a greenish panicle of flowers hanging laxly down—allow it space, you see in dry places the Little Forget-me-not (*Myosotis collina*). Its entire size could be covered by a halfpenny, but you will observe that its clusters of diminutive flowers are of the most delicate sapphire blue. Not far off where the dog's mercury is growing, and covering the bank to the base of the bushes, is the Jack-by-the-Hedge,—Sauce Alone, and Treacle-mustard, as it is known by in different places (*Sisymbrium alliaria*). If you are in doubt about it, you have only to bruise the leaves, and the unmistakable smell of garlic they give out will soon tell you whether you have hit on the right species or not. This plant is one of our earliest comers, brightening the hedge-banks with its cheerful green leaves and white cruciferous flowers, long before floral nature has aroused herself from her winter's slumbers. In former times, the leaves of the "sauce alone" were boiled as table vegetables, or used for stuffing roast pork. The white-flowered Dead-nettle (*Lamium album*) is another early plant, whose whorls of labiate flowers and square stems render it easily recognisable. If not in the green lanes, at any rate in the plantations often bordering them, or in the moist meadows beyond, grows an early summer plant, one of our most beautiful native flowers, the Early Orchis (*Orchis mascula*). It grows to about a foot in height, and nothing can exceed the fresh beauty of its spike of pinkish-purple blossoms. The tubers of this species, like the base of the cuckoo-pint, contain such a degree of starchy or farinaceous matter that it was formerly much sought after, boiled in water, and sold at the corners of the streets in London and elsewhere under the name of "saloop." These tubers have been stated to contain more nutritious matter, according to their bulk, than any other vegetable production; and the statement has gone so far as to assert that one ounce a day was sufficient to sustain a man. Our readers need not try the experiment unless they choose. The same moist meadows where this plant grows—and we have seen fields quite purpled with its blooms—will be sure to yield still greater numbers of the Cuckoo flower, or Lady's smock, as it is also termed—a cruciferous plant with palish lilac flowers, and pungent leaves that remind you of its affinity to the cresses. In the marshier spots you will not have to

look for Shakespeare's Mary-buds—Marsh Mari-
golds we now call them (*Caltha palustris*). They
will obtrude themselves on your attention if they
are within a quarter of a mile, with their great
gorgeously-yellow blossoms and shining green leaves.
Surely a prettier plant than this is not included
in our English flora! By-and-by you will notice
how curiously the capsules shed their seeds, just as
if they knew what they were about.

Let us return to our shady green lanes. In the
northern and midland counties particularly, these
are the places to find that stately flower—the most
imperial of our indigenous kind — the Foxglove
(*Purpura digitalis*). Who does not know its purple
flowers? or what boy has not closed one end, and
after filling the glove with his breath, suddenly
clapt it on his hand, in order to hear the sharp
sound it made when bursting? Its common name
is a good illustration of how such terms have been
corrupted. Originally it was "folks'" glove—that
is, *fairies'* glove. The fairies have given their names
to more than one of our common plants, just as, in
old Catholic times, the Virgin did. The latter may
be recognised in "*mary*-buds," "*lady's* smock,"
"*lady's* mantle," "*lady's* bedstraw," &c. A powerful medicine (*digitalis*) is made from the foxglove.
The hedges in June and July are quite gay with
such plants as the White and Yellow Bedstraw
("*bede*-straw," as it was formerly called), which
grow up almost to the tops of the hawthorn, where

the latter is low. The Yellow Bedstraw (*Galium verum*) has another name ("cheese rennet"), so given on account of its possessing the power of curdling milk. Its spikes of small golden yellow flowers renders it easily identifiable, and the smell of new-mown hay which they give forth is anything but disagreeable. The White Bedstraw (*Galium mollugo*) has its spikes also crowded with blossoms. Another species of this genus, called Goose-grass, or Cleavers (*G. aparine*), is a capital climber, and well deserves its name, for if you cast a fragment of the plant on a person it will "cleave" or adhere to the dress as if it were covered with gum. Its flowers are small, and grow at the base of the rosette-like whorls of leaves, which run up the square stem. Here and there, at the foot of the hedge-banks, are clusters of another species, the Cross-wort (*Galium cruciatum*), an erect plant about a foot high, with whorls of palish-green, downy leaves, and thick clusters of small yellow flowers at their bases. It gives out a faint and rather sickly perfume of new hay. Sometimes, partly climbing at the base of the hedges, is a very pretty plant, with small pinkish, snap-dragon shaped flowers, called Fumitory (*Fumaria officinalis*), which cannot fail to be recognised in the early summer, when the attention is not too much distracted by the superabundance of species. Some people derive its name from *fume de terre* (earth-smoke), from the supposed thin, vapour-like appearance of its delicate green leaves. It is difficult to see how such a name could be given, although the term "earth-smoke" is said to be applied to it in the north of England. Formerly it was boiled, and used as a cosmetic. In June and July, after the first species of Stitchwort has departed, another and even more delicately beautiful one takes its place (*Stellaria graminea*), with smaller, star-like flowers supported on stalks so slender that you can hardly see them. The beautiful Granulated Saxifrage (*Saxifraga granulata*) makes its appearance a little earlier; and in the eastern counties this exceedingly pretty plant grows so abundantly that many of the meadows are white with its blossoms. In the northern counties it is much less common, being deemed almost a rarity in some places by local botanists. The leaves are at the base of the flower-stalk, are roundish, with indented edges, and form a very pretty rosette. The Bladder Campion (*Silene inflata*) is another early summer plant, whose calyx is so puffed out beneath the cleft white petals, that it resembles a miniature bladder. It grows in tufts or patches by the sides of the roads and lanes. The striped pinkish bells of the Small Bindweed (*Convolvulus arvensis*) are now adorning the hedge-backings, their leaves creeping down the banks in graceful festoons. An elegant flower, and a pretty one, with a faint perfume worthy of its connections, is this species!

As the summer advances, the attention of the

young botanist is more in demand. The Valerian, both Great and Marsh (*V. officinalis* and *V. dioica*), have both gone off. The former lined the ditch sides, where its roots were perhaps sought for to attract cats! The latter species was scattered over the marsh, where the difference in the appearance of the male and female flowers (which bloom on separate plants), may have somewhat puzzled the young beginner. It is now covered with seed-vessels, whose light flocky appendages and the withered stem supporting them, give to the plant quite a different appearance. The Black Knapweed (*Centaurea nigra*) is growing in abundance in the meadows, and on the slopes of the hedge-banks in the quiet lanes, and the meadow brown butterfly is flitting about, and selecting them in preference to any other flower. You cannot mistake this plant, with its thistle-like head and purple florets, and calyx covered with black-edged scales (whence its name). The drier parts of the hedge banks are covered with the delicate little Blue-bell (*Campanula rotundifolia.*) You look in vain, however, for the round leaves which give to it its botanical specific name—they have all disappeared, only coming when the plant was springing above ground. We hardly know which of its two popular names conveys the richest associations—"harebell" or "bluebell"—we like them both, and both are immortalised in poetry. The Scotch claim this as their favourite plant, and we admire their taste—as we have

admired the flower when we saw it growing in such
abundance on the sides of the Scotch mountains.
Fairy stories often connect this pretty, delicate little
plant with the antics of the "folk," who are said to
have rung such soft music out of it in the moon-
light.   That, however, must have been long ago! It
would be charming indeed to believe in such associations now.

What of the geraniums? From early to late
summer they adorn our most dusty road sides, as
well as the banks of our sequestered green lanes,
and we cannot afford to glance at commonest British
wild flowers without noticing them. The Herb
Robert (*Geranium robertianum*) was one of the first
to appear, and its beautiful ruddy stalks, delicately-
cut leaves, and light mauve-coloured flowers made it
a prominent object.   Next came the Shining Crane's-
bill (*G. lucidum*), aptly so called, for no one can
mistake its glossy green leaves for those of any
other species.   And now the fields as well as the
hedge-banks and the margins of the waysides are
covered with the soft, elegant leaves, and small pinkish flower of the Dove's Foot Crane's-bill (*G. molle*).
These plants well deserve their name, for the seed-
vessel bears no slight resemblance to the bill of the
bird which has lent them its cognomen.   Similarly
with an allied plant, also common by our road sides,
the Stork's-bill (*Erodium cicutarium*), whose flowers
are of the same colour as those of the geraniums
already mentioned, but whose leaves are even more

elegantly cleft and complicately indented. It flowers more or less all the summer through, and if you obtain a plant bearing a seed vessel, you cannot fail to notice what a comical resemblance it possesses to the head and beak of the stork.

In no group of plants, perhaps, does the young botanist find so much difficulty as with those termed "umbelliferous." They are in flower the summer through, and their number is legion. The above name is derived from the manner in which each flower-stalks springs, from different levels to the same surface, like the whalebone ribs of an umbrella supporting the silk. As a rule, you find these flower-stalks, with their branches, as well as the petals of each flower, multiples of each other. Indeed, it is most singular how the law of numbers is seen in the vegetable world. It is nearly always constant in the stamens, petals, and sepals of the majority of plants. Unfortunately the umbelliferous (umbrella-like) plants bear flowers, generally whiteish, or some shade of yellow, very much like each other. The student must carefully study their leaves, which are exceedingly various, as well as the seed-vessels. These facts, and the time of flowering, smell, habitat, &c., will generally lead him right. Almost the first to appear of this great group is the Earth-nut (*Bunium flexuosum*)—the identical plant which Shakespeare's Caliban offered to dig for the sake of its "nuts." The latter are a granulous, tuber-like portion of the roots, and are far from

B

unpleasant, when freshly dug. The flower umbels are small and thin, and the fine needle-shaped leaves are a good guide to its identification. The Hemlock (*Conium maculatum*) is a sign of the advancing summer. Its soft, dark, elegantly-cut leaves (of which there is an abundance) and spotted stem are good indices to its identity. It grows in the hedges, often as close to the hawthorn as it possibly can. The rather fetid smell it gives out when bruised is also characteristic of the plant, and another means of discovering it. The plant is held to be poisonous, and readers will remember the " hemlock juice " which Socrates was forced to take to produce death. The Fool's Parsley (*Æthusa cynapium*) is another common wayside plant, whose flower-umbels are recognised by the *spurs* which may be seen beneath. It is a pretty plant, with leaves so delicately and gracefully formed that ignorant persons often take them, when the plant is young, for ferns. The Wild Carrot (*Daucus carota*) is also distinguished by its finely-cut leaves, but in this case the umbel of flowers is large and round, and the blossoms so thickly grouped that the surface is depressed in the centre. The outer flowers are white, and the central ones of a pinkish colour. It is an early summer plant, and the above description, and the peculiar carrot-like smell it gives out when the leaves are bruised, readily lead to its identification. The Rough Chervil (*Chœrophyllum temulum*) is another umbellifer common along our waysides.

The St. John's Wort (*Hypericum perforatum*) is a pretty plant, with delicate, heart-shaped green leaves, that seem, when held between the eye and the light, as if they were thickly punctured all over. The yellow flowers, tinged with red, and having the tips of the petals dotted with black, and the thick brush-like clusters of stamens inside them, lead to its easy recognition. Indeed most people know this plant, for it is exceedingly common, especially in our shady lanes and on calcareous soils. Few of our native plants have so many associations connected with them as the St John's Wort. It is one of the oldest and most credited of "vulneraries," and you will find few herbs whose virtues are so persistently believed in by herbalists as this, except it be perhaps the Yarrow, or "thousand-leaf" (*Achillea millefolium*) whose fine leaves cover the hedge-bank in many places, from the centre of which there springs an umbel-like cluster of greyish-white flowers. The yarrow gives out a peculiar and not unpleasant odour, when crushed, somewhat resembling that of southernwood. But to return to the St. John's wort—there are many English species, the commonest of which is that we have just named. It was one of the flowers gathered by our ancestors for the purpose of throwing on the bonfires which were kindled on St John's eve. On the continent it is still considered to act as a charm against evil spirits, &c., and at one time it was worn in Scotland as a protection against witchcraft.

R 2

Another plant, also peculiarly fond of calcareous soils, but which may often be seen blooming on old walls, is the Viper's Bugloss (*Echium vulgare*), a decidedly pretty and even showy species. Its spike of blue and pink flowers, and its stem dotted and prickled all over, are ready means of recognising it. Its vulgar name was derived from the supposed resemblance of its seeds to the head of a viper. As the summer advances, the drier hedge-banks and uncultivated fields are all aglow with the bright yellow flowers of the Rag-wort (*Senecio jacobœa*), a composite plant, quite as pretty as the Michaelmas Daisies we have imported into our gardens, and, in our opinion, both in the shape of its leaves and in the colour of the flowers, far exceeding the latter plant. The advanced summer also brings out the Hawkweeds (*Hieracium*) whose many species puzzle the young botanist almost as much as the umbelliferous plants. The name of the genus is derived from the belief that the hawk fed on these plants, and also fed its young upon them, in order to obtain that clearness of vision which distinguishes them from other birds. The earliest of the hawkweeds is the Mouse-ear (*Hieracium pilosella*), which grows with a single stem, and a blossom almost canary coloured. Its pale green, very downy leaves grow on the hedge-banks in pretty rosettes, and in feel and appearance they are not unlike the ear of the little animal whose name they bear. By-and-by you will have other species of hawkweeds out that you can hardly distinguish from dandelions, both in cut of leaf and shape and colour of flower. The Succory hawkweeds are very pretty plants, which love to grow in the shadier parts of the lanes. The Chicory (*Cichorium intybus*) is also a composite plant, with a flower exactly resembling those of the larger hawkweeds, but of a beautiful *light-blue* colour. It loves a limy soil, and is particularly abundant in the eastern counties, growing side by side with the Dyer's Rockweed (*Reseda luteola*), which you may easily recognise as a large kind of mignonette ; and in company with the bright and attractive Ox-eye Daisy (*Chrysanthemum leucanthemum*). It is the long carrot-like root of the chicory that is dried and roasted and used with coffee. In Germany and Belgium, and even in some parts of this country, it is now cultivated for this purpose. The Willow-herb (*Epilobium*) and the purple Loosestrife (*Lythrum salicaria*) are also summer plants, which you will certainly find growing on the margins of the nearest tarn. The former will be recognised by their willow-like leaves and rosy flowers, whose seed vessels shoot out into long, thin pods. Nothing can exceed the brilliancy of the tall, light purple spikes of flowers borne by the Loosestrife. The plant contains a large degree of tannic acid, so that it is used as an astringent. By many, this plant is believed to be the " long purple " of Shakespeare, who must have seen it growing in abundance on the banks of the Avon.

The Yellow Toad-Flax (*Linaria vulgaris*) is another roadside plant, and a beautiful one too, with its large, canary-yellow flowers, tinged inside with orange. Among some of our country people it is better known as "butter and eggs." Formerly (and perhaps in some places the custom is still carried on) the juice of this plant was used as a cosmetic. The hedges are now intertwined with the dark green leaves of the Bitter-sweet (*Solanum dulcamara*) whose pretty purple and yellow flowers at once show by their shapes that this species is a near relative of our common potato. By-and-by these flowers will be replaced with bright scarlet berries, so attractive to the eye that many have been tempted to taste them, much to their disgust afterwards. The Old Man's Beard (*Clematis vitalba*) grows beside it, but is a stronger climber, so that it fairly covers the hedges with its greenish-white flowers. When seeding, these flowers will be replaced with long feathery arms, like the flocculent " wool " of a seeding dandelion, and then you will see the appropriateness of the name " old man's beard." The hedges in the eastern and southern counties are often covered for hundreds· of yards by this plant. A young microscopist cannot do better, in trying his hand at section-cutting, than begin with the tough stem of this plant. The section is exceeding curious and pretty, and will well repay the labour bestowed in obtaining it.

In no department of natural history, perhaps, is

optical power, whether applied by a microscope or a
good magnifying-glass, so useful or instructive as in
botany.   Beautiful as most flowers appear even to
the naked eye, these beauties are enhanced when
gazed at with such larger powers of vision as the
microscope bestows.   The seeds of our flowering
plants are not usually noticed, but if you carry that
useful object, a pocket-lens, about you, you will
never be in want of most agreeable employment

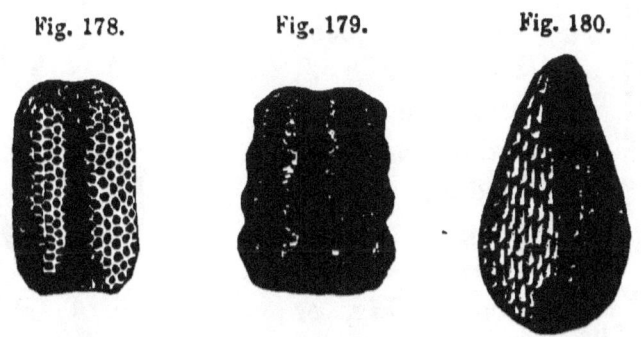

Fig. 178.   Fig. 179.   Fig. 180.

Seed of Foxglove.   Seed of Great Mullein.   Seed of Lousewort.

when out for a stroll.   What plants are not in bloom
may be in seed.   Those of the Foxglove (Fig. 178) are
remarkably elegant ; as are also the seeds of the Great
Mullein (*Verbascum thapsus*), a way-side plant,
especially in the eastern and southern counties, so
pretty that we have seen it grown in gardens in
Lancashire.   Its large pale-green leaves, covered with
down, so that they look like vegetable flannel, cluster
thickly on the ground, and out of them spring a tall
spike of canary-coloured flowers, with pink stamens.

It goes by the name of Aaron's Rod, and High Taper, in allusion to the hollow flower-stalk, which,

Fig. 181.

Fig. 182.

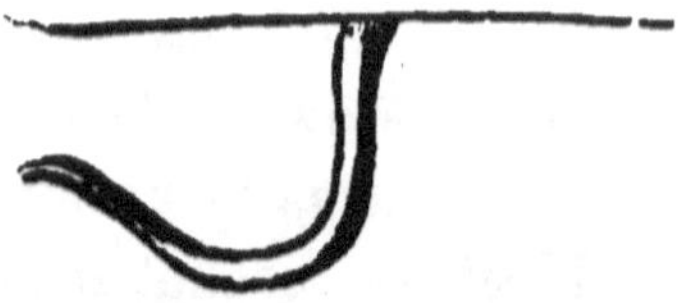

Hair of Milkwort (*Polygala vúlgaris*).

Fig. 183.

when the plant has died off, dries up and can be used for holding tapers. "High," however, is a corruption of *hig*, or *hag*, the Saxon name for the hawthorn. The seed of the Lousewort (*Pedicularis palustris*), a pretty plant with elegantly cut leaves and pink flowers, growing abundantly on the adjacent marshes, is another object worth examination by the young student. Not less interesting are the *hairs*

Hair of Honey-suckle (*Lonicera periclymenum*).

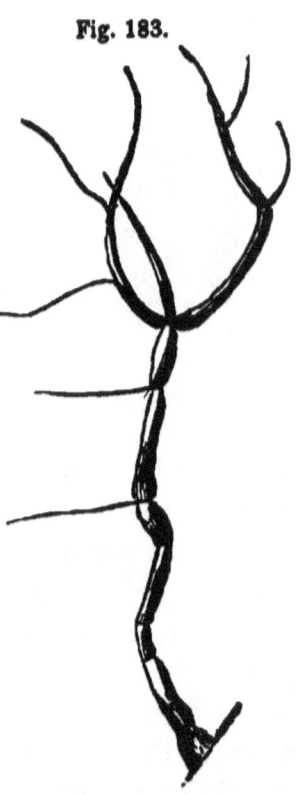

Hair of Great Mullein (*Verbascum thapsus*).

which frequently cover the stems and leaves of many of our flowering plants, and which the student will generally find assuming distinct shapes in various species of flowers, much as they may seem alike to the naked eye. Some of these hairs, as on the common Honeysuckle (*Lonicera periclymenum*, Fig. 181) and the Milkwort (*Polygala vulgaris*) are exceedingly simple. The latter plant is very pretty, although not more than two or three inches in height, and may be found on heaths or on the drier parts of the hedge banks, where its little tassel-shaped, sky-blue flowers will readily recommend it to the eye. The hairs of the great mullein, and mouse-eared hawkweed, on the contrary, are much branched. In the Ragged Robin (*Lychnis flos-cuculi*, Fig. 189 *a*), the common Primrose (*Primula vulgaris*, Fig. 185), and Rib-wort plantain (*Plantago lanceolata*, Fig. 186), the vegetable hairs are formed out of simple beaded cells. In the *Antirrhinum* (Fig. 187) and Fig-wort (*Scrophularia nodosa*)—the latter a common plant by the sides of streams or ditches, where its reddish-green flowers, resembling those of a calceolaria, and its unpleasant odour when bruised, will readily identify it—the hairs assume a peculiar shape, ending with

Fig. 184.

Hair of Mouse-eared Hawkweed (*Hieracium pilosella*).

a little knob.   It is believed by some botanists that these hairs have a peculiar use in vegetable economy in regulating the *electrical* condition of plants.

With a higher microscopical power, the student will never be at a loss for beautiful objects in the pollen-grain of different species of plants.   Indeed

Fig. 185.   Fig. 186.

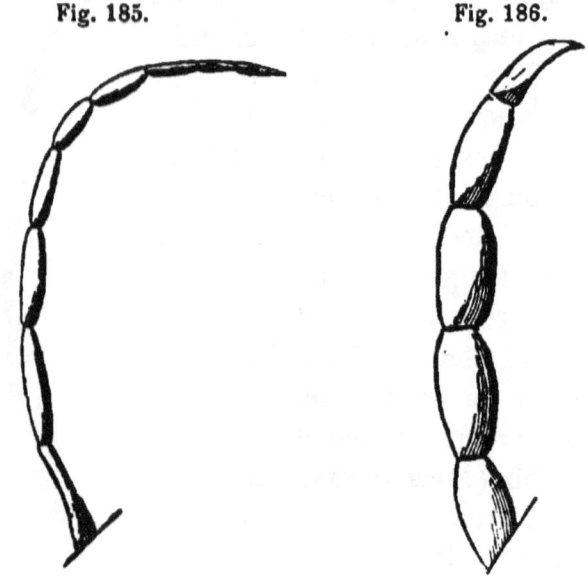

Hair of Primrose (*Primula*   Hair of Rib-wort Plantain
        vulgaris).   (*Plantago lanceolata*).

few natural objects, except the *Diatomaceæ*, can compare with them for beauty, both of form and ornamentation.

In Fig. 189 is given an illustration of the pollen of the Bladder Campion, which, once seen, is not likely to be soon forgotten.   The grains of the Broad-leaved Helleborine are shaped not unlike Savoy biscuits;

whilst those of the common field Knautia or Scabious —an abundant, lilac-coloured plant, growing along the moister parts of hedge-banks, especially in the neighbourhood of corn-fields, form some of the most exquisite of microscopical objects. Scarcely less beautiful are the pollen-grains of another common plant, to be found in abundance on the surface of

Fig. 187.   Fig. 188.

Hair of Antirrhinum (*Antirrhinum majus*).   Hair of Fig-wort (*Scrophularia nodosa*).

any old tarn or pond, and rightly named Pond-weed (*Potamogeton densum*). The pollen of the Great Burnet (*Sanguisorba officinalis*)—a plant with a dark, liver-coloured head of flowers, not uncommon in the meadows of the midland and northern counties — is also of an elegant shape, although not equalling the triangular grains of the common Eye-bright (*Euphrasia officinalis*). This latter plant you may find in the shadier parts of the green lanes, and in the adjoining heaths and meadows. Its height is not above six inches, and its leaves are beautifully cut and densely packed, the pretty little flowers, whitish, and streaked with lilac and yellow, forming elegant clusters. It has long been celebrated, as its name imports, for its supposed cure of eye-diseases,

Fig. 189 a.

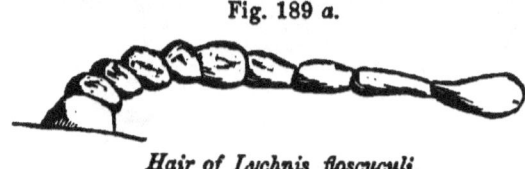

Hair of Lychnis floscuculi.

Fig. 189.

Pollen of Bladder Campion (*Silene inflata*), Broad-leaved Helleborine (*Epipactis latifolia*), and Field Knautia (*Scabiosa arvensis*).

and it is still collected for that purpose and sold by herbalists, although it is difficult to tell in what way it can act as healer. A good deal of the medicinal properties of flowers is hypothetical, and based on what is called the "doctrine of signatures," which taught that most plants bore about them, in colour, shape, or spots, a reference to their healing properties in certain complaints. Hence it was that Lung-wort was believed to be good for consumption, because of the fancied resemblance of the leaves to the lungs. Red flowered plants were fully believed to be useful for blood diseases, and bright-eyed ones, such as the speedwell, eyebright, &c., for diseases of the eyes. We need hardly stop to point out the utter baselessness of such a belief. Science now goes deeper than externals like these. It is possible, however, that the wholesale experimenting on the qualities of herbs induced by such a belief, led to the actual discovery of some species which were beneficial.

Fig. 190.

Pollen of Pond Weed (*Potamogeton densum*), Ditto Great Burnet (*Sanguisorba officinalis*), and of Eye-bright (*Euphrasia officinalis*).

Very curious microscopical objects are the pollen grains of the Spear Thistle (*Cnicus lanceolatus*)—one of our commonest, too abundant, thistles. They are not unlike the toothed wheels of a watch. The pollen of the common rush (*Juncus conglomeratus*) when viewed in a certain light, also forms an attractive object. That of the Common Bitter Vetch (*Orobus tuberosus*)—a most beautiful plant, with pink and red flowers, and grass-like leaves, growing abundantly in the shady lanes of Lancashire and Cheshire, although scarcer elsewhere—greatly re-

sembles the pollen dust of the Broad-leaved Helleborine. The grains of a species of hawkweed usually
found growing near the sea (*Hieracium subaudum*),
which plant has often puzzled the young botanist,

Fig. 191.

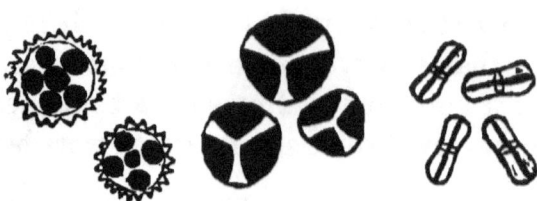

Pollen of Spear Thistle (*Cnicus lanceolatus*), Common Rush (*Jucundus conglomeratus*), and Bitter Vetch (*Orobus tuberosus.*)

Fig. 192.

Pollen of *Hæracium subaudum*, *Erica ciliaris*, and Green Mint (*Mentha viridis*).

perhaps, by the swellings on its stem, caused by an
insect, one of the cynips, having deposited its eggs
beneath the skin—are surrounded by hairy cilia.
The pollen of one of our Lings (*Erica ciliaris*) is
triangular; whilst that of the common green Mint
(*Mentha viridis*) is nucleated.

The microscope, notwithstanding the discoveries
it has made in the investigation and determination
of vegetable tissues, has still much to do before we

obtain a correct knowledge of the natural classification of plants. Professor Gulliver, one of our most distinguished botanists, has shown that many plants are related by the *crystals* formed in various parts of their tissues. These crystals, on account of their being usually needle-shaped, are called *raphides*

Fig. 193.

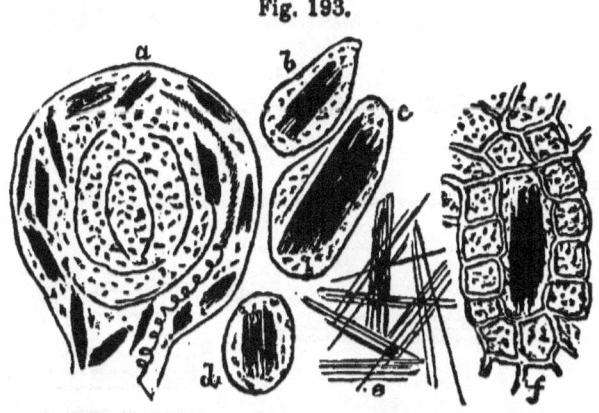

Raphides: *a*, in the ovule of Fuchsia; *b*, in a cell from the berry of Fuchsia; *c*, from the berry of *Arum maculatum* ; *d*, from the leaf of *Neottia spiralis* ; *e*, loose from the berry of *Tamus communis* ; *f*, in an intercellular space of an old frond of *Lemna trisulca* (Duckweed). All moderately magnified.

(Fig. 193); and one group distinguished by other peculiarities goes by the name of *sphæraphides*. Both these groups of plant crystals may be seen with a good student's microscope. Professor Gulliver recommends, as a way to find these crystals in the plants known to bear them, to scrape and mash to a pulp a bit of the leaf, or any other part of the plant, in a drop of water on the object-slide of the microscope; this pulp should then be pressed with a

thin glass cover, and viewed with a quarter-inch
objective. He has shown satisfactorily that these
plant crystals are not diseased growths, but natural
products, and he expresses his belief that they may
ultimately prove useful, as characters, in systematic
botany. In many cases, these crystals assume forms
which are distinctly geometrical, as in Fig. 194.
These prisms are well adapted for the polarisation of

Fig. 194.

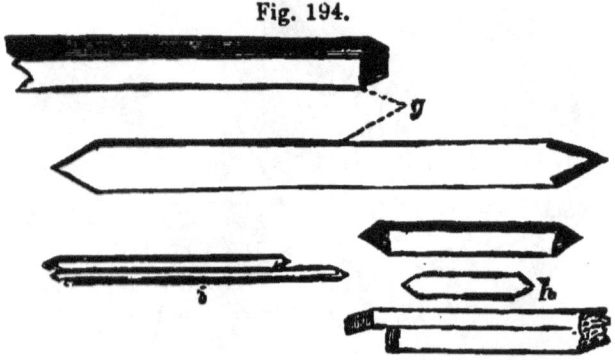

Crystal Prisms, highly magnified: *g*, from *Quillaja saponaria*; *h*, from
the Testa of Milk Thistle (*Silybum marianum*); *i*, from the Ovary-
coat of Spear Thistle (*Carduus lanceolatus*).

light. Generally speaking their chemical composition
is oxalate of lime, though some of them appear to be
composed of phosphate of lime. The Onion and
common Rhubarb are good plants for the young
microscopist to experiment upon in search of these
interesting objects; and, as Professor Gulliver has re-
marked, it is an occupation fit for the drawing-room,
and one well calculated to employ the fair and dextrous
hands of ladies. In no plants are the geometrically
shaped crystals better seen than in the Knap-weed

(*Centaurea*, Fig. 195, *p*) and the Shallot onion. And it is found that these shapes are, in some instances, characteristic of different species in the same genus. Thus their investigation may help in approximating the values of specific differences—one of the most vexed questions in modern botany. The *sphæraphides* are groups or conglomerations of minute

Fig. 195.

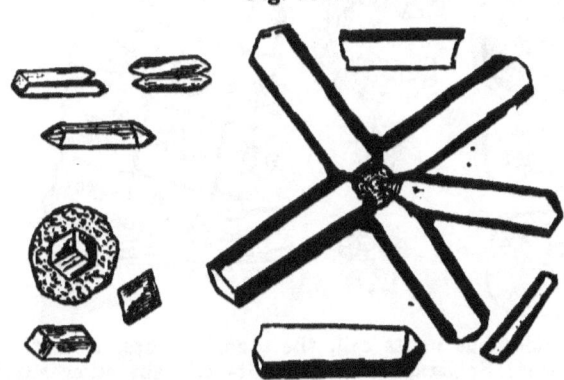

p, Crystal Prism from ovary-coat of *Centaurea nigra*; *q*, different forms, one in its cell, from the same part of *Centaurea scabiosa*; *r*, Crystalline Cross, and three single Crystals, from bulb-scale of Shallot. All highly magnified.

crystalline granules, or angular crystals, frequently smoothish, and often granular or star-like on the surface ; and these are generally contained in a distinct cell. Their usual diameter is about the thousandth part of an inch ; but in our British plants their size is often smaller than this. They reach their largest size among plants of the *Cactus* tribe. The common Nettle, and Marine Bladder Campion — a plant resembling, in flower, the

Bladder Campion already noticed, but with fewer
and smaller leaves—both yield these sphæraphides
(Fig. 196).

Of other structures of plants which a little knowledge of microscopical investigation will yield to the
student, space forbids us to treat; with that instrument a "feast of fat things" is always spread, and

Fig. 196.

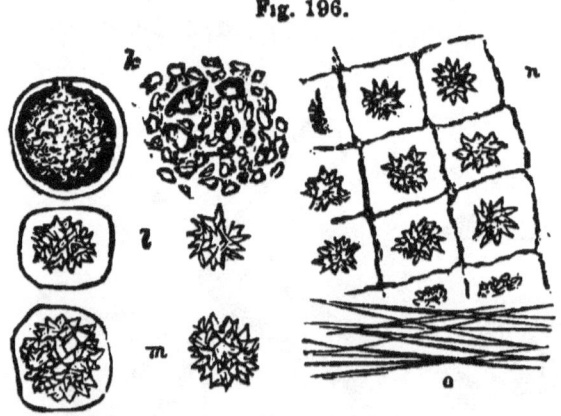

k, Sphæraphides, one in its cell, the other crushed, from the leaf of
the Nettle; *l*, Sphæraphides, one in its cell, the other naked, from
the stem of Dog's Mercury (*Mercurialis annua*); *m*, the same, from
the leaf of Marine Bladder Campion (*Silene maritima*); *n*, Sphæ-
raphid Tissue (magnified less than half as much as the other objects),
from the leaf of *Veratrum*; *o*, Raphides, from the same leaf.

leisure hours may thus be profitably spent and the
mind be relieved of worldly cares, and feel, as a human
soul should feel, freer from the arbitrary shackles
which the stiffened duties of modern civilisation tend
to fasten on a man. We know of no higher or more
congenial occupation than that of investigating the
laws and phenomena of Nature. Surely if *politics*—

the often absurd result of men's follies, prejudices,
or wickedness—are deemed worthy the attention
of great intellects, the grander and more harmonious
inter-relation of the animal and vegetable kingdoms,
their antiquity, and the causes which have led to
their present distribution and arrangement, are as
much more worthy of investigation as eternal things
are above temporal !

CHAPTER IX.

THE RUSHES, GRASSES, AND FERNS OF THE GREEN LANES.

UR English fields and lanes are crowded with a host of objects whose appearance is too modest and unpretentious to obtain even a passing notice from ordinary pedestrians. It requires little extra observation, however, to discover that they really possess beauties and attractions of their own. Without such common objects as grasses, rushes, sedges, &c., what would become of that charming greenness which delights every eye? Their general effect, therefore, if not their individual, is far from unimportant. Nay, they possess a utility also, as food of all kinds of cattle, such as more showy members of the vegetable kingdom have not. These remarks may sound like an apology, when every botanist knows that the delicate, graceful beauty and structure of our rushes and grasses really need nothing of the kind. Ferns have long held a high place in public estimation, on account of their superior attraction of form, and such a fact cannot be wondered at. Our moister and shadier lanes grow them as few gardens can, for more independent and seemingly capricious objects do not exist.

Let us first glance at some of the Rushes and Sedges which may be easily found during an ordinary country stroll. They are usually an index of a hungry, undrained soil, or of hard, clayey ground. In the dry ditches or hollows by the lane sides you cannot fail to meet with more than one species. Among others may be found, in the later summer months, the Hard Rush (*Juncus glaucus*), which well deserves its popular name; its hard, wiry, but slender stems also serving to identify it. The Common Rush (*Juncus communis*) is no less abundant, though you must seek for it in moister places than the previous species usually affects. It is also larger and softer, and its stems have not the same glaucous colour; the flowers, though springing from a similar place in the side of the stem, are more bunchy. It is the pith of this species, and of *Juncus effusus*, that has for such a long time been used as wicks for those candles which go by the name of "Rush-lights." But perhaps the most interesting species is the Toad Rush (*Juncus bufonius*, Fig. 197). This also loves watery places, especially where there is a subsoil of clay or brickearth. You may generally find it in abundance in deserted brickfields, which it is the first to inhabit. It makes its appearance

as a dense carpet of minute, bright green threads,
each tipped with an orange-coloured knob, so that
when they are wet the surface glistens as if be-
gemmed with topazes. These seedlings at this time

Fig. 197.

The Toad Rush.

bear little resemblance to the adult plant, as may be
seen in Fig. 198. A species of plant that is very
common, like shellfish and butterflies, is always
characterised by varietal differences, some of which
are frequently so marked and distinct as to be per-

petuated. The Toad Rush is distinguished as belonging to this class, and its varieties may generally be
found in different habitats in the month of August.
In May the meadows are nearly carpeted by an
allied form, the Field Woodrush (*Luzula campestris*),
—a really pretty plant, if you will only take the
trouble to look at it closely. Its flowers are quite
as regular as those with showy corollas, and their
dark umber is beautifully relieved by the light
yellow of the comparatively large anthers of the
stamens. In the north of England
and midland counties, this species

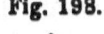

Fig. 198.

goes by the name of "sweeps," in
allusion to its dark-coloured flowers.
A further examination of any
marshy ground will also reveal the
presence of two other common

species of rush, *Juncus effusus*, and
J. acutiflorus. The former will be

Toad Rush Seedlings.

distinguished by its soft stems, which cause it to
go by the popular name of the Soft Rush—the latter
by its flowers, which are very sharp; the stem also
is jointed.

The margins of the banks of streams or of tarns
are the places which sedges most love. Here you
may find the Remote Carex (*Carex remota*), in June,
especially where the trees overhang the moist places.
The Fox Carex (*C. vulpina*), is another abundant
species. It is sometimes called the Great Sedge,
for it not unfrequently grows to the height of

three feet.   All the sedges may readily be identified
by their angular stems, and more particularly by
the separate arrangement of the male and female
organs on the same plant.   The latter are usually
arranged in prickly bunches, lower down; whilst
the former sometimes droop in graceful panicles.
The Yellow Carex (*C. flava*), is also a generally
abundant species, as is indicated by its numerous
varieties.   Its leaves are very grass-like, but its
flower-spike is very graceful, having bunches of
female flowers where the leaves strike off the stem,
the stem being terminated by a slender tuft of
yellowish-brown male flowers.   The student is almost certain to meet with one variety or another of
this sedge in any moist place where sedges are likely
to grow.   The Pink-leaved Sedge (*C. panicea*), a
common species, has an erect stem, slightly curved
when in fruit, which are usually tinged with purple,
hence the common name.   It is a perennial plant,
and may be found in most marshy places in the early
summer months.   The Hammer Sedge (*C. hirta*) is a
very beautiful form, its long grass-like leaves spreading out gracefully, and its spike of pretty male and
female flowers rising from their midst, the contrast
in their light and dark colours adding considerably
to the attractive appearance of the plant.   It is a
common species, possessing several well-marked
varieties, all of which are to be found in our marshes
and meadows.   In those which are swampier and
moister than usual, the young botanist is certain to

meet with at least one species of the so-called Cotton Grass (*Eriophorum*), whose soft, white, silky bunch of fibres (beautiful objects under the microscope) gives to the plant a name by which any one may distinguish it. We have seen the Norfolk marshes almost white with the abundance of this sedge, and not more than two or three years ago a scheme was set afoot to cultivate it for commercial purposes. We have not heard, however, whether anything came of it, but it is hardly likely to successfully compete with the genuine cotton tree, either for quantity or quality, although it does seem a pity that so much utilisable material should not be employed in some way or another. The cotton-like down of one species (*Eriophorum angustifolium*), is often used in the moorland districts of Yorkshire and Lancashire for stuffing pillows. Candle and lamp wicks are also manufactured out of it in various places in the same district.

Our native grasses are now having more attention paid to them, for they are being cultivated for lawns and pastures, which are sown with their seed. Indeed, so well acquainted are some of our seed-merchants with the more important species, that a person has only to name the kind of soil he wishes to have covered with grass, and the seed of the species best suited to it will be sent him. Until very recently, the study of our British grasses had been much neglected by botanists. One species, the Sweet-Scented Vernal Grass (*Anthoxanthum odoratum*, Fig. 199), had, indeed, long been a favourite, even with common people, inasmuch as it is the perfume of this very common and beautiful grass that gives the well-known scent to new-mown

Fig. 199.

a. Panicle of *Anthoxanthum odoratum*.
b. Inner Glumes with Awns containing Ovary, magnified.
c. Inner Glumes, Ovary removed, magnified.
d. Outer Glumes—Styles.

hay or grass. The study of grasses is not so difficult as many suppose, and if it be a trifle more so than the study of flowering-plants so called, like every other out-of-the-way subject, when once mastered, it more than compensates for the little extra pains taken with it. The sweet-scented vernal grass blooms at a time when most other grasses are short and inconspicuous, so that it is doubly welcome on that account. Towards the end of May you may see it in full flower, the flowers forming a spike-like panicle from one to two inches in length. It has been supposed that it is the quantity of pollen thrown off by this species of plant that causes the peculiar catarrh known as "hay-fever." The seeds are highly hygrometrical, and when subjected to moisture, or after being moistened, to warmth, they exhibit a series of very interesting movements. The flowering glumes are awned, the glumes being covered with stiff, brown, erect hairs, particularly towards the base, where the hairs are generally spread out somewhat after the style of a cat's whiskers. These awns, when seen with a low microscopic power, form really beautiful objects. They are also easily influenced by moisture, that of the hand alone being sufficient to make the bent awns screw themselves about in quite a comical fashion. Indeed, the queer contortions and postural movements of these organs must be experimented on to be thoroughly appreciated: and we can promise our young readers no little harmless fun if they will try the experiment.

Another genus of our commonest grasses, to be found by every roadside, is the *Alopecurus* or Fox-tail as it is appropriately called, from the resemblance of the tuft to the tail of a fox. We have several

Fig. 200.

Slender Foxtail (*Alo-
pecurus agrestis*).

native species, of which the rarest perhaps is the slender Fox-tail grass (*Alopecurus agrestis*, Fig. 200). It is a tall, straggling grass, with few pretensions to beauty, and is generally found growing about a foot high. The culm, or stem, usually squats on the ground, and at the joints it is bent. The flower spike is long and very slender, and is of a purplish colour. Its florets are less closely packed together than those of other species of fox-tail. Fig. 201 represents one of the florets as seen under a strong magnifying glass. The Marsh Foxtail (*A. geniculatus*, Fig. 202) is a very ornamental grass, especially when in full flower. It is usually to be found in very moist places, or even in the waters of a pond, if the latter be situated in a shady place. Its broadish leaves cause the plant to appear as if floating. If you should come upon such a shaded tarn, or pool, in June or July (and we have many such fringing our English lanes), you will be almost certain to find this grass. Its rich white and flesh-coloured heads make it a prominent object, one that a young botanist on the look-out for novelties is not likely to hurriedly pass over. Its scientific specific name is a very appropriate one, as it alludes to the bent or *kneed* position into which the purple-coloured stem is thrown at every joint. From the lower joints there frequently spring roots. The sheaths with which the broadish leaves surround the stem are looser in the species of foxtail grass last mentioned. The Meadow Fox-tail (*Alopecurus pratensis*) has a close resemblance to the last species, but you will find it only in meadows, where it grows most luxuriantly. It is more erect in its growth, how-ever, and has larger and thicker spikes, and longer awns. The florets are not unlike those of the marsh foxtail, Fig. 202.

Fig. 201.

Floret of *Alopecurus agrestis*, magnified.

Let us now turn to another abundant species of grass you are certain to find in your walks through the fields and lanes: it is a soft, silky-looking grass, of a white or light-red colour, growing in compact masses among various other kinds, and goes by the name of Meadow Soft Grass (*Holcus lanatus*). It vegetates rather late in the season, but usually produces a very abundant crop, especially on light or moist soils. When in full flower the panicle is very spreading. The florets are two-flowered, the

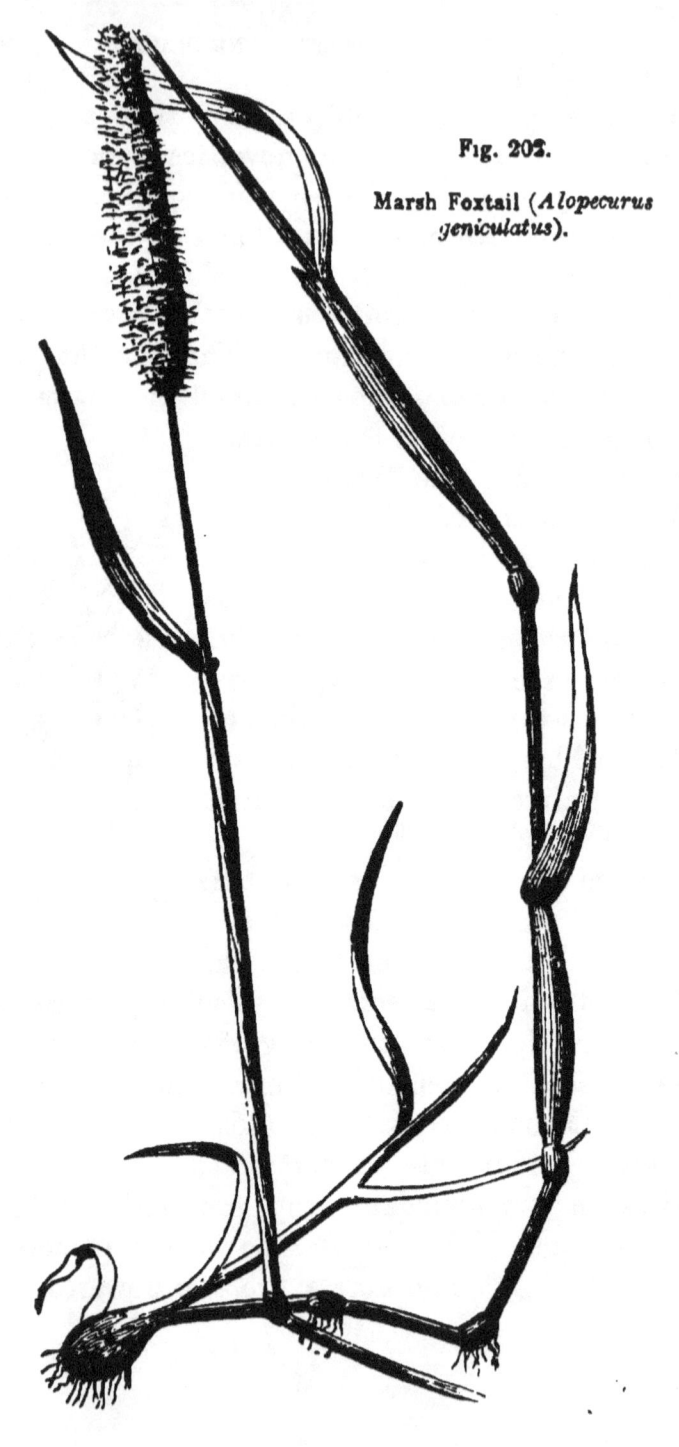

Fig. 202.

Marsh Foxtail (*Alopecurus geniculatus*).

upper and smaller flower, which bears an awn, being
barren, and the lower without awns but fertile.
This occurrence of barren and fertile flowers on the
same spike or panicle in many grasses is of great
importance, as showing the physiological changes
which must have occurred in the life-history of the
species before such a result was brought about. For

Fig. 203.   · Fig. 204

Floret of *Alopecurus*   Floret of *Holcus* divested of the
geniculatus.   outer Glumes.

few people would be bold enough to say that these
barren flowers had been so created—this assertion
would imply an ignorant freak of creative power, such
as we cannot for a moment associate with God's
works. Fig. 204 represents a floret of *Holcus* divested
of its outer glumes or scales. We have only two
English species of this genus, that just described and
the Creeping Soft Grass (*Holcus mollis*), which may

be found in abundance in July or August under our hedges, or indeed in any shady place. The Brome Grass (*Bromus*) also is a genus which includes many ornamental grasses that are both widely spread and abundant in this country. All the species bear a strong resemblance to each other, although the generic type is very marked and distinct. One species the Barren Brome (*Bromus sterilis*, Fig. 206)

Fig. 205.

Floret of *Holcus*.

may be found on almost every piece of waste ground, or along the hedge-banks of our lanes and road-sides. Common though it is, we have few native grasses that can compare with it for elegance and grace. To judge correctly of its pretensions to beauty, you should see it, not where it so frequently grows, on the hedge-banks of our dusty roads, but along some grass-grown tree-shaded, country lane. There it will grow to the height of over two feet, will have soft, downy leaves, and spikelets seated on long slender pedicels which droop in the most graceful of curves. Each spikelet contains about seven compressed flowers, whose long, slender awns give to the whole plant a light and feathery appearance which greatly enhances its beauty. Along the dusty roads, the sterile Brome grass possesses a great capacity for collecting dust, and in such situations the plant is often an invisible green. One of the flowering glumes is represented at *b*, in Fig. 206. Another

Fig. 206.

Barren Brome Grass (*Bromus sterilis*).   *a*, Spikelets;
b, Flowering Glume.

T

species of Brome (*Bromus erectus*) is to be found in fields, where it grows, as its name implies, more erect than the foregoing species. With this exception, and its strikingly yellow stamens, it so nearly

Fig. 207.

Common Rye Grass (*Lolium perenne*).

resembles the Sterile Brome Grass that there is little difficulty in identifying it.

Another of our commonest British grasses is the Darnel, or Rye Grass (*Lolium*), of which we have several species. This grass makes an excellent hay on dry chalk or sandy soils, where it may be cultivated with advantage along with clover. All the species, however, are subject to great variation, thus showing the capability of considerable powers of adaptation to different physical conditions. The Common Rye Grass (*Lolium perenne*, Fig. 207) may be found everywhere. The Bearded Darnel (*Lolium temulentum*), so called on account of its long awns, is supposed by some writers to be the "tares" to which the Saviour alluded in his parable of the tares and wheat. The seeds of this species have a very peculiar intoxicating effect. When malted with barley, the ale brewed from the mixture produces speedy drunkenness ; and if they are ground up with bread-corn, the bread, if eaten *hot*, produces a similar effect. It is usually met with in cultivated fields. Cattle seem to know its qualities instinctively, for they always avoid it.

Fig. 208.

Culm.

Other abundant British grasses are *Aira, Poa, Festuca*, &c., whose numerous species grow in most fields. But we proceed now to notice the very common road-side forms, such as the Meadow Barley and Wall Barley. This genus contains four British species, all of which are easily recognisable. The spikelets in all the species are situated three together or nearly so, in alternate notches in the flower-stalk or culm (Fig. 208). The Wall Barley (*Hordeum mu-*

T 2

rinum, Fig. 209), may be found growing on the top or

Fig. 209.

in the decomposing mortar of most old walls. It is rather a stout grass, the stems being sometimes bent. It may be known from the Meadow Barley (*Hordeum pratense*, Fig. 211) by its panicle being longer and stronger. The bristles terminating the chaff-scales (*glumes*) are called 'awns,' and these in the Wall Barley are of considerable length (see Fig. 210). The meadow barley grows as tall as the wall barley, but it is more slender. The Sea-side Barley (*Hordeum maritimum*, Fig. 213), so called on account of its growing abundantly on the sands by the sea-shore, is a smaller species than either of the two already mentioned. It will also be recognised by its glaucous hue and its spreading awns, which latter peculiarity gives it a remarkably light and feathery appearance. The wall barley may be found growing

Wall Barley (*Hordeum murinum*).

along the margins of our road-sides, in company with the meadow barley, when they frequently

approach each other so much in general resemblance
that it is somewhat difficult to tell one from the
other. Our figures, however, and a little trouble
taken in examining the glumes and awns, will
readily aid in their identification. Some of our

Fig. 210.

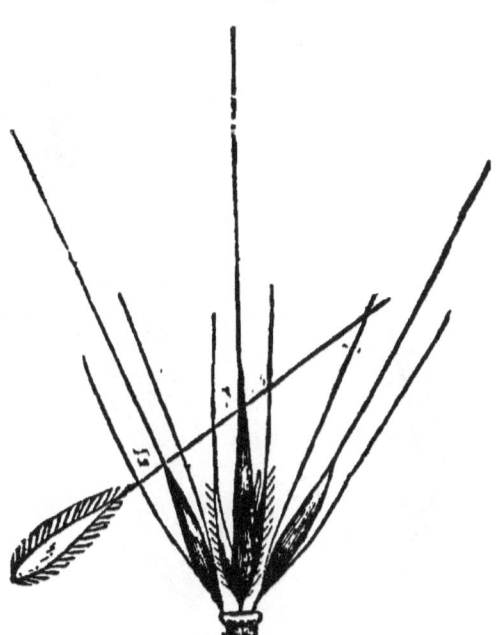

Glumes and Awns of Wall Barley.

common English grasses, as for instance the Millet
Grass, are remarkable for their elegance, causing
them always to be selected when a person is making
up a bouquet of wild flowers. Others, such as the
Couch Grass (*Triticum repens*), are so abundant as to
be troublesome, inasmuch as they *will* replace more

useful plants. The roots, however, have a sweet taste, not much unlike liquorice. The leaves contain a good deal of silica, so that cattle will only eat this grass when it is young. The Crested Dog's-tail Grass (*Cynosurus cristatus*) is also a very pretty

Fig. 211.

Meadow Barley (*Hordeum pratense*).

grass, which flowers in July and August, and is then very abundant in all our meadows and pastures. The leaves of this grass are of the shortest growth of any of the pasture grasses. They grow close together, and are very palatable to cattle, particularly to sheep.   Birds, and especially pigeons, are fond of the seeds, and feed on them when more delicate morsels are not in their way.   The general

Fig. 212.   Fig. 213.

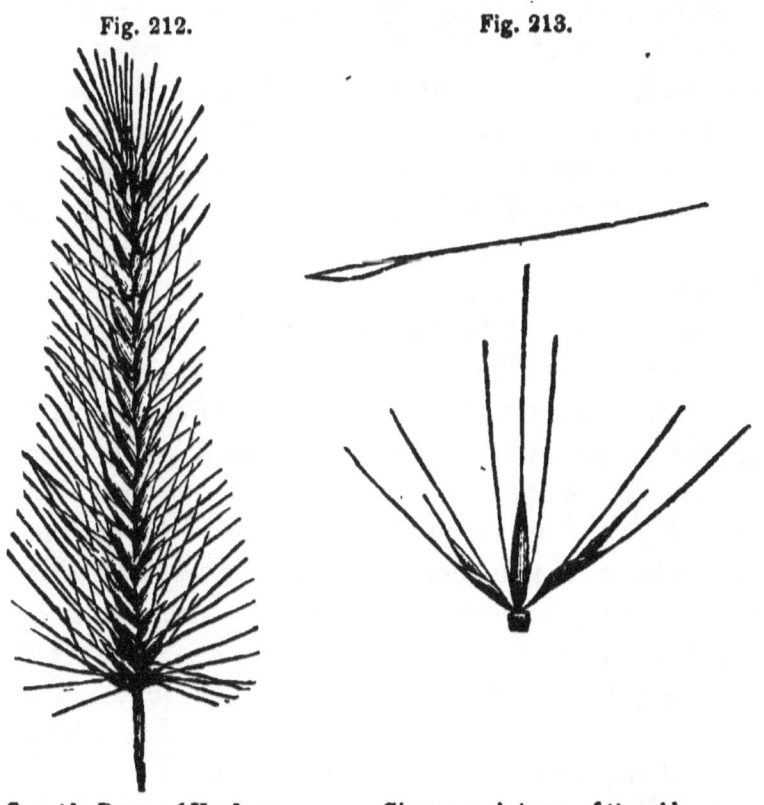

Sea-side Barley (*Hordeum maritimum*).

Glumes and Awns of Sea-side Barley (*H. maritimum*).

resemblance of the flower panicle to the tail of a dog, and its pretty purplish-grey colour, will assist the student in recognising it. Geologically speaking, grasses possess an extraordinary interest, in that they appear to be the oldest of the flower-bearing plants. Fossils have been met with in the Coal Measures which are believed to be the flowers of extinct species of grasses.

Ferns have an antiquity greater still, and second only to that of their allies the Club Mosses. As far back as the Devonian or Old Red Sandstone epoch, we meet with such magnificent examples that we are warranted in believing they are even older than this period, if it be true that the simpler forms always precede the more complex. In the Coal Measures they form the most beautiful, as well as the commonest of fossils, and it is not too much to say that the motive-power of Great Britain, derived from her magnificent seams of coal, is due originally to the ferns and club-mosses of the Carboniferous epoch. From that time to this we never lose sight of ferns, and how much they have been differentiated in the interval is evident from the general similarity of the fossil ferns of the Coal Measures in every country, and the wonderful variety and number of species yielded by the same countries now. More species of ferns live at the present time than during any other period of the earth's history.

We do not propose giving a detailed account of our British ferns. The young beginner will find a pleasant, popular, and sufficiently exhaustive description of them in a cheap and attractive little book written by Mrs. Lankester, called ' A Plain and Easy Account of British Ferns.' One cannot be surprised that this class of plants should have obtained so

much attention. Their elegant forms and fresh
colours make them general favourites. A little care
will cause them to flourish in our rooms, even in
the heart of large cities and towns, the greater
part of the year; and we know of few objects
which cheer the eye more than a well-kept
Wardian case of ferns. But in our rambles in
the woods and lanes, how their presence lends
interest! The very Brakes (*Pteris aquilina*),
abundant and rampant though they be, are among
the most elegant of natural objects. Singularly
enough, though they grow so readily where one
would hardly expect it, in the stoniest places, on
the barrenest soils, and where they have to compete
with myriads of other plants for even a foothold,
the brakes are among the most difficult to rear
artificially. A more capricious fern, in this respect,
does not exist in our English flora. The germination
and earlier development of ferns are better known
now than they formerly were; and, what is very
remarkable, their earlier stages resemble the fully
developed condition of cryptogamous plants lower
in organisation than themselves. For instance, the
earlier stages in the life-history of our commonest
ferns are so like the Liver-worts, and especially the
Marchantia, that we have known them to be taken
for the latter plants, even in greenhouses, where
practical gardeners attended on them! In this
respect, therefore, ferns follow the same law as
universally prevails among the higher classes of

animals, in which the larval condition of a higher group resembles the adult state of a lower.

Out on the Norfolk marshes we have frequently

Fig. 214.

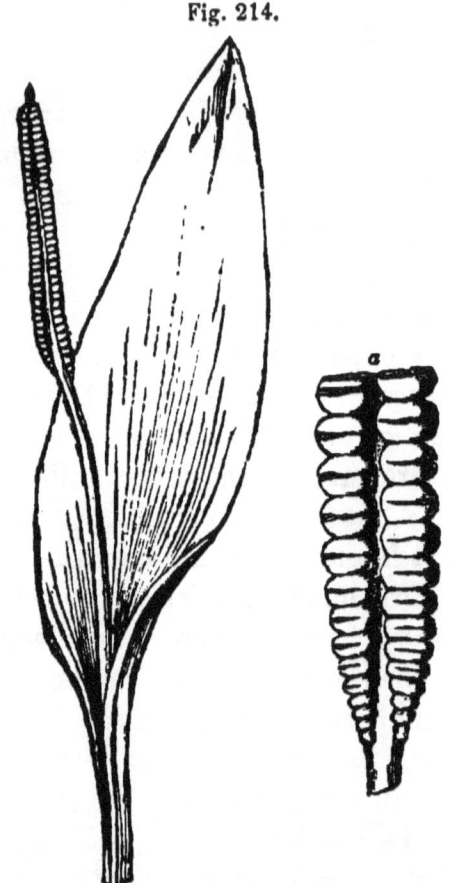

Ophioglossum vulgatum. *a*, Portion of Fertile Spike enlarged.

seen the ground covered for many scores of yards, with the bright-green fronds of the Adder's Tongue (*Ophioglossum vulgatum*, Fig. 214). You would hardly take this elegant little plant for one of the fern tribe, but a short examination of the spike growing from the single frond will soon convince you of the fact. None of the ferns bear true flowers, although sometimes their superficial appearance warrants the popular belief that some species do. And, as a consequence, they do not bear *seeds*, but spores, which differ from them in their power of germinating from any part of their surface, whilst a true seed can only sprout from one part. The spores and spore-cases of ferns are among the most beautiful of microscopical objects, and those with which the young microscopist generally makes his first acquaintance. The ingenious way with which the halves of the spore-cases are held together by a sort of spiral ring, called the *annulus*, is very remarkable. Not less interesting and instructive is the different way in which the spore-cases are borne on the backs of the fern-leaves or "fronds." In some, as in the Common Brake, the edges of the leaves are turned over, and thus form the *indusium* where the spores collect and ripen. In this simple manner we have a differentiation of a part of the leaf taking place when the fern gets riper. The same process occurs in the Common Maiden-Hair fern (*Adiantum capillus-veneris*) and the following figures show the gradual manner in which this is effected. The spores are contained in little vessels called *thecæ*, which are usually gathered in clusters termed *sori* (No. 3, Fig. 215), the indusium covering

Fig. 215.

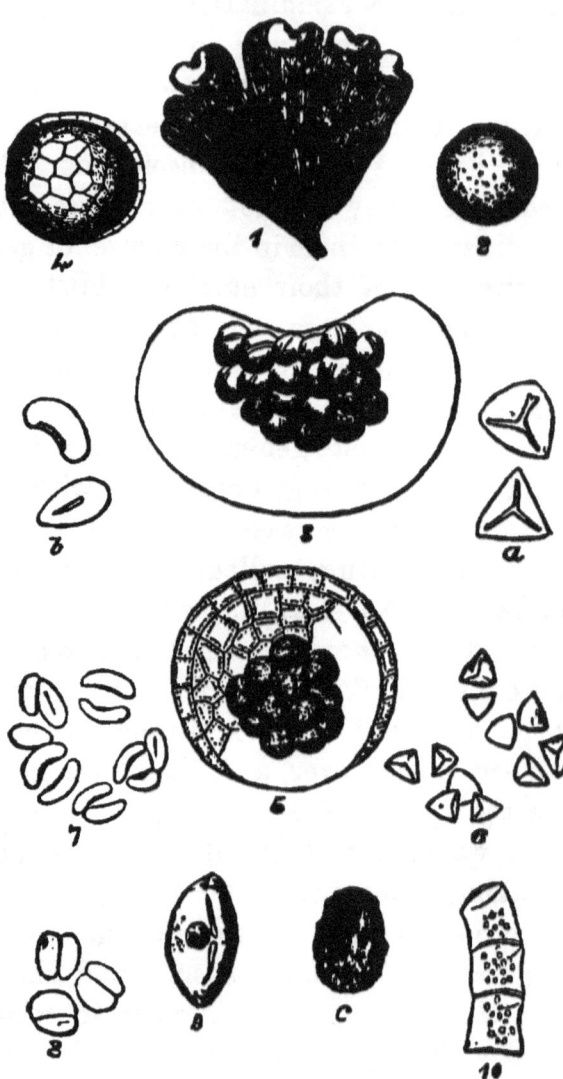

The Formation of Fern Spores.

these being formed of a single layer of cells. Fig. 215 shows at No. 1 the indusium, formed by the outgrowth and overlapping of the edge of the pinnule or leaflet. As soon as this is effected, the *thecæ* appear between it and the leaf as small green cells, full of granular matter (No. 2). In a little while these develop a cellular covering and a peculiar disposition of cells, which afterwards form the spring by which the spores are eventually liberated from the thecæ. As the thecæ advance towards maturity, there appear within them small round cells (No. 5) developed from the granular matter, these by subsequent cell-division become the spores. In their early stage the spores are transparent, but afterwards become opaque and dark coloured. The young spores of the Maiden-hair are represented at No. 6; of the Oak Fern (*Polypodium dryopteris*), at No. 7; and of the Narrow Prickly Fern (*Polystichum lobatum*) at No. 8, in which the formation of the spore from the division of the round cell is very evident.

The genera into which our British ferns are separated are characterised chiefly by the position of the *sori* and their coverings. Thus, those of the Common Polypody (*Polypodium vulgare*) are naked, —that is, the sori are not covered over by any extraneous protection. You cannot fail to find this beautiful and commonest of ferns growing on old tree trunks, or festooning the banks of the ditches by the lane side. It is green, even in the winter time, when hardly any other green thing appears, and then you may see the golden yellow sori arranged in pairs on the back of the pinnules. The late summer is the time to look along the banks of moist dykes, or in old wells, or the crevices of wet rocks for the Hart's Tongue Fern (*Scolopendrium vulgare*). You cannot mistake the long green leaves, hanging down like so many ribbons. This is one of our favourite domesticated ferns, as it will grow readily where there is moisture and subdued light. If you examine the back of one of the mature fronds you will see dark lines running parallel with the veins. These are the sori. In company with the hart's tongue you will find the Male Fern (*Lastrea filix-mas*)—a name given to it when it was believed to be the male form, of which the Female Fern (*Athyris filix-fœmina*) was the female. We now know they belong, not only to different species, but also to different genera. Most delicately cut plants they are, excelling in beauty and elegance many foreign ferns grown in our conservatories. The Holly Ferns are also common (*Polystichum*), and these may be known by the feature which has given to them their popular name, viz., the minute prickles which terminate the serrations of the pinnules.

In a botanical ramble down Growdale Glen, in the Isle of Man, many years ago, we came across a clump of bright green ferns, four or five feet in height, which for a moment made us draw back in admiration. Never before had we seen such a sight

nor since, with the exception of even a more tropic-
looking plantation of the same fern on the shores
of one of the large Norfolk lakes or
"broads," at Irstead, near Norwich.
There was the Royal Flowering
Fern (*Osmunda regalis*), never better
deserving its name. The large light-
green fronds and stout stems covered
at least a hundred square yards
like a miniature forest, each stem
terminating in a spike of brownish-
yellow *sori*, or spore-cases, which
have caused it to be named " flowering." (Fig 216). Not many years
ago the " seed " or spores of this
fern were fully believed to render
the person carrying them *invisible*;
but before they had this effect it
was necessary to gather them at
midnight, on St. John's eve! In
Norfolk we have seen this fern
growing to the height of five or
six feet.

Fig. 216.

Royal Fern (*Osmunda
regalis*).

The limestone walls of Derbyshire are the places for ferns. Here,
in abundance, grow the Maiden-
hair Spleenwort (*Asplenium trichomanes*), with its
shining black stem and bright green, roundish
pinnules. The Bladder Fern (*Cystopteris fragilis*)
will be found associated with it, and when we say it

is one of our most elegant and graceful species, we have described it so that it cannot be mistaken. The Limestone Polypody (*Polypodium calcareum*) grows in the same places, its lower fronds being nearly as broad across the diameter of the fern as the latter is high, thus giving to the plant quite a triangular outline.   Out on the hills above grow the Parsley Fern (*Cryptogramme crispa*, Fig. 217), so named because its habit of carrying the spore-cases

Fig. 217.

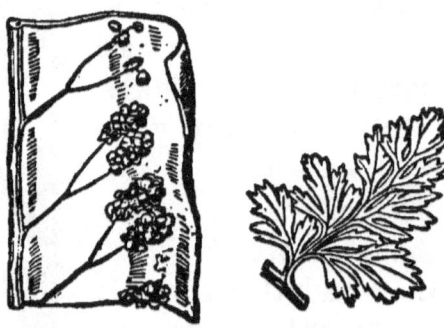

Parsley Fern (*Cryptogramme crispa*).   *b*, Portion enlarged.

clustered together causes it to resemble the parsley grown in our gardens.   On some parts of the Lancashire moors, as at Fo Edge, we have seen this pretty fern covering the rough ground for acres.

Another common fern in Derbyshire is the Rue-leaved Fern (*Asplenium ruta-muraria*), which the student will always recognise by its resemblance to the rue grown in our gardens. It is rarely more than two or three inches in height. The walls of old churches and ruins are places to look for this plant, and it may often be found in such situations growing in thousands.   A rarer fern than this, and perhaps the most beautiful of all our English species, is the Scaly Spleenwort (*Ceterach officinarum*, Fig 218), which, if found anywhere, will be met with in such spots as those where the rue-leaved fern grows.   It is tolerably well scattered over the northern, western,

Fig. 218

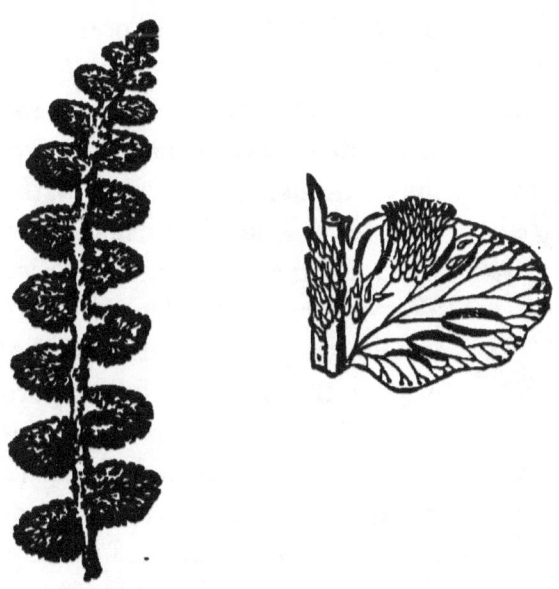

Ceterach officinarum.   *b*, Portion enlarged.

and southern counties of England, but its beauty has sadly interfered with its perpetuity.   The silvery light-brown scales on the back of the pinnules have given to it its common name. Formerly, this plant was much sought after in order

U

Fig. 219.

b

Woodsia ilvensis.
b, Portion en-
larged.

to apply it to wounds and ulcers. Its roots are short, but they possess the power of penetrating the hardest mortar. Another of our rarest native ferns is *Woodsia ilvensis* (Fig 219), which can be met with only in the bleakest and most exposed mountain regions.

The commonest of our road and lane side ferns are the polypody, which may frequently be met with under distinct varietal forms; the Male Fern, Female Fern, and Blechnum. The latter resembles the Polypody in the shape of its fronds, but some of the fronds only bear spore-cases, and these are generally erect and brown. The Dilated Fern (*Lastrea dilatata*) is also a common and most elegant plant, especially abundant in the shady lanes of the northern and midland counties. The Holly Fern is another lover of the northern districts, although it is also common in some parts of the eastern counties. Lastly, in the woods you may meet with the Oak-fern (*Polypodium dryopteris*), a plant

never to be forgotten, for nothing can excel the
beauty of its light green fronds, and slender black
stems.   We have already mentioned the hart's
tongue as another lane-side species. Little introduction is required to the study of this class of
plants, for when once the student has commenced
collecting them he is almost certain to continue.
Few plants keep so well in the herbarium, or look
so natural when mounted.   In this form they
remind one of many pleasant hours in the woods
and lanes and on the mountain sides; and thus
continue the enjoyment of the sunniest and most
innocent spots of one's life!

CHAPTER X.

THE MOSSES, FUNGI, AND LICHENS OF THE GREEN LANES.

BESIDES the more prominent and attractive objects to be noticed in any country stroll, a little extra attention reveals the presence of others whose smallness alone has concealed them. Among these are the mosses and lichens. You find them everywhere, and William Hunt's pretty sketches have shown us what miniature fairy-glens and grottos are distributed over the hedge-banks of our country lanes!

Let us take the mosses first. You find them growing abundantly on the top and in the interstices of any old wall, especially if it be in a shady place. You thrust aside the plants on the hedge or dyke banks, and find other species growing at their roots. The bole of an old tree is a rich hunting-ground for them, for several species have already upholstered the rough bark with those delicate shades of velvety green that artists love to paint. Perhaps in your examination of some of the mosses—especially the

common species growing so abundantly on the top
of the wall (the Screw Wall Moss, *Tortula muralis*),
you will find some of them in *fruit*. Examine this
wall moss with an ordinary pocket-lens, and if you
have not thus looked at it before we will guarantee
you a pleasant surprise. Although mosses and ferns
are *cryptogamous*—that is, they have no palpable

Fig. 220.

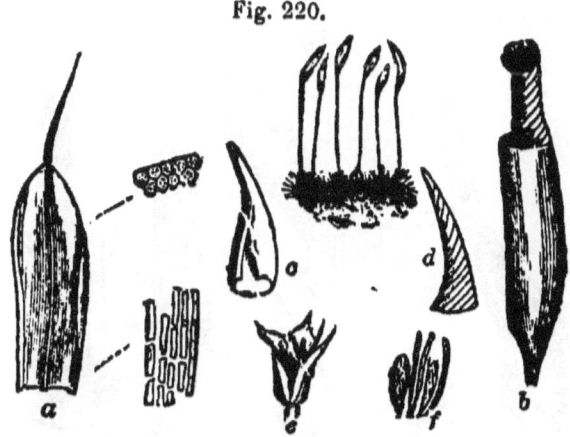

Tortula muralis. *a.* Leaf and its Areolations; *b.* Capsule; *c.* Calyptra.
d. Lid   *e.* Male flower; *f.* Antheridia and Paraphyses.

method of fructification like the true flowering-
plants—yet recent botanical discoveries have proved
that the old idea of there being no analogous male
and female organs is fallacious. Although perhaps
they do not possess them in the same degree, yet
the more highly organised even of the cryptogamia
have differentiated sexual parts. In Fig. 220 *e*, is
given what is called the *male* flower of the screw
wall moss. At the summit of the capsule (*b*) is

seen the twisted peristome, so much resembling the screwed end of an iron bolt, that you see at once the origin of its name. This twisted appearance also is seen on the "lid" (d). The leaves of most mosses are very beautiful objects under the microscope, the cellular structure coming out very distinctly, and showing their six-sided shapes, due to the mutual pressure induced by the growth of

Fig. 221.

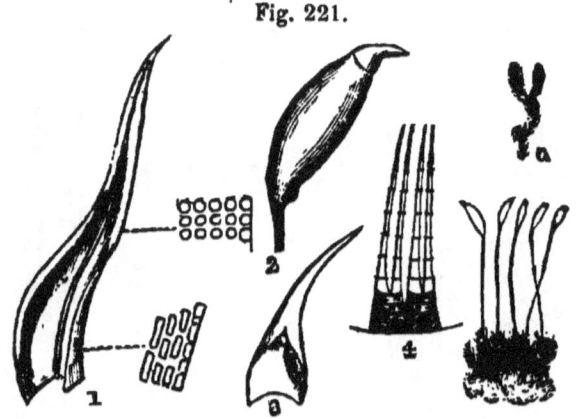

Ceratodon purpureus. a. Male Plant. 1. Leaf and its Areolation. 2. Capsule. 3. Calyptra. 4. Two Teeth of the Peristome.

each cell. On the waste ground by the roadside you may frequently find another species of moss which, at first sight, you would take for the *Tortula muralis* just described. That useful instrument, a good pocket-lens, however, will soon rectify the mistake, and show you that it is quite another genus of moss, called *Ceratodon purpureus* (Fig. 221). In the woodcut are given the chief parts of the moss as seen under a magnifying glass, and, if the student compare these with the corresponding parts of Fig. 220, he will readily perceive the difference. Most noticeable will be the absence of that spiral twist of the lid. The areolation of the leaf, or the arrangement of the leaf-cells, is also different.

It is true that many of our mosses fruit in winter,

Fig. 222.

Fig. 223.

Spore of *Funaria
hygrometrica.*

Spore of *Funaria hygrometrica*
germinating.

Fig. 224.

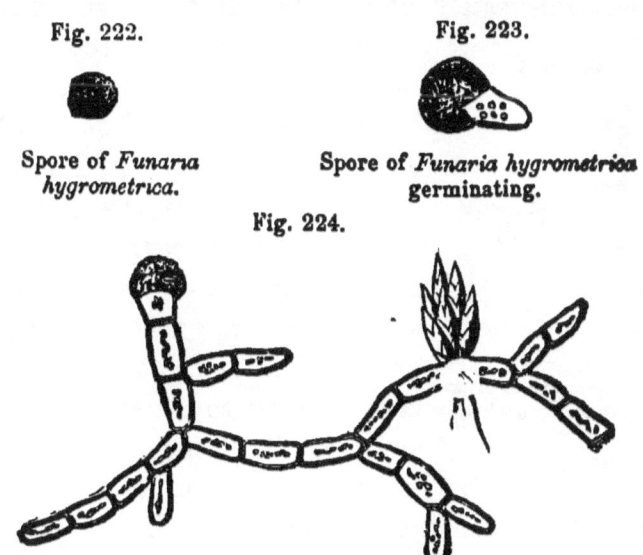

Prothallium and young Plant.

when other vegetation is dormant; but still we have many species, quite sufficient to occupy the attention of the young botanist, which fruit during the summer months. Chief among these are the *Sphagnums*, some species of *Bryum*, *Funaria*, *Fontinalis*, &c. The former may be found in abundance in most marshy places, for it is this genus which accumulates so as to form a good part of our peat or turf deposits. The latter species grows in water, and may perhaps be found in such a tarn or pond as that whose chief contents we have already described.

Should the student wish to become a bryologist, he will have to use the microscope very assiduously. Only by this means can he thoroughly understand the structural beauty of mosses. But he will find his

Pseudopodium of *Aulacomnium androgynum*, with one of the Gemmæ.

labours more than recompensed in the many interesting details brought to light. Let us glance at a few of these. In Fig. 222 is given the spore of the Rope-Moss (*Funaria hygrometrica*) — one of the commonest mosses growing on waste ground, garden paths, &c., and which is remarkable for its sensitiveness to moisture, the stem twisting in a very lively fashion when a shower of rain falls after some long continued drought. These spores are less than the thousandth part of an inch in diameter. You see them sprouting in Fig. 223, and in Fig. 224 you observe how cell has been added to cell, and the filament elongated so as to produce the green films you see, in spring, covering damp walls and banks. This is called the *prothallium*, and it is from it that the young moss-plant will bud, after which it dies away. In some mosses a portion of the leaves are altered into gemmæ, and clustered on the top of a naked stalk, as in *Aulacomnium*, Fig. 225. We have already

Fig. 226.

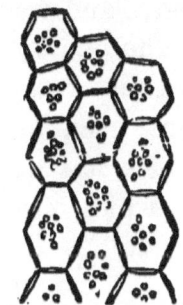

Areolation of *Pottia truncata.*

Fig. 227.

Areolation of *Grimmia apocarpa.*

Fig. 228.

Areolation of *Bryum cæspiticium.*

Fig. 229.

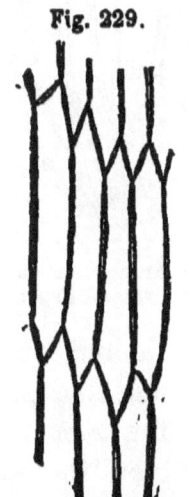

Areolation of *Hypnum rutabulum.*

spoken of the areolation of the leaves of mosses, but we should state that these leaves are always sessile, and have one, two, and even three layers of cells.

It is the form and arrangement of these that con
stitutes what botanists call *areolation*.   It is oi
great importance in the diagnosis of species, inasmuch as it varies in different genera, and frequently
even in different species of the same genus, as may
be seen in Figs. 228, 229.   The cells often contain
granules of the green substance peculiar to all
plants, called *chlorophyl*.   Reference has also been
made to the reproductive organs, which are of two

Fig. 230.   Fig. 231.

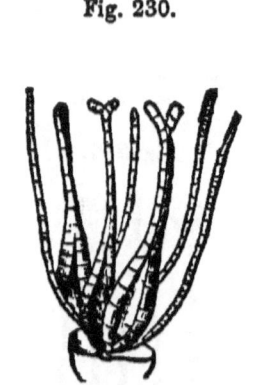 

Three Archegonia and Paraphyses of *Bryum*.

Two Antheridia and Para-
physes of *Polytrichum*.

kinds, male and female.   The occurrence of these is
pretty much like that of the male and female organs
of true flower-bearing plants.   Sometimes they are
combined on the same plant; at others they are
separate, but on the same plant; and frequently
they are separate, on different plants.   The male
organs are usually surrounded by a circle of small
leaves called the *perigonium*.   These male organs
are called *antheridia* (Fig. 231) and they seem

analogous to the stamens of ordinary flowering-plants. Mixed with them are numerous jointed threads called *paraphyses*, which seem set apart for the purpose of keeping the male organs moist, and thus to preserve their vitality. The female organs are termed *archegonia* (Fig. 230), and they correspond to the pistils of true flowering plants. When the antheridia, or male organs, are sufficiently ripe, they rupture, and set free peculiar bodies which move about as if they were living creatures. These are called *spermatozoids* (Fig. 232).

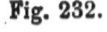

Fig. 232.

Meantime, the female organ (*archego-nium*) has been preparing for their reception, by also rupturing its walls, and rolling them back like the mouth of a trumpet, so that the spermatozoids can more readily enter, and fertilise the germinal cell. The latter then roots

Spermatozoids

itself, and sends up its fruit-stalk, on the end of which it carries the calyptra or veil (Fig. 234), which envelopes the young fruit. Both the veil and the capsule it covers are of different shapes in different species, so that proper attention paid to them will readily enable the student to recognise the various kinds of mosses. The mouth of the capsule, or fruit-case, is covered with a lid, which can be taken off by the thumb-nail as easily as the lids which cover the old fashioned earthenware teapots. In the several species this lid is of different shapes, and hence becomes another aid to their identification. In the genus *Andræa* there is no lid, and the spores have therefore to make their escape by the capsule splitting into four parts (Fig. 239). In those mosses whose capsules are covered with lids, there is frequently a contractile

Fig. 233.   Fig. 234.

Young Fruit of *Orthotri-chum crispum,* showing Vaginula and hairy Calyptra.

Mitriform Calyptra of *Encalyptra.*

ring of cells interposed between the lid and mouth of the capsules, called the *annulus,* or "ring." Fig. 240 shows the different internal parts of a not uncommon species of moss (*Mnium hornum*), and from this the student will gain a good idea of the general structure. When the capsule lid of a moss is taken off, the first thing seen is the *peristome*, which consists of a number of teeth-like edges, which have always a constant number, as four, eight, sixteen, or twenty-four. The forms of these teeth

Fig. 235.

Cucullate inflated Calyptra of *Funaria*.

Fig. 236.

Cucullate conic Calyptra of *Fissidens*.

Fig. 237.

Fruit of *Splachnum ampul-laceum* with small conic Lid, cylindric Capsule, and obovate Apophysis.

Fig. 238.

Strumose Capsule of *Dicra-num starkii*, with rostrate Lid and Annulus.

are exceedingly various, and therefore if attention be paid to them, they afford extra means of identify-ing the numerous species of mosses. One group of mosses have no teeth, and these go by the name of the "naked-mouthed" mosses (*gymnostomous*).

There is an outer and inner peristome, the latter
originating from the outer wall of the spore-sac.
In addition even to the peculiarities of form and
structure just described, there are several others
which the reader will find described in Stark's

Fig. 239.   Fig. 240.

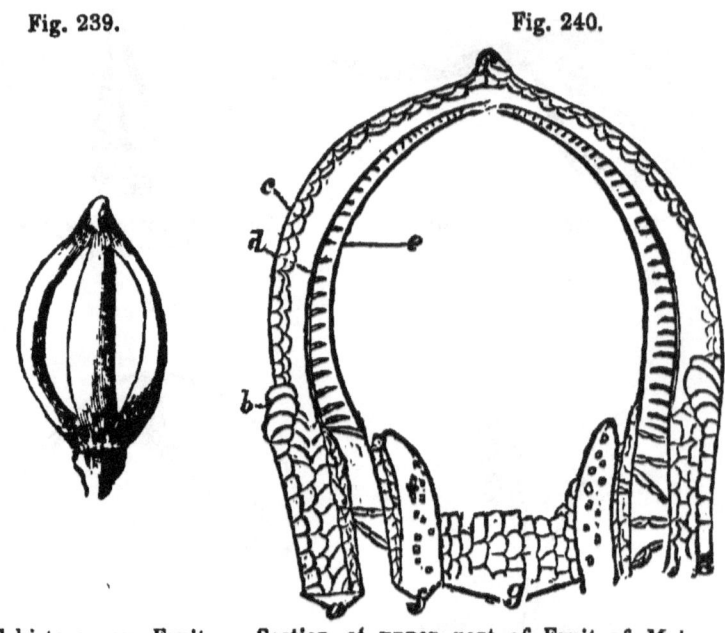

Schistocarpous Fruit   Section of upper part of Fruit of *Mnium*
of *Andreæa*.   *hornum.*   *a.* Wall of Capsule ; *b.* Annulus ;
                             c. Lid ; *d.* Tooth of outer Peristome ;
                             e. Tooth of inner Peristome ; *f.* Cavity of
                             Sporangium and Spores ; *g.* Columella.

'History of British Mosses,' and in the writings
of the best muscologist of the day, Dr. Braithwaite.
    The Scale Mosses are many of them very in-
teresting objects. One of these, the Fringed Scale
Moss (*Ptilidium ciliare*), occurs abundantly in heathy

places, where it forms large purplish-brown patches, which look like ordinary moss. The stems are from one to three inches in length, and prostrate, bearing on the one side a profusion of short branchlets, which are themselves repeatedly divided. The leaves overlap each other, and are placed in two rows on opposite sides of the stem. Each lobe is divided and cleft into two pointed segments, all of which are

Fig. 241.

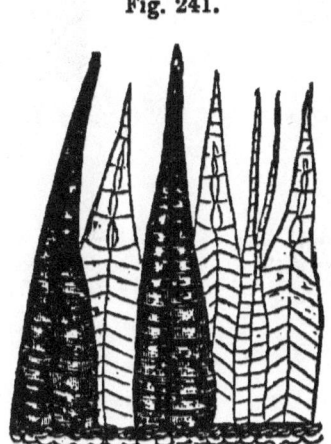

Part of inner and outer Peristomes of Moss.

fringed with hairs. When parts of these leaves are viewed with a magnifying power of three hundred diameters, they are seen to consist of roundish cells, which have the usual disposition to become hexagonal, except in the hairs.

In January or February you will find it impossible to take a country walk without seeing the bark of trees, and the twigs of hawthorn, ash, &c., often covered with *lichens,* of a bright yellow, or silvery-grey colour.   The former is called *Physcia parietina,* and its structure is very remarkable.   Under the

Fig. 242.

Fig. 243.

Fruit of *Tetraphis pellucida,*
Peristome of four Teeth.

Splachnum sphæricum, with
eight bigeminate Teeth, and
exserted Columella.

Fig. 244.

Fig. 245.

Bifid Tooth from Peristome
of *Fissidens.*

Peristome and Tympanum of
Pogonatum aloides.

microscope it appears as follows :—It will be seen
that even these lowly organised types of vegetation
have differentiated parts for the purposes of reproduction. If you cut across the leaf-like layer
(*thallus*) of the common Yellow Lichen, even with
the naked eye you will perceive three different
layers. When these are submitted to the micro-

Fig. 246.

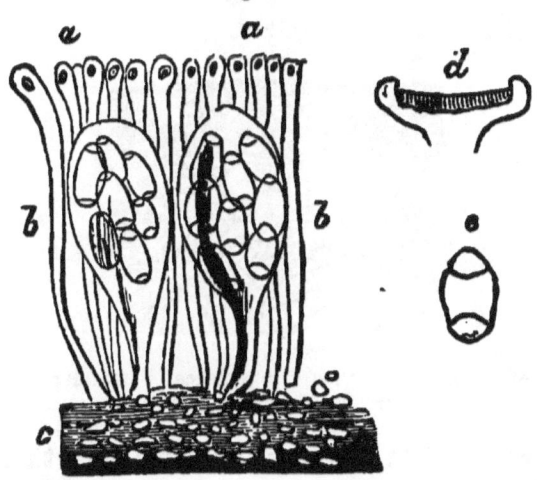

Section of *Physcia parietina.* a. Paraphyses; b. Asci with Spores;
c. Hypothecium; d. Section of Apothecium; e. Spore.

scope, they present the appearance seen in Fig. 246.
Like mosses, lichens are very abundant. They grow
on stones, trees, twigs, hedge-banks, rocks, almost
everywhere. We possess in this country about eight
hundred different indigenous species. Perhaps the
best book you can carry with you in your search
after these very interesting forms is Lindsay's
'History of British Lichens,' in which you will

x

find the leading genera figured and coloured.
Many species of lichens have long been used in
the arts for dyeing purposes; whilst others are
esteemed equally valuable for medicine. They are
the first possessors of the soil, and their decay
often lays the foundation on which plants of a
higher structure can better flourish. Our grandest
buildings, the proudest works of men's hands, are

Fig. 247.

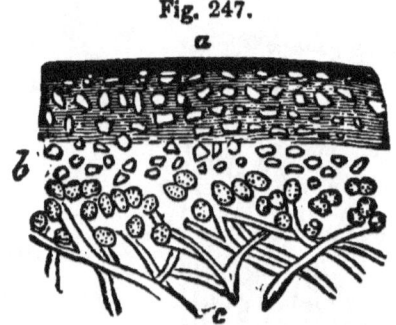

Section of *Physcia parietina.* *a.* Cortical Stratum; *b.* Gonidie
Stratum; *c.* Medullary Stratum.

in time reduced to dust by the slow growth of these
" time-stains."

Whilst treating on objects whose structure can
only be seen by microscopical aid, let us not omit
another class whose occurrence is frequently only
too common. They are parasitic fungi, which occur
as black pustules on dead twigs or leaves. Fig. 248
is an excellent example of these lovely objects as
seen when magnified. It occurs on the twigs of the
beech, where the pustules form small orifices, with
a ragged mouth, within which may be seen a black

mass of spores. Each of these spores is of the
star-shape seen in Fig. 248. When viewed with
transmitted light, they are of an amber colour.
During the summer months these black pustules
may be found on nearly every dead twig of beech or
lime which still remains attached to the parent
tree. The proper way to mount the spores is to

Fig. 248.

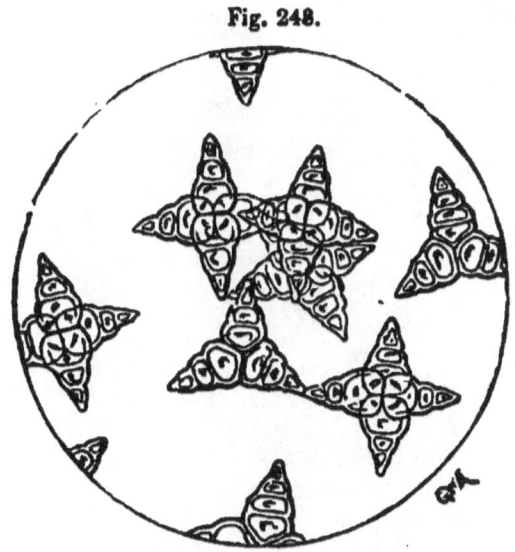

Star-spored Fungus (*Asterosporium Hoffmanni*)

take out a portion with the point of a penknife and
lay it on a glass slide, adding a drop of spirit,
which will break up the mass into individual spores.
A portion of this fluid may then be transferred to a
clean slide, and a drop of balsam placed on it as the
spirit evaporates. The whole should then be covered
with thin glass in the ordinary way. Similar

objects to these may be found on the leaves of
many of our summer plants. Those of the Common
Pilewort (*Ranunculus ficaria*) are especially liable to
beautiful "rust," called "cluster-cups," on account
of their resembling a number of cups closely packed
together, when examined with a lens. The "brands,"

Fig. 249.

The Bramble-leaf Brand (*Aregma bulbosum*, Fr.).

as they are called, belong to the same group of
parasitic fungi. If you examine the leaves of the
common bramble, towards the middle of the summer,
you will frequently see the under surfaces covered
with blotches of yellow dust. As autumn approaches, darker bodies will be found mixed with

this yellow powder, until at last the yellow spores
will scarcely be found, and their places occupied
with large blackish spots. These will be indicated,
on the upper surfaces of the leaves, by reddish
coloured spots. The darker spots are clusters of
spores of the Bramble Brand (Fig. 249), one of our
prettiest microscopic objects. If mounted in the

Fig. 250.

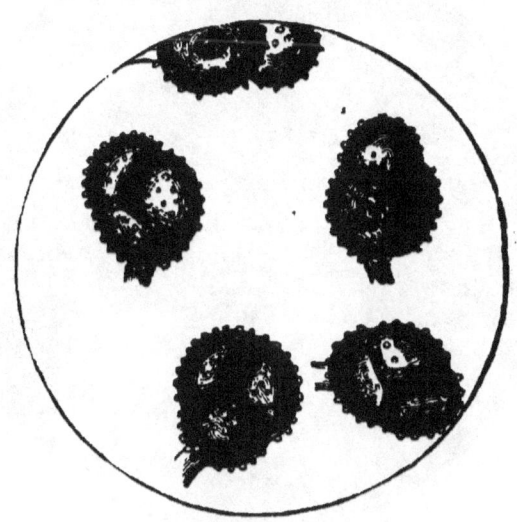

Meadow-sweet Brand (*Triphragmium ulmaria*).

manner already described in the star-shaped fungus,
they will keep for years, and always prove attractive. The leaves of the meadow-sweet (*Spiræa
ulmaria*) are frequently covered with a similar
fungus, of a distinct species called Meadow-sweet
Brand (*Triphragmium ulmaria* Fig. 250). It may
usually be found where the meadow-sweet grows, in

moist situations, and can be readily recognised by
the small black dots, not bigger than a pin's head,
on the under side of the leaves. When examined
under the microscope with a quarter of an inch
objective, the pustules are seen to consist of aggre-

Fig. 251.

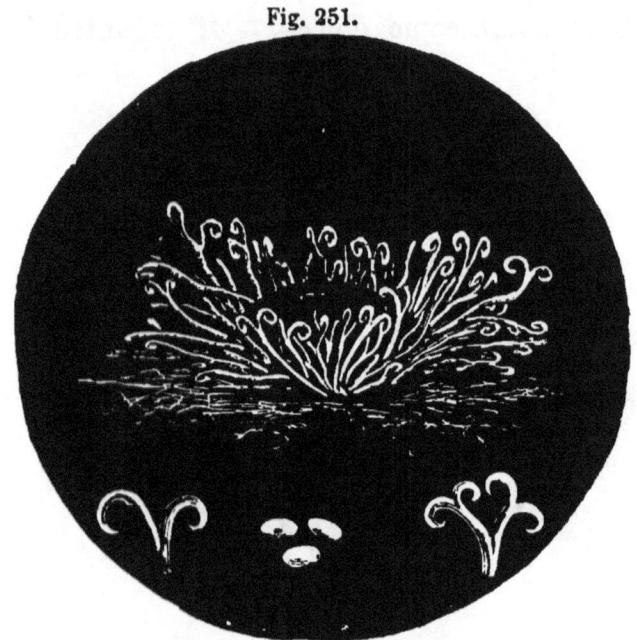

Maple Blight (*Uncinula bicornis*).

gations of three-celled spores, whence their name of
Triphragmium.

Another species of microscopic fungus is the
Maple Blight (*Uncinula bicornis*, Fig. 251). This
may be found, as a kind of whitish powder, on
the leaves of the maple and sycamore during the
autumnal months. If examined with a pocket-lens,

the white powdered leaf will be seen to have a number of minute dots scattered over it. These are the fruit receptacles of the light, and if one be placed under the microscope, and viewed with a one-inch objective, it will turn out a very pretty object indeed. When one of these receptacles is taken up, and viewed with a higher microscopic power, a great number of pear-shaped bags, termed *asci*, each holding eight spores, are visible. These are the fruit of the blight, which is called *uncinula* on account of the hooked appendages. The above figure of one of the receptacles is given as seen under a half-inch objective. The spores and hooks are seen below the receptacle. Should your walk be in the spring and early summer months, you will perhaps have noticed the dead stems of herbaceous plants and the small twigs of trees to be covered with little black pustules, not bigger, if so big, as a pin's head. These are minute fungi, belonging to a group called *Sphæriacei*. The little black spots are perhaps covered by a skin, or epidermis, which later in the season will be thrown off. The pustule is nearly spherical, flattened at the base, however, and having at its apex a teat-like projection (*a*). The centre of this becomes perforated, and out of the perforation the inner contents of the fungus will escape. If a section of the pustule be made, the interior will be found occupied by a minute drop of jelly, which should be taken out with a needle and placed in a drop of water on a glass-slide, if you wish to examine it under the microscope. The little sacks (*asci*) then come out with remarkable distinctness. This structure is peculiar to many of the micro-

Fig. 252.

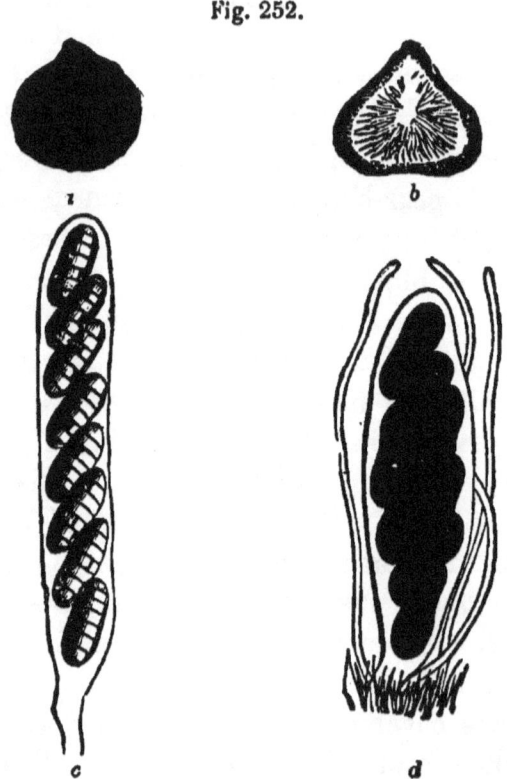

Sphæria herbarum. *a.* Perithecium; *b.* Section of ditto, magnified slightly; *c.* Ascus, with uniseriate Spores; *d.* Ascus, with biseriate Spores and Paraphyses, × 320.

scopic fungi, which a little patience will enable you to find on the leaves of plants more frequently than you had imagined. If you are short of objects for the microscope you cannot do better than turn into the nearest wheat field where the sicklier heads, covered with the black powder called "smut," will afford you microscopic fungi in abundance. The

Fig. 253.

Nostoc commune, nat. size.

Fig. 254.

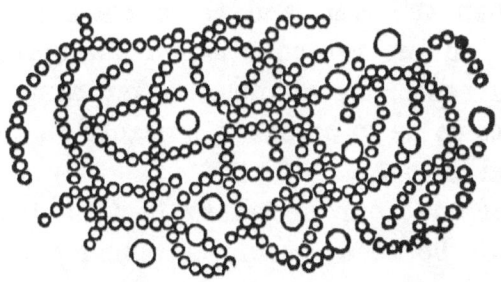

Nostoc commune, × 320, showing bead-like Cells.

study of these minute but interesting forms of vegetation is more fascinating than people suppose, for many of them are among the most beautiful and elegant forms seen with optical assistance. Such books as Cooke's 'Microscopic Fungi' will assist the student, not only in finding the objects, but by the numerous figures, in enabling him to identify them. And all naturalists are now agreed, that it is only by a more intimate acquaintance with the simpler forms of life that we can hope to rise to a thorough understanding of the complex structures of higher organisms. A not unfrequent object met with in our walks is a greenish gelatinous substance, once supposed to be the residue of a shooting-star! It is in reality one of those curious organisms called *Nostoc*, or *Tremella* (Fig. 253), belonging to the *Algæ* family. We have several species of them in this country, whose internal structure is very much alike in all (Fig. 254), consisting of bead-like threads immersed in gelatine. Here and there, when seen under the microscope, one bead or sphere appears larger than the rest, and these are believed to be concerned in the reproduction of the species. The *Nostoc* is especially abundant after rainy weather, sometimes so as to become a nuisance on our garden walks and lawns.

We conclude our necessary hasty notices of the objects to be seen during a country stroll by a reference to the larger fungi. You cannot fail to observe them, for they grow almost everywhere. An old tree, however, is a splendid habitat, and here you may expect to find more than one kind. Out of other trees you see these fungi growing like a series of tongues overlapping each other. If you examine the underside of these, you will find it covered with minute pores, resembling a sponge. This species (*Polyporus*) is not a bad article of food, if properly cooked; but to find out how to do this you must study such books as Dr. Badham's 'Fungi,' Mr. M. C. Cooke's 'British Fungi,' and the coloured charts of Mr. Worthington Smyth, showing forth at a glance the edible and poisonous species. The explanatory notes belonging to these charts are most useful, not only as showing how the edible species are to be cooked, but also as setting forth a practical experience in the determination of what kinds of fungi are poisonous and which are not, which entitles Mr. Smyth to a foremost place among bold investigators.

We have several hundred species of those kinds of Fungus popularly known as "Toadstools." We English as a rule only profess to eat one kind, which we dignify by the name of "Mushroom." Unfortunately for our consistency, in the course of the year we really eat three or four other species, and that under the delusion that we are all the while sticking to our true mushrooms! In the brief space here allotted we cannot be expected to enter fully into the delineation of the several species, nor is it desirable, seeing it has already been done by our best fungologists. The young student, how- ever, may find amusement as well as instruction in the examination of ordinary species of what he considers "toadstools." Those bearing gills are called *Agarici*, whilst the stalked species which are perforated go by the name of *Boleti*. Young specimens of the former are covered over with a thin skin called *volva*. As the fungus grows, this is

Fig. 255.

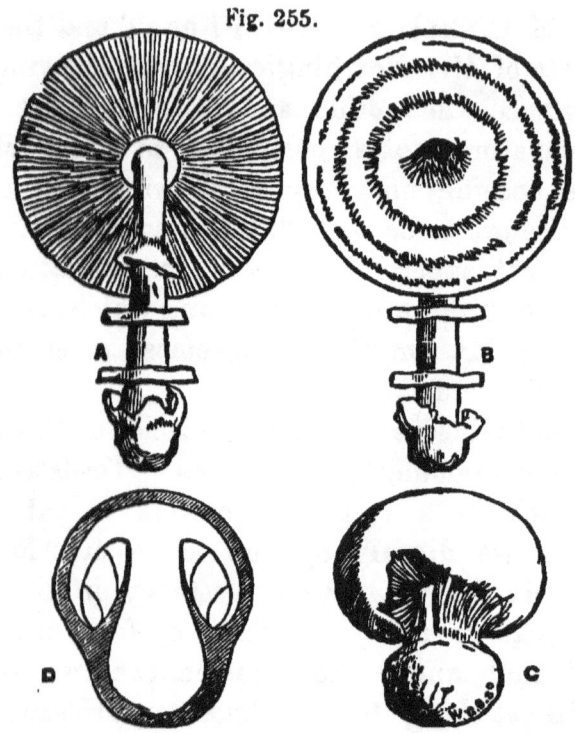

Specimens showing the Gills, Rings, and Stages of Growth.

ruptured, whilst the growing stem carries a part of it upwards to form the *annulus*, or ring, to be seen just beneath the gills of the mushroom (Fig. A. 255).

One species of fungus is too good to be passed unnoticed. It is the Morel (*Morchella esculenta*,

Fig. 256) one of the most easily recognised of all
the fungi. We have gathered this species by scores
in the fir-woods of Norfolk, when April has been a
warmer month than usual. After being gathered,
each fungus should be hung by a bit of string where
there is a current of air, so as to be properly dried.
When thus dried, all you have to do is to powder a
little in soup, or grate the dry
fungus over your chop or steak
whilst cooking, and you will be
thankful ever afterwards for the
knowledge! Another fungus,
hastily classed by us among the
"toadstools," but whose merits
are thoroughly appreciated in
France, is the Champignon
(*Marasmius oreades*, Fig. 257).
This is one of the most dainty
of the Agarics, as well as among
the safest to use for cookery
purposes. You cannot help

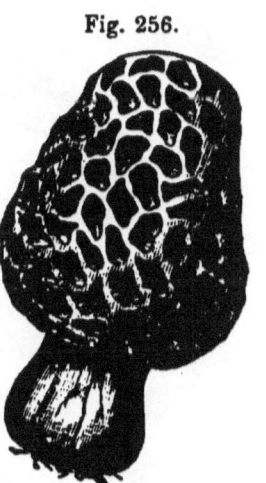

Fig. 256.

Morel.

noticing it in your walks, it is so abundant. Were
it for nothing else, its habit of forming those dark
green rings commonly known as "fairy rings"
would render it a conspicuous species. These rings
are caused by the spores being thrown outward, and,
as the inner ground is tolerably exhausted of its
nitrogenous substances, the spores thus scattered
have a tendency to grow only on the outer or fertile
ground. This fungus is of too dry a nature to

make *ketchup*, but in a stew, or added to other mushrooms, it is a great dainty. Gather this, as well as all other kinds of edible fungi, when young— the younger the better, in all species, for even the edible " mushroom " is bad for food when too old.

Fig. 257.

Fairy-ring Champignon (*Marasmius oreades*).

Lastly, we have another group of fungi of equal abundance to the champignon, to be found growing wherever there are damp pastures. You know them better as " puff-balls " (*Lycoperdon*) on account of their emitting such a quantity of snuff-like powder (spores) when thoroughly ripe and dry. Formerly, the dry Puff-balls made excellent " tinder," on account of the ease with which a spark could ignite it. In Norfolk, these Puff-balls are **very** abundant and very large, frequently growing to the size of a man's head. There they commonly go by the name of "bulfers," and we have been grieved to see them kicked about by the nailed boots of agricultural labourers, who were little aware how they were treating real dainties! Fig. 258 is **a nearly**

Fig. 258.

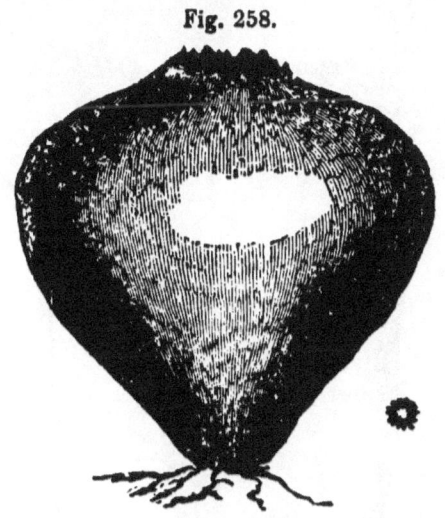

Lycoperdon atropurpureum. a. Spore.

pear-shaped puff-ball, without stem—a feature whose absence will readily lead to its identification. The spores are of a dark purple-brown colour, hence the scientific specific name. The species bearing a stem (Fig. 259) often grows to a height of six inches. The commonest of our native puff-balls, however, is that whose top is covered with a mealy-looking wart (Fig. 260, *Lycoperdon gemmatum*). The scars left by these warts when they are rubbed off are six-sided. The Pear-shaped Puff-ball (*Lycoperdon pyriforme,* Fig. 261) is also common, and may be found growing on old stumps. The spores of this species are of a

Fig. 259.

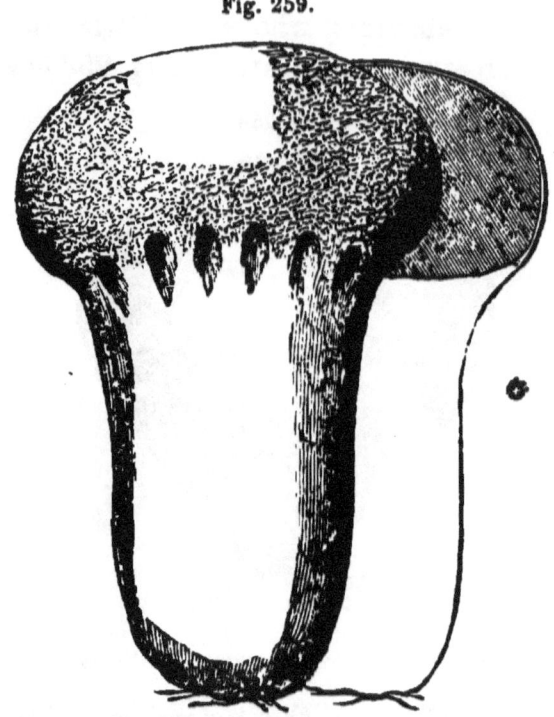

Lycoperdon saccatum.   *a.* Spore.

greenish-yellow colour. Another species is the Little Puff-ball (*Lycoperdon pusillum,* Fig. 262), which grows on hedge banks and in pastures, but it is not so abundant as some of the foregoing. The proper time for collecting these objects, with a view to eating them, is when the flesh is perfectly white. Then you may cut them in slices, and fry them; or use them as you would ordinary mushrooms. This you will do almost without distinguishing the difference.

Our task is now ended. We have endeavoured to make a country stroll more interesting, as well as more profitable. A harvest of material is every-

Fig. 260.

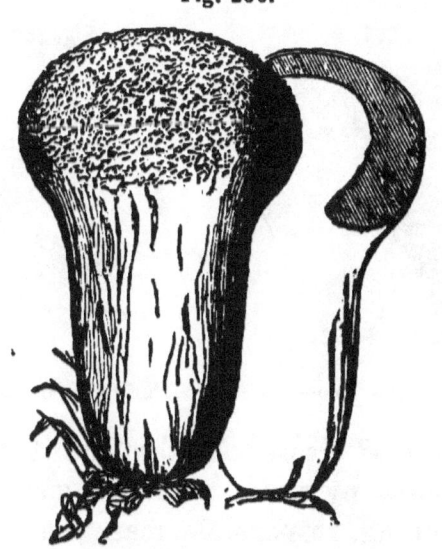

Lycoperdon gemmatum.

where at hand, but how few think of the bounty of the "Lord of the Harvest!" To the young especially, the study of these objects should have a peculiar charm, and it is among the most noticeable features in the education of the present day that the young *are* becoming more interested in natural history pursuits. There are few studies which more completely take the conceit out of human nature

Y

than these, for they reveal to us the presence of millions
of organic forms, none of which can be associated
with any utility to man, but whose vital processes
none the less speak of the Wisdom and Love which
have constructed them, and fitted them to be sharers
of our terrestrial life. In the companionship of that
life we find a higher purpose than mere utilitarian-

Fig. 261   Fig. 262.

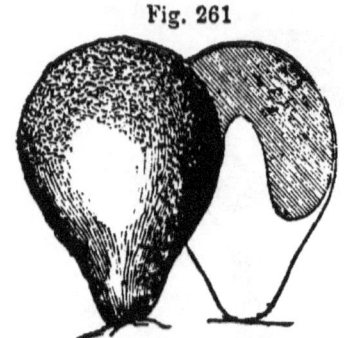

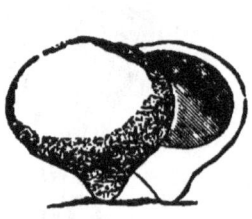

Lycoperdon pyriforme.   Puff-ball (*L. pusillum*).

ism; for, as good George Herbert has it, the natural
world is but a pyramid, at the summit of which
stands reasoning, responsible man, the mouth-piece
and high-priest of the dumb forms which can utter
no song of thanks or praise except through their
gambols—whilst man is permitted, mind to mind, as
face to face, to investigate this great mystery of
life, and pour out in intelligible language his thanks
to the Creator !

INDEX.